The Trinity Constellation

Christ's Rebels Build the Future

by Duane Fleming

PublishAmerica
Baltimore

ISBN: 1-4241-2744-0
PUBLISHED BY PUBLISHAMERICA, LLLP
www.publishamerica.com
Baltimore

Printed in the United States of America

David

my old friend,
may our dreams
be fulfilled to
the benefit of many.

Duane

Table of Contents

Chapter 1
SOMETHING NEW IN ROCADURA

David O'Laughlin mused about his surprise trip to meet five billionaires. He wondered what kind of people they would be. Would they be egocentric, aloof, and strictly out for empire expansion? Or, would they be like Bill Gates and Ted Turner, giving billions to good causes? He had a few clues to go on but they didn't give him the whole picture. He knew from Peter Erikson, the president of his planning company, that they were creating some new and unique economic arrangements, and *that* is what excited David. Erikson sent David and his colleague, Carlos Vega, to visit the billionaires operation and determine whether they should join forces with them to design and build new towns in Latin America.

The billionaires were known simply as *El Cinco*, "The Five." Together, they had over sixty billion dollars in cash, plus other assets. They concealed their operation from the media by not giving interviews and by maintaining a high level of internal security. They chose not to have a web site and they only gave one press conference last year. They were shrouded in secrecy. El Cinco had a large security force to protect their construction operations. You had to be invited to enter their premises. The fact that David was invited made him feel very special. He speculated that El Cinco had a portfolio on him that would surprise his own mother.

On their way to Rocadura, David and Carlos had arranged a meeting at the State Department in Washington, D.C., to learn more about El Cinco.

Carlos Veda glided the van through a large forest. They were 80 miles outside of Washington D.C. Large maple trees and oaks lined the road and the trees had turned crimson and gold. A sun-lit fall canopy hung over the edge of the road. The autumn leaves were changing color and the sunlight danced upon the leaves and through small open spaces with easy, rhythmical waves. David lazily watched the light show of brilliant yellows, crimsons and greens. The sun's rays broke through the trees intermittently, with a hypnotic rhythm. The regular repetition of the sun breaking through the trees was especially pleasing.

"We're about an hour outside of Washington," Carlos said. "I think I'll let you drive the last leg—I'm getting a bit tired."

"Fine. I'm ready to take over."

Carlos gave David a sideways glance, realizing he must have interrupted some deep thought. He said nothing though, as he pulled into a gas station to fuel up and allow David to change places.

"Carlos, doesn't Rocadura mean Bedrock in Spanish, like the hometown of the Flintstones?"

Carlos chuckled. "Yes, but I think the founding fathers of Rocadura were thinking more about establishing a rock solid foundation for the culture, you know, where people could carve out a living in a new land."

"Okay, but Rocadura is about the poorest country in Latin America and it sounds like hard rock to me."

Carlos tuned the radio to a Latin music station playing salsa.

"That's easy to take. It's salsa with passion."

"You have to dance to it," smiled Carlos, "if you really want to get into it. Then, the salsa gives you its nighttime magic."

"I know. I spent a night salsa dancing at a Tito Puente concert in Miami. I was hoarse the next day. It was really great stuff. At one point, Tito started describing things that begin with his initials—like Toilet Paper, Turn Pike and Tough Percussion."

"That old Puerto Rican played lots of parties and made a good living at it."

They drove along in silence for a while, enjoying the salsa beat. David imagined Carlos dancing in some Miami night club. Carlos was built tall and lean. He combed his black hair back with some kind of gel. He was an impeccable dresser, always making a well-tailored appearance and never having trouble attracting the ladies. He would dance with an economy of motion. He gave the ladies a strong lead, and they liked it. *Carlos was a good buddy*, thought David, *we laugh and work well together, but he has this belief that the market economy is the only economic arrangement on Earth.* Sometimes David wondered how they could have such a strong bond and be so different in their economics. Carlos was his Sancho Panza. Carlos was materialistic and skeptical, but he was good hearted. *It would be fun to see how he will react to this new economic structure. He'll ask all of the hard questions*, thought David.

Then Carlos said, as if on cue, "I'm looking forward to our briefing tomorrow. Humberto will give us the State Department's 'inside' about El Cinco's operation. From what I gather, they're building leading edge new towns."

"The thing that excites the hell out of me is that Humberto said it's got some kind of advanced economic structure."

"Yeah, man. They're creating thousands of jobs and we get to explore new life forms on the planet!"

"We're pretty lucky guys," Carlos observed. "I never thought an outfit like ours would be invited to go on an exploration like this, especially in a place like Rocadura."

"Humberto said that they must have a powerful job training system, because they are creating jobs for campesinos, for the poorest of the poor."

"If that's true it could have impact around the globe, because three billion people each live on two dollars a day or less," said David.

"Yeah, and one billion are Muslims and most of them are living on a pile of sand. That's why the Islamic leaders are pounding the table for fairness in the distribution of wealth."

"I read an article published by a Jordanian, Rami Khouri, in 1990 that said the Arab dream will not be denied. They grow up to believe that Islam is the most perfect path to God, but they look at their society and see poverty, a lack of good jobs, education and freedom. They compare all of that to the West and wonder what's wrong. They feel a lack of dignity and it makes them angry. Unfortunately, we've supported too many corrupt leaders who kept people in harsh poverty too long. I guess it drove some of them into madness and the madmen came out of the desert on September 11."

"Yeah, and they haven't stopped coming," Carlos remarked crisply.

"The root of war is fear and extreme poverty leads to fear. We damn well know how to produce wealth. Now, we need to learn how to distribute the wealth," remarked David. "We can win the peace through social justice."

"We need a positive solution to end the violence, that's for sure. Maybe we'll find something of value in Rocadura."

"Humberto gave me some hope about that."

"I'm glad we have Humberto. He wants to cut through the bureaucracy, and get the job done. How long have you known him?"

"I met him two years ago at a conference in D.C. We keep in touch, but I don't know him very well. He's very sharp. In his position, you have to be a wily fox."

Carlos thought about David, compared to Humberto. David was about as far from a wily fox as you could get. In fact, Carlos thought David was not skeptical enough, perhaps a little too nice sometimes. He was wise, but he just wanted to believe people were better than they were. Carlos always looked for those "feet of clay" and usually found them pretty damned quickly. But David was bright and insightful. He weighed in at about 180 and was a typical Irish dishwater blond. David was a handsome man, according to the many girlfriends Carlos had dated. He had a bit of the rogue in him and tried a mustache for a while, but decided people didn't really trust a man with a mustache, so he shaved it off. David enjoyed being Irish, full of life and good humor, and seemed to carry most of the faults and the virtues associated with his heritage. David liked to drink, like most of his buddies. He worked hard during the day. Three or four times a week he would quaff a Jameson on the rocks and a beer. But David drank moderately and he was never intoxicated. Carlos wondered what was driving him. David was definitely on a quest. Well, there was the Irish thing about justice. He had pointed out to Carlos that the British kept their foot on the necks of the Irish for 300 years. They shipped them off to penal colonies as slave labor. The Irish developed a powerful demand for fairness from that experience. The incredible number of priests that flowed out of Ireland for a hundred years will attest to that. David said these priests had turned their backs on hatred and revenge. They went straight to the source of goodness and learned to love their former enemies, as Christ had taught them. They stopped railing against evil, were given grace for their faith and went for creative pursuits. They simply pushed aside the evils of the world, saying, "Let the unquiet be as unquiet as they will." But Carlos also read about the anger of the IRA. The good and the bad, they flow from the same human experiences. *You've always got to keep your eye on that,* thought Carlos, with self-satisfaction at the insight. And David had an Irish temper. He was as mild-mannered and easy-going as they come, ninety-eight percent of the time. But once in a while, he sensed that two percent of Irish temper that lurked below the surface. David used that to his advantage with men who wanted to test his mettle. He was a "standup kind of guy." In the main, however, Carlos thought David was a good man and fun to be with. He had this idealistic belief that an economic system could be created beyond the market economy! What a dreamer! *Not in* my *lifetime*, thought Carlos.

David's thoughts turned to his own commitment not to merely sit around producing words and ideas. He wanted to find solutions to the core problems—the over-arching problems caused by wrong-headed economic theories. From the beginning, he knew he was traveling a long road. He steeled himself with perseverance by remembering the poverty he'd seen in his own family and around the world. He had watched his father move from one job to another as a carpenter and block layer. There were many periods of unemployment where a bare existence was all that his father could provide for the family. National economic recessions always hit construction first. During one long recession, the only work his father could find to put food on the table was picking apples for 50 cents an hour. He was trapped picking apples for two years before construction started up again. They lived with his grandmother in the country in order to survive. David carried wood and coal for winter heating and cooking. There was no indoor plumbing. He hauled drinking water from a neighbor's well, 200 yards away. Bathing water was taken from the creek to fill a tub or two on Saturdays. At 20 degrees above zero, you really didn't want to go out to that two hole john and freeze. In the summer, you had to keep an eye out for the black widow spider. There were more than a dozen bites a year, the newspaper reported. This kind of experience gave David a great appreciation for modern conveniences, especially showers. David loved showers.

To overcome poverty, David made education his highest priority. He worked his way through undergraduate school as a computer graphics specialist. Just after he earned his Bachelor of Arts degree at Loyola University, he was fired by the architectural firm that employed him.

He remembered getting the call to come to the director's office. It was not unusual to be called in for a new work assignment, so David suspected nothing was amiss—except, this was in the 90s when no job was secure. *No*, thought David, *my work has been good. I meet all of my deadlines. Relax. Old man Peters just has another new job for you.*

The door to the director's office was slightly ajar. David tapped on the door.

"Come in," Mr. Peters said. "Have a seat."

David sat down and got his pad ready to take notes.

"The company has decided to 'outsource' some work," Peters began.

Upon hearing this, David felt a sense of anxiety and extreme alertness.

Peters continued. "Our consultants have advised us to transfer the entire division's work to China to take advantage of the cheap semi-professional labor there. I'm sorry, David, but we'll have to let you go."

David was stunned. He couldn't believe what Peters had just said. A minute passed in silence as the thought of being unemployed during these hard times raced across his mind. At first, he thought, *I've got a college degree. I'll make it okay.* Then, David's Irish broke through the surface. He looked at Peters, sitting comfortably behind his desk in his expensive suit and cuffed linked white starched shirt. He was part of the smug upper class. *They have suffered so little,* thought David, *they don't realize what they're doing to people.*

"So, hard work and talent don't mean anything to you. Hell, *people* don't mean anything to you, do they?"

"Now wait a minute, David…"

"No," said David in a calm voice, "*you* wait a minute. I've got something to say."

David's mind raced ahead to find some way to penetrate Peters' smug, self-assured arrogance. And then, it came to him.

"Forgiveness is what you need. I forgive you for what you're doing to me and the whole division. I mean it. I forgive you as a person, but you need to reflect on what you're doing to people and take it to heart. You need forgiveness from God."

The impact was instant. Peters' face turned to David in shock.

"Now, David, it's out of my hands. I'm just doing what is best for the board of directors and the shareholders."

"Then, you all need to start bending your knees," he said calmly. "Give me a call if you want to go to Mass with me someday. You might be surprised what good it can do for you."

Peters froze in his chair, bewildered and dumbfounded.

David struggled for a year, living on part-time consulting work. Finally, he won an assistantship at the University of Oregon and used his GI Bill to finish graduate school. Armed with a master's in planning, he worked in long range planning for a large electric utility company. After two years, the company brought in a cruel CEO to quickly fire 10,000 workers "to save the company by becoming more competitive in the global economy," the newspaper said. David felt he was lucky not to have a wife and kids to support when he was fired for the second time in his life. He was young. He would make it, he thought, but he hated the arrogant corporations that were throwing families into the street as if they were dogs. In four years, corporations had "downsized" 10,500,000 people into financial despair. Economists had no solutions. It was just the way the "free" enterprise system works. What a joke. As if nothing could be done about massive layoffs. Meanwhile, the stock market was soaring to astronomical heights because many large corporations were achieving new levels of profits by reducing labor costs at the expense of millions of families.

Why does life have to be so hard? David asked himself. *It shouldn't be so damned tough to make a decent living. Why do we allow a dog-eat-dog economic system to rule our lives?* It didn't have to be that way. David had a fire in his belly to discover a much better way. He would fight to move beyond the market economy to a new kind of economic structure. He longed to deliver something wiser, kinder and closer to the human heart. He thought about what an incredible task that is—to create a new, more human economic system. Was it extreme arrogance to think he could deliver such a thing? Then, one night, he was in bed reading a very small book by Buckminster Fuller: *Operating Manual for the Spaceship Earth.* Suddenly, he was overwhelmed by a vision that it could be done. He felt a surge of awesome insight, a connection with something much larger than himself. Fuller had seen that, with rapidly developing technology, we could produce much more for much less, and pass the benefits to everyone without loss to the rich. With wrenching speed, David had crossed over into a new plane of knowing a truth beyond his comprehension. Yet, somehow he understood that he was really onto something totally transcendent and totally real. In a deep flash of recognition, he knew in his gut that "Bucky" Fuller was right! David reveled in the insight. With splendid clarity, he drifted into the full knowledge that he was going to participate in delivering a new economic system with beautiful values. His whole being was seized by a creative insight of new possibilities. He was instantly overwhelmed with this inner discovery that was at once powerfully convincing and totally unthinkable. It scared the hell out him.

He refreshed himself with the knowledge that he was a city planner, which is a field that enables broad, generalist thinking toward comprehensive solutions. He was strongly hoping that he would find some of those solutions to build on in Rocadura.

David's reflections were interrupted when he realized that they had approached the exit ramp to their hotel.

The two men checked in, threw their bags into the room, and hastily made their way to a nearby restaurant named Hello Hialeah. The bar area was awash with pictures of race horses. There were huge murals of horses pounding down the stretch run, their jockeys in bright silks, lashing with their whips. There were numerous photos on the walls of a man, apparently the bar's owner, posing with horses in the winner's circle.

"What would you like to have?" asked the bartendress.

"I'll just have a Jameson's on the rocks."

"And I'll have a Cuba libre."

"Okay," she said, with a pert bounce and then glided smoothly to her mixing station. She returned with the drinks.

"Will you be staying in Washington long?" she asked, in a way that was only mildly suggestive.

"Just tonight," said David. "We're moving on to adventure in Latin America."

She gave a little gush of semi-disappointment with a toss of her hair, then, drifted like a dream to the other end of the bar.

The Jameson was as smooth as ever, and David began to feel revived a bit from the long trip to Washington.

They ordered fried grouper fingers with a Caesar salad and ate at the bar. They decided to watch a little TV and retire early.

The following morning, David and Carlos went to the State Department to visit Alfredo Humberto, the director of Economic Analysis for the consulates in Central and South America. They found the State Department office and told the receptionist that they had an appointment with Humberto and they were led to his office. Humberto was a dark-haired man with an extraordinary handle bar mustache. It was very carefully kept, with the ends waxed and curled. He stepped in front of his desk as they entered the room.

"*Buenos dias, amigo,*" he said to Carlos, shaking his hand. Then, turning to David, he added, "It's a pleasure to meet you, Mr. O'Laughlin. I've read your work on energy planning—it was right on target. That's part of the reason why you were selected to visit El Cinco's operation."

"Thank you," said David. "I had a lot of fun researching that piece."

"Our consulates in Central America have been following their operations for about seven years," Humberto began. "They're a group of wealthy entrepreneurs who have bought thousands of acres of land and are creating new towns built onto existing villages. In fact, they're employing entire villages in their projects. This is very good, as you know, because the large cities can't offer them good jobs, housing or sanitation. They just go to starve or get killed in some rotten shanty town. The people from the villages are much better off when they can remain in the countryside."

"This sounds like quite an undertaking. Just how wealthy are these folks?" Carlos enquired.

"They are five billionaires. Together, they're worth something around 60 billion, in American dollars," Humberto responded, with a winning smile. "The villagers refer to them simply as *El Cinco*, 'The Five.' Their corporation is called Livelihood Systems, Inc., or LSI, for short. They made a lot of friends because they provided thousands of new jobs and we hear they pay good wages. They sponsored fiestas and paid for the entertainment and bussed hundreds of farmers in from the hinterlands. Every year the villagers saw new towns under construction, rising from the ashes of the last devastating hurricane. They are renewing the land and giving a new life to the people. Now, they are a legend. The villagers renamed them 'The Amazing Five,' then, 'The Daring Five' or 'Those Mysterious Five.' They couldn't agree on one way to praise them so they finally settled on El Cinco. To the villagers, El Cinco are a mysterious bunch. They rarely make public appearances. They grant the press one or two interviews a year with their spokesperson."

"Sounds like El Cinco are building the Third Way," said David. "What do you think about that?"

"That's my take, exactly," said Humberto, with an intense gleam in his eye. "They are definitely combining economic efficiency with a new kind of human development."

"Fascinating," Carlos mused, "but they must have made some enemies along the way. How could they assemble all of that land to build new towns without ticking a few people off? You know that the richest ten percent of the population has more income than eighty percent of the population in Rocadura."

"We don't know how they acquired so much land, and of course, that's for you to find out."

The customary smile in Humberto's eyes disappeared when he said, "But I must caution you that LSI does have some powerful enemies. One of their villages was attacked by the right wing organization called 'Freedom's Way.' It was reported in the Rocaduran press that this is a new guerilla group which is based in the mountains northwest of El Cedro. They attacked the Las Faldas new town and managed to destroy some ethanol storage tanks, before they were repelled by LSI security forces. You'll need to keep on your toes a bit."

"I knew it was all too good to be true—I mean about LSI," Carlos growled. "Something good comes into the world and something bad rises to meet it. I'm glad you told us. We'll take some precautions."

Carlos paused, then asked warily, "Are there any other visitors we should know about?"

Humberto smiled a knowing smile underneath his immaculate handle bar mustache.

"Why yes. We haven't gotten inside their organization, but we have high quality external surveillance. They have been visited by major bankers from Brazil, Columbia, Venezuela and Argentina. They have also been visited by representatives from the Vatican."

"No kidding," mused David, "the Pope is onto them already?"

"Oh, yes. But I've saved the most interesting visitor for last. He's an Islamic leader with high-level credentials."

"Okay, so the CIA checked this guy out, right?"

"You can believe we checked him out, right down to his shoe size. His family has strong ties to the U.S. Politically, he is well-known as a peacemaker. He's the Jimmy Carter of Mecca. We believe he came to find out what the Constellation is all about, just like you guys. He spent most of his time with a Catholic priest who helped found the Constellation."

"Well, that's a relief! The last thing I need to hear is that the Constellation is under attack by Islam," asserted Carlos.

"No problem, friend," smiled Humberto. "They're looking for solutions, and the Constellation offers something of value to them."

"I understand LSI agreed to let us visit them for a few weeks because they're ready to share their technology and planning principles," said David. "Why are they beginning to open up to outsiders, at this time?"

Humberto smiled. "I can only guess, but after our consulate reported the attack on Las Faldas, they may be looking for friends of an international nature. One way to acquire friends is to share what you have. Besides, when you're doing something as big as LSI is, things *will* get political, sooner than later."

"But why did they choose our firm?" asked David.

"According to their chief planner, Fredrico de la Chica," said Humberto, "you share some common planning principles and Europa has a goal of creating job opportunities in new towns instead of merely building more bedroom communities. Secondly, Europa has built many fuel ethanol plants—so you're familiar with that technology. Lastly, we recommended you two specifically. Then, El Cinco no doubt ran a background check on you, which you must have passed, although, I'll be damned if I know how," chided Humberto.

"It's because I know how to dance at fiestacitas," beamed Carlos, "and *El Gringo*, here, wrote three articles on why the latest solar cells are the best thing since the samba."

"We know little more, except that they are definitely creating livelihoods," said Humberto. "Let me show you a video. This is a press conference with El Cinco. The enchanting lady is Conchita Seguras, their spokesperson."

Humberto inserted a video into the player.

As soon as David saw the "enchanting lady," he knew what Humberto was talking about. She stood on a stage with a microphone. She had dark hair with soft brown highlights. Her eyes were also soft brown. She was a tall woman with the kind of easy dignity that comes to those who know who they are and what they're about. David watched her every move, hardly hearing her words. When he finally regained his self-awareness he heard her speak of the number of jobs being created in the new towns they were building.

"In the last four years, we've created one hundred and twenty-two thousand jobs," Conchita Seguras announced. "Now, we're creating jobs at the rate of twenty-four thousand per year, and growing. El Cinco have seven more new towns under development and fourteen more in preliminary planning and land acquisition. We're planning buildout of each new town with a population of 60,000 people. If all goes well, we'll build an economic structure that will support over one million people in 21 new towns. And we'll do it Constellation Style!"

There was an immediate ovation as the camera panned an audience of thousands of exuberant people. There were colorful decorations down the street and a banner that read, "*Viva La Constelacion*" and another that read, "*Feria de las Faldas*."

"As Robert Redford said in *Butch Cassidy and the Sundance Kid*, 'Who are those guys?'" David asked. "And what is Constellation Style?"

"I don't know," said Humberto. "Believe me, I am as curious as you are, and I'll be waiting with no patience at all until I get your first report. Our consulates can only go so far with El Cinco. Well, friends, I've got a ten o'clock meeting coming up, and I need to prepare. You can pick up an information packet on El Cedro from Marge, out front. Good hunting, gentlemen."

Chapter 2
THE BEST KEPT SECRET IN ECONOMICS

The flight left Washington thirty minutes behind schedule. David and Carlos changed planes in Houston and were soon flying over the Gulf of Mexico.

"I'm glad that we have good weather," said Carlos, "I've had some bumpy trips in the past…" He stopped in mid-sentence, thinking that it would be unwise to start telling horror stories on the way over.

David showed no concern. He was looking out the window at a magnificent scene of towering cumulus clouds, billowing high above the airplane.

"These clouds remind me of Emmanuel Kant's essay 'On the Beautiful and the Sublime,'" David explained. "He said when we see the awesome creative power of nature, like a star-studded night sky, we can be overcome with a feeling of the vastness of nature. We can't grasp it in its totality, the mystery of nature, so it transcends us and we're awed. When we relax and accept it, this emotional state may transform into a feeling of the sublime. When the sublime is combined with the valuing of Beauty, Kant defined that feeling as 'splendid.'"

"That sounds like something worth reading. Where did you come across *that* piece of work?" Carlos wondered.

"Well, you know how the Jesuits are on philosophy. They want you to sample what the major philosophers have said, so you learn how to make distinctions about what is true and what is false. At Loyola, Kant was required reading."

David thought back to those days in Chicago, and how he struggled with Kant's writings. He decided that if he could grasp what Kant was saying, no one would ever "snow" him again. Sure, it was a presumptuous boast, but it sounded good at the time.

"I've never had a peak experience like that," Carlos said, feeling he had missed something important in life. "How does it happen?"

"Well, you can't make it happen. It just happens to you. I've had two in my life and I understand from the literature that it's not all that rare. It seems to happen with people who are creative or striving for self-fulfillment. Many people have peak experiences during really good sex with someone they deeply love. That's the most common way it happens."

Carlos reflected. "Oh, well," he said with a rakish grin, "I guess I *have* had a peak experience or two."

I'll bet not, thought David.

"I'm not talking about knock your socks off sex with a lusty vixen. Not to say that it can't be really mind-blowing. A peak experience in sex is most often found when two people reach a new level of sweet security and deep love with each other. Peak experiences always involve the whole person, which means there has to be a spiritual dimension because we are body, mind and soul."

"Well, now you're getting into that thing I call total commitment territory. I'm not ready for that yet."

As the long flight over the Gulf of Mexico continued, David's thoughts drifted back to his first peak experience—the love of his life, his wife, Linda. They had been dating for a year and had fallen deeply in love and were engaged. They had just spent a weekend at his parents' house. She had apparently gone into the situation with some apprehension about how she would be received. As the weekend advanced, Linda grew to know she was very happily embraced by both his mother and father. More than simply approving of her, they warmly wanted her to join the family. She was overcome with heartfelt affection and a huge relief from her anxiety. David only discovered this in perfect hindsight. In Linda's heart, mind and soul, all of the barriers had fallen away. At last she knew that he was hers and she was his.

When they returned home, David and Linda immediately found themselves in bed together. David was astonished by her radiance, her pure lovingness. He sensed she was transported into a new realm of love even as he approached with his first caress. Then, gradually, he was transported with her. All was unconsciously understood in the most perfect way. There was no holding back, as all of their being was given to each other in that moment of everything is just rightness, everything is full and complete. David could still envision her transformed beauty lying out before him. She was glowing with warmth, lush, giving her whole self to him in those extraordinary moments. They had gone into a state of sweet oblivion, where all cares vanish and all consciousness is lost, except in the act of loving. That was the day when the real wedding vows were given to each other. The formal ceremony would be a gift to family and friends.

David was brought out of his reverie by the voice of the captain: "We'll be landing in Las Palmas in twenty minutes. Thank you for flying with Latin Express."

The plane landed in Las Palmas on the steamy hot coast of Rocadura. As they stepped off the plane onto the runway, the impact of the heat and ninety-eight percent humidity was instant. Sweat formed on David's body in places he'd forgotten existed. The airport was surrounded by palm trees and dense jungle covering the hillsides.

This was a point of entry into the country, and everyone had to go through Customs. David was ahead of Carlos in the line. The sign over the door read: "*Departamento de Salud.*" As David entered the tiny room, he was greeted politely by a heavyset woman in a white uniform. She was seated next to a cabinet with a countertop stocked with syringes. She motioned for him to sit down in the chair beside the cabinet. She asked to see his vaccination record. When she told him he would need a smallpox vaccination, David protested; he'd been told in the United States that they no longer required smallpox vaccinations in Rocadura. He knew there were more cases of smallpox caused by vaccinations than were occurring naturally, and David had been forewarned by a fellow passenger on the plane that he might have to bribe his way out of a vaccination.

Holding his billfold conspicuously before her, he said in Spanish, "I don't think I really need a vaccination, don't you agree?"

"Ah," she said, "you understand *Contrabando?*"

David offered her five dollars.

She asked, "Do you have any friends behind you who do not need vaccinations?"

How enterprising, thought David.

He said, "Yes," and described Carlos. She held up ten fingers. He gave her the ten dollars American and left.

He said quietly to Carlos as he passed him, "Tell her you are Carlos and she'll let you go."

When Carlos emerged, David asked him, "What did she do?"

"She put her finger over her lips and very gently rubbed my arm with a cotton swab. Then she said I was finished and waved me out with a coquettish little smile."

"Ah, bribery, it's the blessing of the bureaucratic class," laughed David, "but I didn't believe it when they told me it was a way of life here."

"Now you are a believer, hey, amigo?"

"Amen. And it's a real rush the first time around," said David, who was still musing about the fact that he had just broken the law and escaped without someone blowing a penalty whistle. He was relieved when their plane took off for El Cedro.

The next morning, David and Carlos were escorted to the LSI offices near the heart of downtown El Cedro, the capital of Rocadura. Their escort was Jaime Martin, a Costa Rican who was educated as a city planner at the Massachusetts Institute of Technology.

"MIT—'the Vatican of Engineering,'" David remarked.

"Yes," said Martin, "in those days it was the University of Georgia for administrators, MIT for technical knowledge and Hunter College for advocacy planning with the folks. I chose MIT for new town planning. I guess you'll be spending some time this morning with Fredrico de la Chica. He's LSI's chief planner."

"That's an unusual name," Carlos remarked, with a big smile, "*Chica* is colloquial for 'girlie.' Where is he from originally?"

"Fredrico is from Guadalajara, Mexico. He has been with LSI since the beginning. He is a rare combination among men: both a doer and a man of vision, and he has 'gracia.' But you will see for yourselves."

As they drove along, David gave a questioning look to Carlos and silently mouthed "Gracia?" with a shrug of the shoulders. Carlos waved him off until later.

LSI headquarters was a modern office building. In the lobby, Martin checked David and Carlos through security. The elevator required a voice code.

"This takes us to the main planning offices, which have special security. El Cinco visit here occasionally, and after a recent attempt to breach our security, we tightened things up a bit."

David and Carlos gave each other a look that said: "Hey, this could get rough," but they said nothing. Little did they know how rough it could get.

Martin led them to the main conference room where five men were getting their day started with coffee. Fredrico de la Chica recognized them and approached with a warm smile.

"Welcome to LSI. Please have some coffee, if you like. I'm here to spend the morning with you and much of the week ahead. I must visit Las Faldas, where this year's Feria will be held. I'd like for you to join me on that trip because you'll learn more in the field than in the office. And, of course, I'll be available to guide you through the Constellation."

Fredrico was a robust type. His big brown eyes looked as if they were spiced with taco seasoning—and they were laughing *with* you. He had a large, roundish head, black hair and the manner that was at once both gentle and deeply wise.

"That's very generous of you," Carlos said. "We're here to learn everything you want to tell us. It's our understanding you want to share your technology and planning techniques at this time."

"That's right. We've established a new urban development process and we want to share it with others. We believe it's time to establish communications with other new town planners and global corporations."

"Well, as you know," David said, "the president of Europa Development, Peter Erikson, has given us an indefinite leave of absence to learn all that we can about your work. We're very excited about the prospects of creating thousands of new jobs each year and in knowing how you've been able to accomplish that."

"Good. You've hit upon the driving force of LSI: to create sustainable employment with promising rising wages. We want to create millions of jobs in a system that advances human development."

"You're building the Third Way, aren't you?" asked David, revealing his excitement.

"The Third Way is many things to many people. The Constellation incorporates several concepts espoused by Third Way advocates, but it is much more. It is unique and still unfolding before our eyes."

"Fascinating!" David exclaimed, struggling to conceal his passion, but still holding back, as he looked for the whole picture.

"That's heavy stuff if you can pull it off," said Carlos.

"I have this wonderful feeling that you have already pulled it off," David said with a heartfelt Irish smile.

"Well, I can see you are somewhat motivated to work with us," smiled Fredrico, with obvious pleasure.

"How did you get started on this path?" David asked.

"About nine years ago, we held a major planning conference in Sao Paulo. We looked at the world from a spiritual and economic perspective. We asked the hard questions about the future of South America, Central America and Mexico. The conference was planned for one week. Then, with everyone's enthusiastic consent, it was extended for another two weeks. We reached some very strong conclusions back in 1998 about global competition that stand to this day. Global competition has clashed up against strong human values like love of the family, a sense of community strength, and happiness in the workplace. We found that in industrialized societies, forty percent of the workers who possess the highest intelligence and skills are fully utilized and paid with comfortable, but declining wages. The middle thirty percent are in various states of anxiety about their security, with lower-paying jobs or they're the working poor with two jobs. The lower thirty percent are shoved aside into the welfare state—or starvation. They are told: We don't want you or need you. We'll pay to keep you away from us. Don't expect more from us, we're engaged in more important pursuits. We decided that this is no way to run a society—and it is up to planners and economists to solve these problems."

David liked Fredrico immediately. On initial contact he could read him instantly because you sensed the inner dignity of the man. Now, David understood what "*gracia*" meant.

Carlos said, "Capitalism, the free enterprise system, has been accepted around the world as the best way to create more jobs. Are you talking about some form of improved capitalism?"

"No. We have to go beyond capitalism if we're going to decrease the suffering in the world. There are too many people who are living on the margin, barely surviving. As things are going, capitalism will simply never reach them, or if it does, it will enslave them at the bottom of the economic pyramid. We have to build an economics of self-reliance and permanency, with jobs that have promise for a better future."

"You're painting a pretty bleak picture of capitalism here," Carlos allowed.

Fredrico looked at Carlos with a knowing smile, as if he had heard that assertion before and knew the answer well. "Once a year, the United Nations and the World Bank present this picture of unattended poverty and world suffering in their annual reports. Then it's quickly forgotten by the media in the industrialized countries. The reason: no one had a solution, so it was swept under the carpet. But sixty percent of the world's population is experiencing this agony on a daily basis."

"I've been tracking these conditions for so long that I find myself in full agreement with what you're saying," David affirmed.

"The driving force of the western industrialized economies has been how to direct capital to produce goods that people will buy, thereby making a satisfying profit for the producers while creating jobs for enough people to ward off revolution," Fredrico continued.

"Capital was supposed to create enough jobs so that enough money would trickle down to the lower levels of society. The result has been that three billion out of seven billion people enjoy a decent livelihood. But two billion out of seven billion people on the planet live in desperate poverty. Another two billion are barely surviving and have little hope for the future. And here is the kicker: by 2020, estimates project we'll have eight billion people on this planet. The conference representatives decided that there had to be a better way to create and sustain livelihoods—and it was our job to do so. The basic concepts were conceived, and after nine months of intensive work and creativity, the Constellation was born!"

David broke into laughter. "I'm sorry. I totally agree with what you're saying, but when you said nine months was the birth period it was just too coincidental!"

Fredrico laughed with David. "That is funny. It just never occurred to me."

Carlos was taken aback. "That's one helluva program to take on!"

David leaned back in his chair and instinctively put his fingers on his chin. "In a few words, what is the Constellation?" he asked.

Fredrico thought for a moment. He reached for a pitcher of water, poured a glass half full and took a drink. David and Carlos could see his concentration and intensity level gradually rise, then fall into self-assuredness.

"The Constellation is a set of seven or eight new towns that are economically integrated for self-sufficiency. That is to say, each new town provides what the others do not produce—and together they have all of the basic necessities of life. They export twenty-five percent of certain products to buy some luxuries. When three Constellations combine, with twenty-one new towns, they are freed from the market economy. They can produce or buy anything they need and plenty of luxury items. They are freed from the global market economy. They have transcended the rat race, with all of its anxiety and human suffering. They have a new freedom to enjoy life with family and friends. They can be true to themselves and they have the means to unfold their unique package of talents. The folks in Las Faldas that you are about to meet have promising livelihoods and no fear of losing their jobs because worker/entrepreneur cooperatives don't fire themselves. They find ways to move into the future together."

"Is the Constellation a product of liberation theology or Marxism?" asked Carlos, with his style of skeptical bluntness.

"No one in our planning conference espouses Marxism," Fredrico stated flatly. "I have never read Marx. Communism is a dead straw man. Socialism has not come forward with any viable alternatives. What we have designed is a journey to self-sufficiency. It goes beyond socialism and capitalism. The Constellation is a new phenomenon in the world. It is built on a strong understanding that in order to have 'the good person' you have to have 'the good society.' They are fundamental, as Abraham Maslow observed. You must have both or you have nothing worth sustaining. That's why conservatism is in awesome decline. Unbridled market forces have thrust a continual revolution of change on people, without solutions to achieve the values of equity, compassion, promising futures, stable family life and a good society."

"What about liberation theology?" asked Carlos.

"Liberation theology is primarily concerned with meeting the needs of the long suffering poor, or as the theologian Leonard Boff wrote: 'Liberation theology does not reflect on a theory but on the screaming, bloody reality of poverty, oppression and premature death.' Dealing directly with poverty is a valid necessity—in any human society or economic structure—okay? Unfortunately, liberation theology doesn't say *how* to accomplish that. The Constellation is a whole new approach to full employment. It is designed to meet human needs and self-actualization at several levels."

Fredrico received a telephone call. He listened for a minute, and said, "Good, thank you, Alberto." Then turning to David and Carlos, he said, "The video on the foundations of the Constellation is all set up in what we call the War Room. We do our strategic planning there."

"I've really been looking forward to this!" exclaimed David.

They walked down the hall and entered a huge multi-leveled room with very large video screens clustered in different areas. Computer control panels were everywhere and video map displays covered several walls. One section of the room had ten video maps mounted from floor to ceiling. One of the maps showed the Ethanol Production System, planned for seven new towns.

Another map showed twenty-one new towns with connecting lines showing rapid transit systems and expressways.

"This reminds me of Strategic Air Command Headquarters," said David. "No wonder you call it the War Room. All you need is a bank of red phones!"

Fredrico smiled knowingly.

"El Cinco continuously gives us everything we need to do the job. As you can see, they spared no expense."

Coffee and scones were provided as David and Carlos were seated in the viewing room.

"As you are about to see, the Constellation is built on one of the strongest foundations in the world—the Mondragon Complex in the Basque Province of Spain," Fredrico explained. "This video is an updated BBC documentary."

The title flashed on the screen.

JOURNEY TO SELF-RELIANCE: THE UNQUALIFIED SUCCESS OF MONDRAGON

The story began many years ago, in the northeast part of Spain, after the Spanish Civil War and the repressive years that followed.

The announcer began with a story about a priest and five young engineers. Old photographs were used to depict the scene.

"A priest named Jose Maria Arizmendiarietta established a technical school to train engineers to pass their exams at the University of Zaragoza. In 1952, eleven students passed their exams and after graduation, four of these engineers worked for a local foundry. When they rose to managerial positions, the engineers tried to institute democratic reforms that would place more control in the hands of the workers. The owners rebuffed the idea and expressed no desire to relinquish any authoritarian control. In 1954, these four engineers were joined by a fifth and they wanted to buy a small, bankrupt factory near Vitoria. Having no capital, they turned to the villagers to finance the new company. They raised $100,000 from approximately 100 villagers and founded Ulgor. They used the first letters of their names to form the name of their company. The villager's loans had no guarantee beyond the talents and personal integrity of the five engineers. After operating briefly in Vitoria, they moved to Mondragon in 1956 and built a new factory to manufacture Aladdin space heating stoves. The Aladdin space heaters were perfect for Mediterranean winters, where forty degrees required just the right amount of heat for a few months, not an expensive central heating system."

David and Carlos were entranced. They realized that what they were seeing had power, because of the incredible amount of money raised by the engineers in a small town.

"In twenty years, the Mondragon Complex created over one hundred worker-owned and managed cooperatives with nineteen thousand jobs. Instead of being 'dwarfed' by under capitalization, they broke the rules: they established their own bank to provide a steady flow of reliable investment capital. By 1998, Mondragon employed twenty thousand people, with revenues exceeding six billion dollars a year and assets of almost fourteen billion."

The bank appeared on the screen, a magnificent modern building sculpted into a hillside on the edge of Mondragon.

The announcer continued. "The Mondragon complex built most of Spain's household appliances, including washing machines and dryers, refrigerators, and stoves. Their industrial cooperatives manufactured electrical goods and machine tools. Mondragon exported twenty-five percent of their products to Europe. Out of the ashes of the post Civil War poverty years, Mondragon eventually rose to serve a region of over 100,000 people. They built their own schools with more than 50,000 students enrolled today. High school students can work their way through college or the Mondragon technical school in a cooperative called Allecoop. Other industrial cooperatives farm out work to Allecoop."

On screen, young people were shown working with loops of multi-colored wire, to form components for appliances.

"They have their own schools, businesses, banks, a Housing Division, and a chain of retail stores. They took control of their lives, their workplaces and their communities."

A chart appeared on the screen showing the structure of the Mondragon cooperatives.

MONDRAGON COOPERATIVES:

INDUSTRIAL	107
AGRICULTURAL	10
SERVICE SECTOR	6
RETAIL	5
HOUSING	15
EDUCATIONAL	46
SUPPORT	10
	199

David found himself entranced as the film unfolded the wonderful story of Mondragon. He realized he had finally found what he had been looking for all of these years. Mondragon was a fantastic springboard into a new and exciting way for people to live happier lives, to have personal validity and a friendly, solid community.

The film's announcer continued.

"Jobs were created in rapid order. The cooperators have an Empresarial Division at the bank responsible for establishing new businesses and guiding them to success. When a group of local people come forward with an idea for a start-up business the Empresarial Division works with them to draw up a business plan. Research and design of the plan can take up to two years, including the potentials for exporting."

"That's impressive," said Carlos.

The announcer continued.

"The bank then loans them the start-up capital and closely monitors their progress. At the first signs of trouble with inventory or cash flow, the bank steps in to help the company to make the necessary adjustments. The system has an exceptional success rate: only three businesses have been lost in the first forty years."

The screen displayed the bank's graphic tracking system for each business. Flat television screens wrapped around the room, forming a band of colorful computer graphics at waist height, up to the ceiling.

"The bank rapidly increased its capital in this manner to carefully protect its investment, to maintain full employment and conserve capital. As we know, a large percentage of all start-up businesses in the U.S. fail in the first five years. The main reason for this is lack of capital when it is most needed. Bad management decisions are another major problem. How did the

Mondragon bank get around that? First and foremost, they have a policy of protecting the people in their businesses. They have very few layoffs. If the group requires a new manager one is hired, but the retired manager is retained in the firm. If the product is not selling, the bank helps the group design a new product. If they need more capital, the bank provides it, if it makes sense to loan more cash. They are a highly flexible, democratic cooperative."

Carlos whispered to David. "It surprises me that I haven't come across Mondragon before. You would think that an economic model *that* successful would have been all over the news."

"Carlos," Fredrico said, "it's the best kept secret in economics. The first BBC film on Mondragon was out, I believe in 1982. It should have been shown on TV over and over again. The fact that it wasn't shown, tells me that the media was controlled by those who refused to believe there is a real alternative to the rat race."

"The top rats like it that way," smiled David.

"Mondragon has had a web site dating back at least to 1999," Fredrico informed them.

A chart came on the screen showing how the cooperatives use their profits to drive their economic engine:

PROFITS/SURPLUS:

RETIREMENT   70% (AVAILABLE FOR INVESTMENT)
CAPITAL RESERVES 20% (AVAILABLE FOR INVESTMENT)
CHARITY/COMMUNITY 10%

The announcer resumed. "Mondragon uses its own capital to create new jobs. Seventy percent of profits are set aside for retirement and these funds are available for investment in new cooperatives as well as for modernizing existing ones. When combined with capital reserves, fully ninety percent of profits are available for reinvestment. This guarantees a strong, well-financed group of cooperatives that can weather the storms of national and international depression, inflation and other hard times.

"The average worker-owner retires after twenty-five years and receives a $100,000 lump sum payment and a pension of seventy percent of average earnings for the last five years of employment."

Another chart appeared showing pay scales and the gap between the lowest paid entry level and the highest paid worker.

MONDRAGON PAY SOLIDARITY

"The Co-ops will practice both external and internal pay solidarity. Internally, the pay factor between the lowest paid and the highest paid member shall not exceed a factor of 1 to 6.

"As Jose Maria Arizmendiarrieta, a founder of Mondragon wrote: 'Cooperation is the authentic integration of people in the economic and social process that shapes a new social order; the cooperators must make this objective extend to all those who hunger and thirst for justice in the working world.'"

"And just think," whispered David, "American CEOs pay themselves 140 times, or more, than the entry level wage!"

The announcer continued. "The Mondragon success story has two major achievements to share with the world at large: first, it shows what wise, good-hearted investors can do. There is a world of difference between a capitalist that is solely seeking bigger profits and a wise capitalizer who has the best interests of people and families at heart. Secondly, under Spanish law, the worker-owners were classified as self-employed. In the beginning, they had to set up their own health care, pensions, and unemployment insurance, without Social Security. Combine these achievements with their banking capability and it is clear that Mondragon is a complete, self-sufficient economic system. It stands today as a splendid alternative to the global competition economy."

The film ended with a panoramic fly over view of the sprawling Mondragon Complex. Ultra modern designs showed the forward vision and creativity of the Mondragon people.

"It's a mind-blowing self-sufficient economic system!" David exclaimed as he rose from his chair with a burst of energy. "I love it! Amazing! It *is* the best kept secret in economics!"

"Yes," said Fredrico, "and now you have some insight into El Cinco. They are the wise and good-hearted capitalizers. They're a new breed of bankers with a providential vision of community building."

"This story is too powerful to stay hidden for much longer," said David. "I love the way they accumulated so much working capital to achieve independence."

"You know, many people have seen a Mondragon film," Fredrico said, recalling his past efforts to spread the word about its undeniable success.

"The cooperative folks told me some key senators were so charged up by it, they showed it to some of President Johnson's cabinet. But, nothing came of it and I think I know why. The power structure didn't believe such a system was possible in the United States. They were frozen by political gridlock and their loyalties to business interests. Otherwise they would have explored this providential alternative to business as usual."

"Since it was a film about cooperatives, I can imagine that many corporate executives would not be too interested," offered Carlos.

"While there are some really big cooperatives in the U.S., they don't have your mainstream corporate interest in bigger and better profits."

"No doubt about that," said Fredrico. "The decisions of corporations put profits and stockholders first. The decisions of Mondragon put people and families first."

"Exactly," smiled David, "and I'm beginning to see that as a worker-owner, you're going to be a humble boss and a cocky worker!"

"That's true in the Constellation!" laughed Fredrico. "But you couldn't see that level of freedom in the original Mondragon film. They just looked like very hard working souls. I personally showed the Mondragon film at four American universities. In the discussion period afterwards, it was clear most people were in favor of the ideas offered, but were skeptical that anyone could make it work in the United States. Some thought the Basques were successful because they were one homogenous culture with the same religion, but that's just a cheap cop-out. Mondragon flourishes while free enterprise jobs get lower pay, reduced pensions, and far fewer family-life rewards. Capitalism equals Anxiety with a capital 'A' for most people now."

"I can see where Mondragon has worked for the Basques, but overall, I think free enterprise is still the best system when it comes to creating jobs on a worldwide basis," said Carlos.

"That, I'm afraid, is an argument from the past," said Fredrico. "When global competition came on the scene, free enterprise was transformed into a 'downsizing machine' resulting in lower paying jobs. Many analysts concluded that creating secure jobs with adequate pay is the main thing that global competition can't deliver. Clearly, we need a new approach. Don't you see the possibilities of Mondragon as a basis for a totally new economic system?"

"I see the possibility," answered Carlos, "but globally, it's a long, hard road. I see implementation problems that, to me, are virtually insurmountable."

David smiled. "Not if enough people want to shift into a more happy economic structure, with sweet security for the basic necessities of life, and demand that it be put in place with all due haste. It'll be interesting to see how the Constellation compares with the Mondragon story."

"Well, we've added a few new tricks," Fredrico said, with a smile that lit up like Times Square. "Gentlemen, it's time to take a break. Allow me to buy lunch downtown at the Alcazar, one of those old-world Spanish restaurants. It has a spectacular view of El Cedro."

"Ahhhhhhh," crooned Carlos, like a famished animal, "that sounds delightful."

"Let's go!" said David. "I can hear my little fat cells calling out to me now."

Chapter 3
THE CORNERSTONE CONSTELLATION

David and Carlos strolled through narrow cobblestone streets, amidst the high-pitched, late morning activity. The vendors were doing a good pre-lunch business. They worked out of stalls full of produce, which lined the sidewalk for a full block. There were huge baskets brimming full with avocados, plantains, peppers, and long rows of dried beans.

"This must be the largest farmer's market in El Cedro," said David.

"I think you're right. Humberto told me that much of this produce comes from huge farms in Rocadura owned by transplanted Mennonites from the U.S."

"What a pity!" moaned David. "I was just thinking, that at least the Rocadurans have a strong domestic farming economy. How would the Mennonites get such a large market share in a strange land?"

"They grow very healthy crops and package them nicely at competitive prices. That's why the restaurants favor them. I'm guessing that it was just a matter of free market economics."

As they strolled, David's soul was filled with richness, joy and the full assurance that he was, here and now, participating in that vision he first experienced when he read "Bucky" Fuller's book. Mondragon was such a powerfully personal experience. He felt so alive. It was a new romance of his soul. He knew that Mondragon was just the beginning of a new adventure. He was thrown back to look at his roots, his reason for being, his path in life. To begin with, he had listened to the words of Christ and had found the ring of truth—the only truth that mattered to him. Nothing else rang so true. He had learned from philosophy to focus on goodness, truth and beauty, the eternal triad of fulfillment all wise men have embraced as the highest values of humankind. But Christ taught the meaning of love. "Love and do what you will," wrote Saint Augustine. *Still, be very careful how you define love,* David added. It is well known that St. Augustine began his life as a womanizer. He had gone through the door of lust and come out on the other side, having learned about God's love for us.

The death of David's wife was a flashback that he did not want, but it came in this rush of things to see and face and grow with. He envisioned the truck rolled over on its side. Once again, he saw the ambulance and the medics at the roadside. For the hundredth time he relived the moment when he saw she was dead, her body laid out on a stretcher. David pulled himself back into the present as fast as he could. Be here now, be here now, he repeated to himself, be here now. Be here now. He began to look around. Tears rolled down his cheeks. He remembered where he was, walking to the restaurant with Carlos.

"What's the matter, man?" asked Carlos.

"Flashback," was all he could say, as he wiped away his tears.

"Oh, Linda," said Carlos softly. He had seen this happen to David before.

They walked along in silence, while David pulled himself back together. Carlos tried to think of something comforting to say, but dealing with death and God were not his strong suits.

"They say it takes two years to get over it," said David. "I'm just about there."

"Hang in there, man," was all Carlos could say.

"Thanks. I'm okay now."

As they walked along, they saw that the buildings were all finished with stucco and painted in pastel colors. Balconies with wrought iron lined the street, with occasional flashes of red geraniums hanging gaily out of flower boxes. Wrought iron gates opened into inner courtyards with water fountains or statutes. David thought this was just like being in Seville and he was amazed at how the Spanish style had been transported halfway around the world. It was the same, identical model for the entire city, he thought, as if whole towns had been lifted from Spain and placed in Rocadura, Columbia, Venezuela. It was such a pure design. It worked very well in the warmer climates. It was beautiful. *Why change for the sake of change?* he thought.

Located on a small hill, the Alcazar restaurant was an old, weathered establishment in a setting of green palm fronds and flowering bougainvilleas. There were signs of wear and tear, which added to the old-world ambience. There were cracks in some of the tiles, and places that had been worn down with time. As they entered, they saw three men sitting at a large tiled bar drinking dry white wine. David and Carlos passed through three archways, decorated with Baroque Spanish tiles colored with blue and green on white. David felt at home in the Alcazar and he imagined it to be the home-away-from-home of many men and women. They were greeted by Fredrico, who stood in the waiting area. He led them to the second floor to a table on the balcony. From this elevated vantage point, they had a clear view of a massive tropical green hill rising above the city.

"Excellent choice, Fredrico," said David. "And I'll bet the cuisine is as good as the view."

"Thank you, David. We're on a working holiday, so I hope that you will you join me in some wine with the meal?" David nodded enthusiastically.

"*Como no, señor?*" Carlos asked.

"Please call me Fredrico. And would you like red or white?"

"Red would be fine with me," David said. Carlos nodded.

"Would you bring me a bottle of *Gran Sangre de Toro?*" Fredrico said to the waiter in Spanish.

They had all ordered a cup of *Caldo Gallego*, a hearty soup of cabbage and potatoes, from Galicia, in the northwest part of Spain. Fredrico insisted on ordering an appetizer of fried chorizo sausage, scallops and shrimp. They all agreed on the house specialty, *Paella Valenciana*, for the main dish.

"So, Fredrico," David said, "you were telling us that the Constellation concept began to crystallize at the planning conference in Sao Paulo. How do you feel it compares to Mondragon?"

"The Constellation has many facets, like a diamond and Mondragon is the foundation of those facets. Mondragon had become a forgotten island unto itself in the world of economists. It didn't fit their global competition models, so they conveniently forgot it existed! But LSI is using virtually everything in the Mondragon system. The Constellation has its own banking system with an entrepreneurial division, just as in Mondragon. It has a cooperative structure and an internal management system similar to Mondragon's, with one person, one vote. The general manager of each cooperative is elected by the entire organization. It's a democratic arrangement with top-flight management that has creative freedom."

Fredrico paused for a sip of wine. He smiled approvingly.

"That's a hearty wine, but it is smooth," David said.

"Yes, it's one of my favorites," Carlos agreed, but you must be careful to order the *Gran Sangre de Toro*, rather than the *Sangre de Toro*, unless you want a very strong wine."

"I'll remember that."

"The Constellation goes well beyond the Mondragon model," continued Fredrico. "It produces more wealth for each individual and family and makes more provisions for the future."

"It provides economic permanence, rather than cowboy capitalism for a few?"

"Precisely. Remember, we had to focus on the lower sixty percent of the world population who are struggling to survive."

"But they have just as much opportunity as everyone else," said Carlos. "They just have to roll up their sleeves and go to work."

"I think it was Mortimer Adler who said, 'the problem with capitalists is that there are not enough of them!'" Fredrico said with a robust laugh.

David thought a minute. "There are too few capitalists who make big bucks and too many people who don't."

"Exactly," Fredrico answered. "And even the jobs that are created are often taken away at the whim of the corporations, who use mysterious market forces to explain every manner of cruel action against employees."

"No permanency," responded David. "Great sport for the higher echelons...anxiety for those in worker hell."

Fredrico's eyes lit up. "But when we realized we could go beyond the Mondragon model and that we were on the verge of passing over a new historic threshold, we were magnificently energized. We were alive, working in a new dimension. We could envision the flowering of a whole new way of making a living."

Fredrico smiled with his now familiar, joyful, knowing look.

The waiters brought the *Caldo Gallego* and the fried seafood appetizers.

"Man, this is delicious," said David, as he lustily lapped up the soup. "They have another hearty soup that I learned about during a visit to Santiago de Compostela. It's called Fabada Asturiana. It's a white bean soup made with chorizo sausage, ham, onions and saffron. Mighty fortifying. Those Gallicians know how to feed a person with simple fare turned into a gourmet meal. The climate is much like Ireland's, so it's hot cabbage and potato soup and the like, to warm the soul."

"I've read about it, but never had a chance to visit," Fredrico said. "Did you see the great cathedral which holds the remains of St. James?"

"Oh yes! He is the patron saint of Spain. He is enshrined in Cathedral of Santiago de Compostela. I'll never forget the column at one of the entries. I think it's called El Portico de Gloria. It has a hand print sculptured right on the stone. Pilgrims for centuries have placed their hands onto that place until it has become so hollowed out that you place your hand way *into* the hand print. When I was there, it was about half of an inch deep. It gives you an incredible feeling about the millions of souls who touched where you have, and lived and died. You get this unearthly feeling of unity with past lives. The place is filled with mysticism."

"Spain is so full of historical experiences that you get caught up with the souls of the past," said Carlos. "You can travel for years in Spain and never touch all of its treasures. Even James Michener, with his fifty researchers and his nine hundred page opus *Iberia* could only highlight the depth of Spanish history."

"Fredrico," said David, "when I was in the cathedral, they told me this incredible story about the Miracle of the Botafumero. The botafumero is a four hundred pound incense burner. It was almost five feet tall and plated with silver. They would swing it from the ceiling, with a great arc across the nave of the cathedral. In the 12th century and beyond, pilgrims came from all over Europe to visit the shrine of St. James. They got within two days of the town after weeks of traveling and they wouldn't stop to take a bath. As they entered the cathedral, you can just imagine…the stench was incredible! So, the priests would swing this gigantic incense burner to mask the awesome odor. Well, the legend goes that, at the very peak of the arc, the chain broke! It could have hit the wall and dropped, killing five or ten people, but it didn't. The botafumero sailed out an open window at its apogee. It was considered a miracle that no one was hurt."

The waiters arrived with a huge paella pan and served it steaming hot in shallow bowls with a Spanish flair, typical of the mother country. David noticed all the waiters were male, as in Old Spain. The soft sound of a Spanish flamenco guitar playing nearby enlivened the mood of the three men.

"What about buying enough land for all of your new town needs?" asked Carlos. "How did you deal with the rich land owners?"

"It was very tough in the beginning. And this is the story of how the first Constellation got started. We call it the Cornerstone Constellation and its center is the new town of Las Faldas del Cielo. The five billionaires had been brought together by Padre Parejo. Each of them had a major industry that was critical to building the new towns. They hired me and several other planners to design new towns and we all soon agreed to follow the Mondragon model. When we began to buy the land, we were confronted with the usual government regulations over land use. There was a blockade of bureaucracy, corruption…demands for bribery."

"A way of life I hear," David smiled wryly.

"Yes, and even worse, the rich land owners wanted twice what the land was worth. Of course, they went to their old friends in high places to make sure they would make a huge profit on the land we wanted. Frankly, they had all of the power to stop our progress. We were stymied then, and it's an ongoing problem."

"It's the old Latino triad of power and influence," smiled Carlos with self-assuredness, "the government backed by the army, the rich landowners and the Church."

"Well, not quite," Fredrico corrected. "The Church was caught in the middle, trying to defend the poor. In those days the government needed desperately to find solutions to poverty, crime, and disease. Forty-five percent of the nation was unemployed or underemployed. The army was as poor as everyone else. This caused dangerous unrest among the young soldiers and officers. The young leaders demanded land and jobs for themselves and their friends, and they almost succeeded with two coup attempts. The breakout of threatening violence from within the Army was imminent. The government needed solutions."

"Desperation and fear of being trampled, eh?" asserted Carlos.

"That was about it for the ruling elite. And so it happened that Padre Parejo hit upon the idea of producing ethanol to gain leverage with the government. We showed them how we could use the Ingram process to produce ethanol vehicle fuel more cheaply than gasoline."

"The Neal Ingram process uses vegetative waste instead of expensive corn," said David. "How do you supply your feed stock for ethanol production?"

"We give our plants haircuts. We use cornstalks, rice husks and sugar cane stalks. It's very cheap. We can produce ethanol car fuel for 1.10 cents a gallon out of the refinery gate," replied Fredrico, "and then we add on our 15 cent profit and the government adds on taxes."

"We guaranteed the President that we would build enough ethanol plants to completely eliminate Rocadura's trade deficit from importing oil, which was about two billion dollars a year. In exchange, they would help us buy land at a reasonable price and most importantly, they would help us get clear title to the land. That was a major breakthrough, because it would ordinarily take years to get clear title. In exchange, we would create hundreds of thousands of jobs with the new towns, and dramatically increase the government's tax base. Also, they would let us establish worker-owned cooperatives and banks without a lot of government red tape. It was an offer they couldn't refuse. That is how we set up the whole system in Rocadura."

"I know why the land owners wanted that much for their land," said Carlos. "My family was in the same position once. The government wanted to buy my grandfather's estate for a land reform project. Ah, yes, and whose ox gets gored in the process? I'll tell you who gets gored: those families who worked for generations to build their fortunes; the people who used their wits to beat the competition and get ahead in life. When land is taken like that, people should be well-compensated…because the land is the wealth of all future generations of that family."

"And so they should," said Fredrico, disarmingly. "We paid them twenty-five to fifty percent above the market value of their land."

"Are they sorry they cut that deal now?" asked Carlos.

"Oh, I don't think so. They're all multimillionaires living like kings and queens. They don't have to work. They live off of their investments. If they don't squander their huge wealth in overindulgence, their children and grandchildren will live in luxury. Carlos, they could not deliver what we could deliver with the use of the land. The right and the left have failed to stand and deliver what's needed, while more and more people suffer and wait without hope. And don't forget that a billion people are still being gored by unemployment every day. How can anyone put the comfort of the top ten percent of a country above the ninety percent below? Well, of course that's untenable. Even the rich could see they would soon be crushed if they didn't find a way to create and establish decent livelihoods for the nation."

"Yes," said David, "I was just reading about how that happened in another Latin country. The rich finally woke up to the fact that they had to do something, but they didn't have any good ideas except jaw-boning about their goals…and no solutions."

"It was hard work, but now we have the solutions. We know how to produce much more for much less on the land—and how to distribute the wealth of the producers back to themselves. We can increase our buying power within the Constellation, in spite of the outside inflation rate. And,

Carlos, you can not turn back the clock. Too many people now know we can make a better life together, economically, socially and technologically."

Carlos was stunned silent. He had no answer for a moment. Then, as if to defend a point of honor, he said calmly, "The old ways die hard. The new ways must prove themselves ten times over, if they are to replace the way we do business now. Many corporations will go under if this new system is put in place on a large scale. To build something new, you must destroy the old."

"Not exactly," said Fredrico. "It's possible to work alongside of each other. Only a few corporations need to be replaced, and corporations die every day anyway, from failure to compete in the dog-eat-dog system. Many of the global corporations will be only marginally affected, except they must understand that their employees are living human beings, not a 'human resource commodity' to be used, abused and thrown away at the first opportunity."

"So, you want to create a perfect society…Utopia," Carlos asserted.

"You are very fond of labels, aren't you, Carlos? No, we have no illusions of creating a utopian dreamland. Are men and women perfect? We all must still work hard to produce what we need to have a comfortable life. In the Constellation, we all must work through the democratic process of determining salary increases for each other. We are struggling with that peer group evaluation process. We must determine how much we all want to give to those poor suffering folks that are desperately waiting to get into a Constellation. Should we give ten percent of our salary or eight percent? What do you do with slackers who drag everyone down? This is no Utopia, it's real."

"I understand what you're saying better now," Carlos said. "I think you've got something pretty good going here and I'm eager to see more."

"Good," Fredrico said as he paused and took a sip of wine. He looked out the window at the view of the forest green hillsides of El Cedro.

"Well, let me tell you about the fun we've got planned for you over the next week," Fredrico said, with a big smile. "Tomorrow morning, we'll have a little strategy session in the War Room. Then, in the afternoon, we'll join El Cinco in a workshop and you'll get to meet them personally. In the evening, I'm told Anita Avilar will give us one of her classic parties. Anita made her billions in hydroponics. You'll love her house. It's on a mountain overlooking El Cedro."

"Great!" said David. "I've been wondering when we could meet El Cinco."

"And party time, as well!" Carlos beamed.

"Then, we'll take a drive out to our prize new town, Las Faldas," said

Fredrico. "We'll be just in time to catch La Feria de Las Faldas. It's a major annual event."

"Ah!" smiled Carlos. "Another party in a town called 'The Skirts'?"

"Yes, and much more," Fredrico said, laughing at Carlos' boyish exuberance. "By the way, the full name of the town is Las Faldas del Cielo, the Skirts or Foothills of Heaven. You'll like La Feria de Las Faldas. You see, about twenty-five percent of our people prefer to work in farming, food processing and food sales. At harvest time, many of the villagers go to the farms to help bring in the crops and have harvest celebrations. It lets people stay close to the earth. They see firsthand how their food is raised and they love being in the country for campfires, pig roasts, and dances in the moonlight. The harvest takes about six weeks and the celebrations take two weeks. People come and go from the town to party with old friends and meet many new ones. You'll see for yourselves next weekend, that's when the harvest celebrations begin at Las Faldas."

"That reminds me of La Feria de Sevilla," said David. "They have a street party for over a week, with thousands from Europe attending. I mean, people actually backpacked in from Germany."

"Okay. Let's start planning together. See you at 9:00?"

"That's perfect," said David.

"Sounds like one helluva great schedule to me," said Carlos.

"Oh," said Fredrico, "I've been having so much fun with you fellows, I forgot to tell you about a certain risk factor. There's this organization called 'Freedom's Way.' They blew up one of our ethanol tanks with a truck bomb a few weeks ago. We've got some intelligence agents in the field trying to ferret them out of their snake hole. Until we do, we are on alert for another attack."

"Yes, Humberto told us about the guerillas during our visit with the State Department."

"Good. I didn't want to lead you into a situation that could be life-threatening without your full knowledge of the situation. If our agents report trouble ahead, I'll be sure to warn you in advance."

Fredrico gave Carlos and David a book and some recent articles on Mondragon, so they convened for the afternoon. David and Carlos agreed to meet for dinner at the hotel.

When he got back to his room, David unpacked some articles he had brought with him from the U.S. He came upon a photograph of Linda and immediately, his mind flashed back to the scene of the accident. She was so beautiful and only twenty-eight. She had tried to pass the truck, but she was in his blind spot on the right hand side when he swung in front of her. After he identified her, he had to drop to his knees to keep from passing out. Their love was so deep that he felt as if he had been hit in the head with a two-by-four.

"Put your head below your heart," said a voice nearby, and he unconsciously obeyed the voice. He felt the dizziness subside and disappear.

His mind flashed to the funeral, and he remembered how surprised he was that so many people came. He was deeply moved by their compassion. Afterwards, he went to Mass to receive grace from Holy Communion eleven days in row. It was his only consolation and his source of strength. David believed in the real presence of Christ in the Eucharist. He experienced direct and deep love from God when he received communion. To David, it was the easiest and most direct way to receive grace from God, and he often wondered how many people knew how easy and awesome that gift could be.

He thought that his faith was so strong that it would pull him through, but he underestimated the enemy and overestimated his inner strength. He cried each morning for days on end. The flashbacks would not go away. He had to live with her in his heart and soul even though she was gone. When love is deep, the price is very dear. Now, at last, the most horrific flashbacks were fading. He didn't wake up in the morning with that queasy, rocky, vulnerable sensation. He didn't have to brace himself against the shower wall to keep his knees from buckling. He knew it was all a psychological "bad think machine," but it took all of his spiritual courage to prevail against it. Now, he didn't have to fight with the gnawing anxiety of facing his own death head on. He had faced it and found his peace in God's unconditional love. Grace and healing time had finally won. He was strong again. He felt whole. David wondered if he would ever court another woman. Maybe it was best to stay single. Then, again…

His mind drifted to the video at the State Department of Conchita Seguras. He remembered how her dignity showed through her beauty.

Chapter 4
COLONEL SALDANA'S LAND WAR

Meanwhile, just sixty miles from Las Faldas, Colonel Victor Saldana was enjoying a holiday in the Hotel San Sabastian. Operating under the extreme right wing "Freedom's Way" cover, he was especially happy with his plan to destroy the entire Energy Technoparc at Las Faldas.

Saldana was a product of a harsh military life. He had worked his way to the top as a colonel by doing the dirty, cruel jobs. He had become an oppressor who took pride in his power and influence at each step up the ladder of rank. When it came to forcing the village peasants to fall in line, Saldana had few equals. His reputation for cruelty and vengeance on all who opposed him had become legend in the army.

As a demonstration of power to a small village, he once took two of the village's young men and forced them to dig two graves, six feet deep, for the first to oppose his rule. Then, he forced them to dig two more graves, six feet deep, until weak from exhaustion, they passed out. He told the villagers that he would not kill them, because they did not consciously disobey his orders. Instead, he ordered his men to lower them into the graves and to throw dirt upon their bodies, leaving their heads uncovered. Saldana left them to wake up, under guard, in this demeaned condition. Saldana had his men take photographs of people who protested openly at public events. Those determined to be conspiring against his rule were immediately shot. The attractive women, he arrested, raped and turned over to his men for more abuse. He used the ancient methods that most cruel men use: pushing the buttons of fear and hate, and attempted degradation to control not only the villagers but his own men as well. In his own mind, he had performed very well to "keep the lid on the cauldron" to ensure that economic growth could be continued to the benefit of the wealthy landowners and the government.

Just when Saldana was satisfied he had conquered all the competitive forces, the Catholic Church and the government had aligned with El Cinco to build a different kind of economic system. They claimed it was counter productive to have the Rocaduran army interfere with the domestic situation, except to protect the rights of individuals to build their own communities.

Saldana recalled how the Rocaduran army was left with no outside enemies. Communism had long since died. Guerrillas were no where to be found. Thus, for men like Saldana, the glory days were gone. His dreams to be a general and the undisputed head of the army were derailed. Even the leaders of *La Guardia Delantera*, the "Advance Guard," a rebel force led by a college professor, who originally had noble purposes, of a social democracy, lost himself in the headiness of raw, absolute power and had been captured. He allowed his organization to be financed by the drug cartel of Cali. The days of the Advance Guard, and their kind, were numbered, leaving the army in the most threatened position possible: there was no enemy left to fight! Saldana gave up hope in his career and retired from the Army with a full pension—even though he was strong for a man of fifty-five years. As he sipped a scotch at the hotel bar, he recalled his recent past and how he had been saved from a desperate situation. He was a man with a passion for extravagant living. He wanted to contact the guerillas in Columbia and work for the drug trade, but he knew that was extremely dangerous. One mistake and he could be eliminated at the whim of the leader. He was used to being the leader, with the power to kill those in his way, so that was not an easy choice for him.

It was during this distressing time that Saldana received a most welcome telephone call. He was invited to dinner by Raul Echeverria. Echeverria was a billionaire with vast holdings of Latin American real estate. He, too, had a reputation. Among the elite of Rocadura, Echeverria was known as "The House Dealer." He always entered negotiations from a strong hand—with the probabilities on his side. Saldana knew such an invitation meant that he was in a good, if not very strong, bargaining position. After all, he was invited with no solicitation on his part. It was a memorable evening for Saldana. The words that passed between the two men were emblazoned on his memory.

Saldana was greeted at the door by an armed security guard who was six feet four inches tall and a lean two hundred and twenty pounds. The guard recognized the colonel immediately, and flashed a comradely smile, as if to say, "We are in the same business."

"Mr. Echeverria is in the study. Go straight down that hall...second door on your left," said the guard as he motioned Saldana to lead the way. The guard walked behind Saldana and they entered the study together.

"Welcome! Welcome! Colonel Saldana," Echeverria announced with energy and warmth, as he extended his hand. "Please join me in a drink. I'm having twenty-one-year-old scotch..."

"That would be delightful," Saldana said, with his toothiest smile.

"Thank you, Jose, please pour the colonel a drink, and that will be all for now," said Echeverria to the guard. Jose handed it to Saldana.

"Chivas Regal?" Saldana ventured. "It's extraordinarily smooth."

"I know. It's so smooth, you don't realize how much you've had. I love to serve it to the young ladies at my parties."

"My sad experience is that most of them stay with champagne or wine."

"All too true. Well, how are things in the Army these days?"

"Pretty damn boring. The only action I've seen lately is when the young soldiers mount a protest against the poverty and unemployment of their friends. But I don't have to deal with that because I'm retired. I can tell you that nobody under my command would have been foolish enough to involve themselves in some stupid protest."

"I see," Echverria nodded, "that's what I expected to hear. The Army has had a long tradition in Rocadura of defending the property rights of the large landholders...wouldn't you say?"

"Yes, of course," he agreed, with a good idea of where this conversation was going.

"Well, now, the government doesn't defend all landholders like they did in the old days. As you know, they are picking winners and losers. The administration favors El Cinco, and they see to it that they can keep building those damned new towns everywhere—on everybody's land. They use several kinds of 'persuasion' if El Cinco can't get the land at their ridiculously low prices. They should not have done that—it's a violation of the capitalist system." His voice rose to a passionate tirade. "It is the unjust seizure of land!"

"I couldn't agree more," Saldana hummed. "The government is in bed with El Cinco, all right. This administration must be floating in their bribe money. They are whores, pure and simple. They just take the highest bribe and go with it."

"But this time is different. I offer more cash up front, and they tell me no. They will collect more, they say, from the new towns because they are creating jobs by the thousands. They will collect new tax revenues and pay themselves well, and legally. They claim that the new towns are the wave of the future and that I should join in a contract with El Cinco to develop my land. But I, for one, do not intend to stand by and watch my family's hard-earned twenty thousand acres be taken for a song and dance by El Cinco."

"Do you need someone to devise a plan?"

"I have some ideas. I have lots of friends who will join me. What I need is a strong man to do the detailed planning and to lead men in the field."

"Señor Echeverria," smiled Saldana, "you are talking to the right man. I hate their guts. Those bastards have ruined my career. I would love to bring them down."

"Good!" said Echeverria quickly, with an instantly satisfied expression. He sensed he had found a man to do his bidding, filling him with relief and elation.

The two men stood and shook hands. Then in a moment of emotion, reached out and embraced, briskly slapping each other on the back.

"All right, we have lots of work to do. First off, I want you to plan an attack on their ethanol storage tanks in Las Faldas. We must show them just how vulnerable they are and scare the hell out of them. Then, when they think they have secured their facilities, I want to hit them again, with a total wipe out of their damned Energy Technoparc." He gestured with a quick, motion of his hand, like a karate chop.

"I see. After the first hit, you want to let them rest for a while in a false sense of security, then take out their entire industrial capacity in one fell swoop," he said as he smashed his fist into his hand.

"That's right," Echeverria elated, with his passion kindled to a high pitch. "I want to play cat and mouse, and make them wonder who is after them, then forget that someone is after them…except for that dim uneasy feeling in the back of their minds."

"Well, then, I will hit them first with a truck full of ordinance, just enough to wipe out one or two ethanol tanks."

"Good!" shouted Echeverria. "I can hardly wait to read the newspaper!"

"Then, in about three or four months, depending on our intelligence, we'll attack from across the border with two helicopters armed to the teeth. In a matter of minutes those gunships will level the place with rockets and clear out."

"This will have to be a very well-kept secret," he cautioned. "You must tell no one that the attacks will be on Las Faldas…and you must not tell anyone that you know me."

"Of course," Saldana answered, reassuringly. "I'll be at total risk with you. From now on, we are as one. But tell me, why is Las Faldas the most strategic target?"

"It's their pride and joy. Of all their new towns, this one is the heart of it all. It is their favorite fiesta town. Wipe out their jobs in Las Faldas and you demoralize the entire group they call El Cinco. From then on, they will be forced to rebuild at huge expense. They will spend millions on security forces. We will slowly bring them to economic ruin. Then, it will be like the old days. My family wealth will be handed down from generation to generation and the peasants will always be with us to work the land."

"It's a good strategy. The Americans brought the Russians to disaster by forcing them to spend themselves into bankruptcy."

"We think alike, my friend," smiled Echeverria, "that is where I got the idea."

With that, the two men shook hands, made their goodbyes, and parted company. They would meet again in two days to work out details.

The first strike on Las Faldas was a tremendous success. With the element of surprise, Saldana loaded a truck with explosive charges, wired the accelerator to the floor and sent it through the wire fence surrounding the ethanol storage tanks. The flames shot up two hundred feet into the air while Saldana escaped to his car in the confusion on foot through a wooded area. He then boldly drove into Las Faldas, undetected, took a hotel room and went directly to the bar to settle his nerves. *To strike with violence is*, he thought, *a fantastic experience.* He knew from his past missions, it would take days to settle down from the enormous quantity of adrenaline that pumped through his system. After drinking three scotches, he relaxed enough to consider eating something. He had not eaten since breakfast. Still, he decided against it and went to his room to sleep.

Echeverria and his rich land holder friends were ecstatic when they read the morning newspaper. They held a party the following Friday that lasted until Sunday morning. The newspapers were full of stories about the new and mysterious guerilla group that claimed responsibility for the bombing, calling themselves "Freedom's Way."

Two months later, Colonel Saldana was ready to prepare for the second attack on Las Faldas. Unbeknownst to him, however, he had made one critical mistake. He had a series of flyers printed to build up the illusion of a large guerilla force, ready to pounce on El Cinco if they tried to "confiscate the people's land." The idea was to establish a reign of terror with a continuous flow of propaganda. Saldana was able to use an underground print shop that specialized in passport forgeries.

When Echeverria saw the printed flyers, he was delighted with the message that they were sending. However, in keeping with his patrician background, he insisted the flyers to be printed in royal purple. It was expensive and much more impressive, he thought.

El Cinco, in the meantime, had hired two ex-CIA operatives, Tom Foley and Steven Rankin, to track down the source of the flyers. They analyzed the ink on the paper, which was rarely used because of its expense. They traced the sales to all known sources. Eventually, they found the underground printing shop and went into their stake out mode.

Within four days, one of Colonel Saldana's most trusted lieutenants paid a visit to the shop to pick up flyers. Foley and Rankin sat in their van across the street from the print shop when a car drove up to the store and parked. A man got out of the car, looked casually around, and slipped into the store entrance.

"Did you check out the shoes?" Tom asked. "He's wearing 'civies' and Rocaduran Army issue boots."

"Very good! I missed that detail. He could be a gun for hire."

After a short wait, the agents watched the man load several boxes into the trunk of his car.

"What do you think? Looks like there are way too many boxes there for passports or driver's licenses."

"Yeah, unless you are providing for a full scale CIA invasion with a cast of thousands. There he goes. Let's check it out."

They followed the lieutenant to Saldana's headquarters, now operating out of the Hotel San Sabastian. Saldana had selected this particular hotel as his base of operations for two reasons. One, he had leased a secluded room on the roof that could be used for military operations meetings without being overheard by hotel employees or guests. Two, it was the perfect place for a military club—which provided the cover for his more important work.

And so it happened, on the following weekend, that Tom and Steve met Saldana in the luxuriously appointed lobby of the Hotel San Sabastian.

Saldana had taken his usual table at the bar, from which he caught a glimpse of something large and extraordinary floating in the lobby.

"It's a blimp!" Saldana gasped, as he grabbed his scotch and rushed into the lobby for a better look. Sure enough, it was a blimp, five feet long and floating right at him about twelve feet above the floor. The blimp stopped abruptly...took a ninety degree turn and revealed a sign on its port side which read: "SURPRISE ATTACK! TAKE THE CHAMPAGNE AND RUN!" Then, Saldana noticed the bottle of champagne that was hanging from the bottom of the blimp.

Saldana chuckled gleefully, as his eyes searched around the lobby. Quickly, he spotted Foley and Rankin with their hand-held remote controls. They were turning it again, revealing the sign on the other side of the blimp: "EXECUTIVE COMMITTEE MEETING—FOLLOWED BY OPEN BAR."

Saldana approached them and said, "What a piece of work! I *love* it! Are you here for a conference?"

"Well, yes, actually, we are," Steve smiled broadly. "We're here to sell this beautiful, floating, hunk of toy to any and all conferences that might come along. Hi. My name is Harry and this is Al."

"It's my pleasure to meet you, gentlemen. I haven't seen anything this much fun for a long time. What does one of these things cost?"

"The recommended sales price is five thousand American."

Saldana thought for a minute. He was flush with cash since his deal with Echeverria. He had a nearly unlimited expense account. But this would probably have to come out of his own pocket, since it was, after all, a toy. "Hmmmm," he said, "that's a bit dear."

"Well, let's see," Steve responded, "we have two demonstration models that have a few miles on them, but will last about three to five more years. We could sell one of those for a mere thousand."

The ego trip of being the "Remote Control General" at parties, meetings and conferences was too much for Saldana to bear. "You've got a deal. I'll take it!"

The deal was made. Foley and Rankin gave careful instructions to Saldana about the control of the blimp and exited the premises. They had just sold a blimp worth $5,000 to Saldana for $1,000. The value of the transaction for them was that these blimps were wired to pickup sound and transmit it over a considerable distance. Best of all, the bug could not be detected easily, since it was wired into the very structure of the blimp. They were counting on Saldana to examine the engine and passenger compartment very carefully, but not to destroy the blimp to find the bug. Immediately, Steve Foley made a telephone call to Fredrico.

"I have some really good sales news. Our product was purchased by our very favorite customer today."

Fredrico asked, "You mean those…" he hesitated, not wanting to give away information on the phone. "You mean those really expensive toys?"

"That's right. Research pays. We expect to send you a full accounting soon. Just thought you'd like to know. I think we could have sold two of them, but then we realized one could be dismantled for spare parts, if you know what I mean!"

"That's fantastic!" Fredrico shouted, not being able to muffle his excitement. "You're quite a salesman. We'll have to look into a bonus if the product is as successful in operation as it is in the salesroom."

"Well, we have every reason to believe that it will be and the timing is right."

"Wonderful!" Fredrico elated. "I'll look forward to your full accounting of the sales details."

"We'll have to be on our way now. Pleasant dreams tonight."

"Thanks again, Steve. And give my thanks to Tom. Good night."

That whole week, Tom and Steve monitored the meeting of the "military club." Finally, their persistence was rewarded in full, pressed down, shaken, overflowing. For what they heard was the final meeting before the major assault on Las Faldas.

"This is the last rehearsal," Colonel Saldana said, with calm understatement, looking around the room with his wild, hot, black eyes on each man. "On Sunday morning, two weeks after the Feria, our two helicopters will reach Las Faldas at thirty minutes after sunrise. They will close on the Energy Technoparc and fire at will until everything is destroyed. They will then fly to the hangar off Highway 11 and mysteriously disappear from the sky. El Cinco will send search helicopters immediately to look for us, but they will find nothing. We will be in our advanced camouflaged site in the mountains. The helicopters will be dismantled and loaded onto small trucks. While they search for the helicopters, we'll drive them across the border…here," he said, pointing to the location on the map. "The hangar will be converted back into a logging camp. If they come there they will find nothing but a logging operation. We can come back and use this site as many times as necessary to put an end to El Cinco. Any questions?"

No one responded. As Colonel Saldana was speaking, his voice was being audio taped by the blimp that was floating near the ceiling of the meeting room. Steve and Tom were receiving his every word in their van, parked within 500 feet of the hotel.

"Remember," he said, "the key to this attack is the element of surprise and a well-planned escape route. Never forget that. Your lives, and the lives of your comrades, depend on how well you execute your part of this campaign. Be strong and we will succeed."

Steve and Tom took off their headphones and looked knowingly, at each other as the meeting was dismissed. They gave each other the "high five" hand slap and laughed with full abandon.

"The CIA was never this much fun," said Steve as he shook his head, while he poured a Jack Daniels on the rocks.

"You got that right! I still can't get over how much he wanted that blimp!"

"Yeah, when they're as bad as they want to be, they have a whole bunch of weaknesses that they can't even see."

"But we still have to identify the exact site Saldana called off Highway 11."

"Hey! Research pays!" Tom strongly asserted, as he took another slow swig of Jack and swished it in his mouth. "Tomorrow we'll visit the land ownership files. We already know from following Saldana that Echeverria is the attacker. We'll look up the land ownership records and find out if there is a logical strike base from any of his properties."

"Echeverria owns several different sites ranging from six hundred to five thousand acres. Will we have time to find the launch site before their strike date?"

"Hell! We *have* to find it and we will!"

"Okay, okay, we'll sleep on it tonight and tomorrow we hit the deck running."

"Yes, my fearless partner, that's the program."

"Hey, come on, lighten up. We just got *their* fearless leader to lay out the entire plan to us—on tape!"

"Yeah," smiled Tom, "are we a piece of work, or what?"

"We *are* good at what we do," replied Steve, with a totally cocky grin and a twist of an imagined mustache. "Good night, my friend. Rest tonight that we've got 'em."

The next morning, Steve and Tom ate breakfast together and then paid a visit to the province's governmental center, where the best record of land ownership was kept.

Steve was studying a map that revealed a largely mountainous area.

Suddenly, he did a double take. "Tom, take a look at this…"

Tom looked at the place on the map where Steve was pointing. He read: "La Sierra Cueva." It was three acres of mountainous land owned by Echeverria, with a dirt road leading off of Highway 11. There could be no doubt. It was the only site that fit all of the criteria. They made a photo copy of the map and left, to call Fredrico.

"Hello, Fredrico. We have good news and other news," Steve said musically. "The good news is that we've discovered the plans of our client and where he lives. I'll drop off the details for you tomorrow."

"Good work, Steve!"

"The other news is that our client plans to visit Las Faldas in the not-to-distant future. So, you'll want to have a beautifully organized surprise party for him when he pays you a visit."

"You can bet on that! Are we talking a week or two?"

"No. It's about three weeks away. If you like, Tom and I will be happy to assist you in preparing your extravaganza."

"By all means. I'll tell Garcia to team up with you and get plans in place as soon as possible. Oh, yeah. Payday is on Friday. I'll get Garcia to cut a check for you guys with a ten percent bonus for outstanding work."

"Thanks, Fredrico. We'll give it all back to you at the Feria, and, man, will we get our money's worth!"

"I can't thank you guys enough. That's a real piece of work. I'm really looking forward to the details. I know I can sleep better now."

Chapter 5
THE SANDBOX

The morning sky was clear and bright as David and Carlos walked to LSI headquarters. The sweet smell of orchid trees was carried on the cool morning breeze. David and Carlos had never seen an orchid tree before. They stopped to examine the multitude of flowers.

"They look like orchids," said Carlos, "but they're smaller and they aren't as perfect as the orchid show variety."

"But it's still incredible to see a tree filled to abundance with small orchid flowers."

The trek between the hotel and LSI led them down a steep run of stone stairs, and along a paved walkway through lush gardens of philodendron and other tropical plants.

They entered LSI headquarters and they were immediately joined by a security guard who checked the I.D. cards Fredrico had given them. Once their clearance was approved, they were escorted to the War Room.

Fredrico rose from his seat at a conference table and greeted them with a heartfelt smile.

"Welcome aboard," he said, grasping their hands robustly. "I've looked forward to having two of the best planners in the U.S. to strategize with. It's going to be fun."

"I'm ready for some creative action," David said. "I just hope we're experienced enough to keep up with you."

"You're experienced enough, but that's not why LSI selected you. You two are *thinkers*. You have a foundation in philosophy, human values, and economics that few planners have. That's why you're the options men for Europa Development Corporation."

"Well, I have to tell you that I've been preparing for this opportunity my entire life," said David. "The anticipation of designing new towns with vast employment potentials is like a peak experience!"

"Hey," Carlos said, "it'll never be as good as a peak experience in sex, but at least it'll last longer!"

"The opportunity to create freely makes a person feel alive…it's pure play!"

"All right," beamed Fredrico, "I can see that you're both primed for a wide-open strategy session. Let's take off!"

There was a thoughtful pause, as the three men settled down to the creative process. In their practiced minds, they scanned the factors and examined the key driving forces involved in building first class new towns.

Carlos made the first offering: "If the Constellations are going to succeed, they need to find a way to be inclusive with the rest of the market. The global corporations are entrenched and they have powerful, far-reaching control structures established throughout the world. The question is, what's in it for them?"

"Well," said Fredrico, "as I mentioned earlier, it's possible to work alongside corporations. Only a few need to be replaced, we all know that corporations die every day anyway, from failure to compete by their own rules."

"Let's look at the corporations as our suppliers," said David. "We maintain our own economic and political freedom within the Constellations, but we invite corporations to sell us the tools and equipment we need to build new towns. Many corporations will treasure the business we can provide. There are thousands of new towns to be built around the world, Constellation Style, and thousands more waiting to be uplifted with a new economic life. Hell, it's a global market in new computers, ethanol fueled gas turbine engines producing electricity, hydrogen powered fuel cells, heavy equipment to excavate and move earth, and so on."

"That's good, David!" said Fredrico with passion. "I like that a lot!"

David elaborated: "Instead of everybody serving corporations in a master-slave state, the corporations serve the needs of people to become self-sufficient and still make money!"

"Now we're cookin'!" said Fredrico, fully enjoying David's contribution.

"Banks will have what they love the most: banking certainty," suggested Carlos. "The Constellation is comprised of hard physical assets built onto a sound, long-term infrastructure. These are bankable assets of the most solid order. You can build one Constellation and borrow on its future productivity to build the next."

"Then, there is the multiplier effect on the national economy," said David. "If we structure everything in the right way, we can create jobs that serve the Constellations on at least a one-to-one ratio. God, I love this! Think of it. Every time Constellation workers cash their paychecks, they go out into the economy and spend their money. This creates jobs supporting families with a newfound wealth, which they desperately need!"

"That's the spirit of Constellation planning," Fredrico said with heart. "It's to expand ways to make a decent living for all and to create sweet security for people to be free from economic anxiety."

"Man, you said it there!" said David. "People around the globe are yearning with all of their heart for an economic system that is *home*! They're weary to their bones from the anxiety of uncertainties. They feel like they could lose everything they've worked for with one stupid mistake on the job. One lapse of performance—you name it—the flu, a sick child, a medium-sized blunder and you're out! Sorry, says management, you are replaceable and we don't give a damn about you or your family. The bottom line is the *only* thing that counts to most CEOs. It's no wonder people around the globe are going on strike, rebelling, acting out their justified anger at totally insane economic systems."

"Padre Parejo gathered us all for Mass one day—I mean the five billionaires and the LSI staff," Fredrico smiled. "He said the economic system we are designing should be a blessing to everyone. No layoffs if at all possible, no intimidation. People suffer enough in this life. The workplace should be a blessing, where we work in happy relationships for a common purpose. More than anything, we should remember that Constellations will be built as a *blessing* to people."

"That's a great way to start the sandbox," said David. "It sets the tone perfectly."

"The sandbox?" asked Fredrico.

"Yeah," said David with a big smile. "That's what I named my experience in physical design classes in the school of architecture. We'd work and play for twelve hours at a stretch. It took so much time to draw plans and graphics and get it right. We would go sleep for five hours and do it all over again. The creative process was addictive. After a while, we were so giddy and loose that play took over completely. We became children again and we'd play until we couldn't think and then play some more!"

"A playful dash into creative heaven," suggested Fredrico. "Well, I've been there. I'll tell you later."

"That's what it is—nonstop creativity," enjoined Carlos. "You just *run* with it! Well, I've had some great experiences in that sandbox and I love it too!"

"Okay," said Carlos purposely, "we have a handle on the philosophy and some of the main assets of the Constellation. Now, what about acquiring the land?"

Then, Fredrico's eyes lit up, and he smiled in a way that suggested he was sure his audience would enjoy his answer.

"Buying the right kind of land in the right location has been one of our major adventures into creativity," he said with new vigor. "Early on, we discovered there was no rule stating all of the land owned and operated by a new town had to be in one big piece. We learned this when we first set out to supply seafood to the new towns. We established an aquaculture complex off of the Lemon Islands. Everything produced by this fish farming operation is dedicated to benefit the new towns. At the moment, we are exporting fifty percent of our daily catch but that will be reduced to around twenty-five percent as the new towns mature, and increase in population. We also have fish farms on nearby land that produce fast growing Tilapia and large Asian Shrimp. The families that work in fish farming are all part of the Constellation structure, in terms of salaries, fringe benefits and economic permanence. So, we buy as much land near a village as we can and then reach out into the hinterland as required. This dramatically lowers our land purchase costs because you are not compelled to buy many pieces of land at speculative prices. It raises transportation costs, but with very inexpensive energy, using our own ethanol, this is not really a problem."

"Outstanding," exclaimed David. "We need to use that technique in the U.S. as well. But what happens when you just can't make a deal, and the price is too high to make the numbers work?"

"Well, sometimes we can make a long term lease deal, but there are always the hard cases, where they just want far too much money. The big land barons own thousands of acres. They're the hardest cases. We're working with the governor of Viscaya Province to use eminent domain to acquire 10,000 acres or so. It will be a test case with enormous impact. If we succeed, it will establish precedents in law that are absolutely necessary to the development of future Constellations. But even if it succeeds, we will need fallback alternatives."

There was a pause while everyone considered the problem. Carlos and David began pacing around the War Room. David looked at the maps depicting the seven new towns of the Constellation. Finally, he had an offering: "The Constellation doesn't need to control the deeds of all properties in order to create an economy for human development. Once the entire community sees the huge benefits of what we're doing, they'll want to become a part of the Constellation. We then simply sign agreements with local landholders to come on board and enjoy the party. We have to design a deal they can't refuse."

Carlos said, "And when you own the only bank in your village and region, and you are *the* major employer, you find yourself in a very strong position. The Constellation can become a hero to the village community, and the town's people will encourage the local land owners to join in the economic opportunities."

"We just sign 'em up!" shouted David, rubbing his hands together with pure joy. "I love it!"

"I never thought of it like that!" answered Fredrico. "That's a major breakthrough. We just go out to those small businesses and landowners and we sign 'em up!" Then, Fredrico paused and reflected. "But, in the final analysis, people have to understand the enormous value of the Constellation before they'll join the cooperative structure."

"That's right. We design like hell, produce the blessing, and then it evolves into a big education project," David said.

"Fredrico, tell us more about your own new town design philosophy," Carlos enquired.

"I believe our new town designs should flow from the needs of the people," said Fredrico. "This is not an economic problem, it's a socioeconomic problem. The solution is to design a 'win-win' economic production *and* distribution system. To do this, you have to go outside the corporate competition and wealth distribution model. In a word, the Constellation transcends the concept and practice of 'global competition.'"

"That's quite a leap. How can you possibly avoid global competition?"

"By becoming self-sufficient. You do it by global cooperation instead of mutually destructive and unfair competition. Now, it's virtually impossible to make one new town self-sufficient. What we did was design seven new towns that supply each other in the basic necessities, a few luxuries and a permanent workplace." Fredrico paused to sip his coffee. Then, he reached into his desk drawer and pulled out several maps and graphics. "Let me show you," he said, as he laid the material out on the table. "One new town supplies timber, paper and cement, and housing construction; another, steel, appliances and sea food; a third has cotton, corn, soybeans and a chocolate factory; a fourth builds cars and transit systems, and makes wine and brandy. All of them provide vegetables, protein, and fruit. They're integrated vertically and horizontally, using the natural resources that are available. Finally, as I told you, they export twenty-five percent of their products and buy things that they can not easily produce—*for now.* Eventually, a complex of twenty-one new towns will produce or import anything that they really need."

"Ah, I see!" David said. "It's a woven cloth!"

"It's a powerful concept," Carlos allowed.

"With twenty-one new towns, we have a trading block of one and a quarter million people. The Constellations are designed to operate with the same economies of scale as the big corporations. We'll be able to absorb the downsider risks of farming and market forces, but we do it with compassion. We make sure everyone is provided for when the going gets tough."

The telephone rang and Fredrico answered.

"Hi, dear heart. Yeah, we're having a grand strategy session. These guys are good." Fredrico gave a quick aside to David and Carlos. "It's Conchita." He turned his attention back to his favorite colleague.

"How did it go in Sao Paulo?"

"Pretty darn good!" said Conchita.

"You and Gail are something else."

Fredrico chuckled while he listened to Conchita tell him about her trip. "Okay, great. Take your time. We'll see you when you get here. Bye for now." He hung up the phone and smiled at Carlos and David.

"I guess you overheard, Conchita and Gail got back from a fundraising trip to Sao Paulo," he explained. "They have about two hundred and seventy interested investors for the Constellation who took our prospectus home with them."

"That's impressive," David said. "Did I hear you say she's dropping by here?"

"Yeah, pretty soon, I imagine. Anyway, where was I? Oh, yeah, our new town system is designed from the inception to raise the standard of living while lowering the cost of living. We found that there are hundreds of ways to do this in almost every economic sector and we're learning new ways every day. These seven new towns are actually competing with each other to raise their standard of living while lowering the costs. When Las Faldas had a breakthrough that increased ethanol production by twenty percent, they immediately passed it on to the other new towns, and believe me they took credit for it. They've got braggin' rights for a while."

"Bucky Fuller's scheme at its best," said David, nodding with affirmation.

Carlos was beginning to see the impact of the mechanisms Fredrico was describing. "But how can these new towns be insulated from global competition? What if a huge multinational agribusiness can sell corn for twenty percent less than the new towns? You simply can't compete with something that big. People naturally buy the cheapest product they can. Then your whole system starts to unravel."

"Well, that's where the cooperator's education becomes very important. All of the workers in the new towns have learned what happens if they buy that cheaper corn. The agribusiness grows and buys more farmland. The farmers are kicked off the land and left jobless. They can't find work to buy corn at *any* price. We won't let that happen to each other. We don't have to compete with the market. All we have to do is feed each other, house and clothe each other, and provide things at a price we all can afford."

"So, you can do this by trading among yourselves?"

"Yes. We also sell to others within the region. It's a large enough market to support our self-sufficiency system. People throughout the region save money in our bank, because we pay one half percent more interest than other banks."

"But like Mondragon, you export some products in the open market. What are they?" asked Carlos.

"Primarily, we export ethanol fuel, solar cells, hydrogen fuel cells, spices, sugar and coffee. We are among the low cost producers, and we don't need a twenty to thirty percent profit! We are satisfied with seven to ten percent above the inflation rate. That gives us enough. It's greed that drives the outside market to its own destruction—and, more importantly, the firing of its workers by the millions. We treasure economic permanence. We want our families to be secure and content with this simple good life—God's good, sweet, joyful life."

There was a long pause around the table. David and Carlos needed to assimilate the vision of the Constellation and reflect upon its implications.

Finally, David said, "In the meantime, the global corporations of the world are competing with each other to take the largest market share for themselves! What a waste of human resources! One gains and one must lose. It's the stupid Darwinian dinosaur theory 'the survival of the fittest.' How can anyone fail to see the fallacy of such a mutually destructive system? People treat their dogs better than dog-eat-dog economics."

"So," Carlos said, "you've transcended the old economic theory that there must be winners and losers. You've created a 'win-win' situation. You have a set of integrated new towns, with wealth increasing internally, because of the way you distribute wealth among yourselves and between new towns. Does this mean everyone gets reduced to lower-middle class level?"

"No," answered Fredrico firmly. "The dream of becoming reasonably wealthy or famous is still a possibility. We just take care that everyone has the basic necessities, a few luxuries and a four-day workweek. They are not slaves to their jobs and they earn enough to provide well for themselves. They can use their three days of free time to become musicians, artists, philosophers, writers, you name it. And if they just want to get richer, they can take a second job in the luxury sector, or create their own business and work seventy hours a week. But the cooperator's spirit is usually satisfied with economic permanence and the understanding that there is more to life than making more and more money. You'll find that our people are pursuing the art of living. They love relaxing and dining with their family and friends. They know how to make a good life for themselves. And remember, we are continually learning how to produce and distribute much more for much less."

"I had no idea the Constellation was so different from classic economics," David remarked. "I love it!"

"It's incredibly seductive stuff," Carlos affirmed, "but does it allow for human freedom?"

"The five billionaires provide the start-up capital, an economic structure and a dynamic process so that people can take charge of their own lives. They work their way into becoming worker-owners with one year's salary, paid over a period of time. They're enabled to be effective, and to exercise personal freedom to create their own manner of being. In fact, Carlos, it provides the most freedom of any economic system in the world."

The phone rang and Fredrico answered: "She's here? Okay, this is a good time. Please tell her to join us in the War Room." He glanced over at Carlos and David. "It's Conchita. She wants to get to know you two so she can introduce you at the meeting with El Cinco tomorrow."

Conchita rapped lightly on the door, then let herself into the War Room. She was a vision in white, wearing a trim fitting business suit with a flaming red scarf to match her lips. Her dark brown hair fell loosely onto her shoulders. David was once again stunned by her beauty and he knew his eyes were giving him away. He and Carlos quickly rose from their chairs to meet her.

"Hello, there." She waved, as she and Fredrico greeted each other with a friendly smile and a warm hug.

"Conchita," Fredrico announced, "this is David O'Laughlin and Carlos Veda. You know they've just joined us to plan new Constellations and they call that creative process the sandbox."

"The sandbox? How playful," Conchita said with a tone of delight in her voice.

David's pulse quickened at the thought of a chance to be playful with her.

"As you know," said Fredrico, "Conchita is my dear friend, and she is also the spokesperson for El Cinco. We've been through the wars together, and you won't find a better co-conspirator than Conchita, especially when the going gets tough. I'm going to check out a few things. I'll be back shortly."

Fredrico left the War Room.

Conchita stepped across the room and extended her hand to David, and then to Carlos. David immediately noticed she wasn't wearing a ring on her left hand. Conchita observed the same thing about David.

"A pleasure to meet you both," she said with a very warm smile.

"I first saw you on a videotape at the State Department," said David. "You do a wonderful job as spokesperson. How long have you been with El Cinco?"

"Just three years, and I love it! Sometimes, I think I'm living in a dream."

She's a living dream, all right, thought David.

"Now, I need to know a bit more about you than your resumes. My understanding is this: Europa Development Corporation sent you down to visit LSI at our invitation, to stay and work with us for a while and possibly become partners. How long will you be with us?"

"Well, it was only going to be for a few weeks," David answered, "but we want to negotiate with our boss, Peter Erikson, to stay for the full design cycle for the second Constellation—the Viscaya Constellation."

"Wonderful," said Conchita. "We were hoping Europa would see the value of what we're doing and join in the effort."

"Well, Conchita," David said, "I have to say that it's the best thing that's happened to me in a long, long time. It's what a city planner dreams about, creative heaven."

"Carlos, what do you think of the Constellation so far?" asked Conchita.

"The creative potentials are mind-blowing," he answered, "but the barriers to advancement of the Constellation are formidable. I have to balance my creative juices with what's out there, if you know what I mean."

"So, you have some constructive doubts. Well, they say if you don't have some doubts now and again, you're not alive!"

"Well, for my part," said David, "I just want to work to advance the Constellations with good design. God couldn't have given me a more splendid role in life."

Conchita was joyful with David's response, as this was her feeling as well. She just smiled and they looked into each other's eyes with the knowledge that this could be the start of something very good.

"After the meeting with El Cinco," Conchita continued, "we'll all be going to La Feria de Las Faldas. I think you'll find it to be a wonderful experience. I know I have, every year."

"The Feria de Las Faldas reminds me of the Feria de Sevilla," said David. "I lived in Sevilla for two years," smiled David, "and I learned how different America is from Spanish-speaking countries. I saw close up how people are economically oppressed. I had culture shock when I went back to the States and witnessed extreme wealth with new eyes. With the Constellations, we have a real shot to end the suffering."

"Well then, you'll understand what I am about to say," Conchita said with more than usual intensity. "One of the greatest lies of our times is that people can not *design* livelihood systems for everyone. Those who make that claim have not lived long enough in the presence of extreme, grinding poverty, or they have not suffered enough themselves to have compassion, and mostly they don't know how good God is to all of us. With seven billion people on the planet and growing, we need Constellations. Otherwise, there is no way to sustain a decent life for everyone. It will be a trip through hell for every nation. The rich and near rich will personally experience violence, terrorism and war."

"I feel the same way, Conchita. Thank God you've got some answers," said David.

Conchita rose from her chair, and as her intensity changed to warmth and a full smile, she took David's hand in hers. "I'm glad you've joined us for this journey. We need your talents. I'll see you at the policy session tomorrow." Then, turning to Carlos, she shook his hand and said, "Thanks for joining us, Carlos!" With that, she left the room, waving to Fredrico as she passed him near the doorway.

David checked his watch. Play time in the sandbox had lasted three hours.

"I'll need some time alone to assimilate all of this. I think I'll take a stroll around the park and go back to the hotel from there."

"Fine," said Fredrico. "I've got plenty more to show you. Meet me here tomorrow at 3:30 and we'll go to the policy session together."

Carlos agreed to meet David back at the hotel for dinner, then David strolled alone toward the great sprawling park he had seen near the center of El Cedro. As he walked, he thought back to his graduate school days. Ever since he earned his degree in city planning, he longed to design a *real* new town. Now, the Constellation offered an endless pathway to totally new and creative designs. He was overwhelmed with his release of inner joy. He began humming the "Blue Danube Waltz." Not caring if there was anyone nearby, he began to dance the waltz along the sidewalk. And...*1-2-3, 1-2-3.* He continued dancing until a couple turned the corner and looked at him like he was nuts. *Okay,* he thought, *so I am nuts. I love this kind of nuts.*

He sat down on a bench in the park, his mind racing ahead to planning a Constellation in the U.S. Many of the problems had already been dealt with in Rocadura. In the U.S., it would be quite a challenge to convince people they can step into a whole new economic enterprise and leave the only way they know behind.

Back at the hotel, David ate a light lunch, then, went to his room to think and make some notations. He thought about financing a Constellation in the States. Would El Cinco help back it? Would Erikson even want to develop it? Where would they start? California? The Midwest? *Yes,* he smiled to himself, *the Midwest, where friends are real friends and will give more to each other.* He would write his report to Erikson and Europa after the trip to Las Faldas. Then, Erikson would decide. This would require every ounce of Irish charm he could deliver. *It has to be a real piece of work,* he thought.

At 4:30 p.m., David took a refreshing swim in the hotel pool. There were only four people on the pool deck. *Tourists,* he thought. He swam laps for twenty-five minutes and paused to enjoy the clouds in the sky and the flowering trees around the pool. Then, he went to his room to shower and dress for dinner. He stopped in at the hotel bar to wait for Carlos.

A well-dressed couple entered the hotel bar and sat down across from David. The lady was an attractive woman. She was smiling, laughing and full of life. David's thoughts turned to Conchita Seguras. *She'll be coming to Las Faldas!* He would see her there! She had a clarity about her. David intuited that she had been through some hard times but had met the challenges. She was exciting. *Damn, what am I thinking? She can take her pick.* He was just another guy in a long line of desperados.

Then, Linda flashed in his mind. Maybe he should just stay single and throw himself into his work. It had been a good way to live so far. He was enjoying a peace and joy in his soul he had not known for years. His spirit was going from strength to strength, from laughter to laughter. Life was on a rising curve. How could he be happier? He and Linda had their ups and downs. She was such a huge part of his daily life. He woke up every morning thinking about her and what they had said the day before. There were those glorious mornings when they woke side by side and cherished each other. And he remembered those long nights. Being that close to a woman was a very hard thing to forget and not want again as part of your life.

"Be a man," he told himself. "Just step right up and make your gentle move. You've got everything to gain—and…" The cliché fell apart in front of his eyes. *I've got a lot to lose if she shuts me out. Okay, that's possible, maybe even probable, but a fellah has got to try.* So, he lifted his sherry to Conchita. He felt good. He could see the path opening before him.

Carlos never arrived. David assumed he had met an attractive lady and had gone his own way. David ate dinner and retired a happy man, his heart full of hope for the future and his creative role in building Constellations around the world.

Chapter 6
FIVE BILLIONAIRES WITH A PLAN

Fredrico caught up with David and Carlos at the War Room. They had thirty minutes before the meeting started with El Cinco.

"How many billionaires are there in the world, Fredrico?" David asked.

"Well, let's see, I think it's in the neighborhood of a thousand to twelve hundred."

"Of course, that means El Cinco represent a tiny fraction of all the world's billionaires. A good friend of mine used to say that all a town needed was thirty-eight good souls."

"You know, I've often had that same thought," Fredrico said, his eyes lighting up to the thesis. "It's truly amazing that it took only five good souls and a few dozen friends to design and deliver the Constellation!"

"Of course," Carlos quickly inserted, "we're only talking about five of the richest people in the world teaming up to do a project requiring about everything they own, plus other people's money."

"Okay, five billionaires and a few friends," David chuckled. "We know that you and Padre Parejo have been right up there in the top two of those friends, and I take my hat off to you, Fredrico. The padre is the spiritual force and you are the advisor to the kings."

"Yes," Carlos smiled sagely, "we're on to you. You are the options man. You define the best alternatives for El Cinco. We know about that, because that's what David and I do at Europa."

"No, no," Fredrico resisted. "El Cinco are different. They all know their own minds. They often have better ideas than I do."

"We know what you mean," said Carlos, "but who has to sort out the best answer when they can't agree, or don't have a clue as to what to do next?"

"Okay," Fredrico said with firmness. "When that happens, Padre Parejo is the spiritual and intellectual guide and I am the options man."

"Exactly," said Carlos, with the satisfaction that he had gotten Fredrico to confess the truth.

"And some damn good options, at that," said David, just to bring the compliment home a bit further.

"So tell us some more about El Cinco," said Carlos. "Who are they and how did they meet?"

"Well, I told you about the planning conference in Sao Paulo. That was the beginning. Of course, Padre Parejo created the opportunity for them to meet. He knew something about all of them and he set the stage. He cued them into the fact that this conference was about human development, economics and a sustainable growth that protects the environment. Actually, looking back on it, I'd say Padre Parejo pre-selected these folks based on their willingness to work on these compelling economic and social issues."

"Good, but who are they, and what do they do?" asked Carlos.

"Let's start with the big picture. They act as executives, and by 'executives' I mean they oversee the general managers of their worker-owner cooperative. In addition, they meet as a body with the staff to make major decisions. Beyond that scope of work, the worker-entrepreneurs take charge of their own divisions. Once the Cornerstone Constellation is more firmly established, the worker-owners will run their own show—one person, one vote. El Cinco have already moved on to financially establish the Vizcaya Constellation, even as we are designing its new towns."

"That's the clever way to do it," interjected Carlos. "Let the crack troops set up the program so it can be run by the natives."

"It's the only way," said David.

"Well, that's what we decided early on, remember? The best and brightest have to design and implement a superior economic system for those who can't," said Fredrico, with a shrug. Let me tell you a bit about them. I'll begin with Arturo Estebar. He's Brazilian and directs all energy projects, including solar cells and the ethanol development program. He became very wealthy utilizing the full scope of the Neal Ingram ethanol process while others lagged behind. He took the technology that could turn vegetative waste into ethanol production using sugar cane stalks, leaves, and corn stalks to produce ethanol, in addition to some sugar itself. Then, he found his stride with El Cinco when they asked him to take on solar cell production as well. It gave him a new mountain to climb and he likes to scramble up those vertical faces. He's a really strong-willed man."

"Yes, I've read quite a bit about his operations," said David. "He was using cars that were built by General Motors back in the 90s that could run on one hundred percent ethanol. Most Americans didn't know such cars existed."

"Next," said Fredrico, "there is Teng Hisung, from Japan. He's director of all aquaculture and fish farming operations. His Asian complex is extraordinary. He really enjoys the teamwork style of the worker-owned cooperatives. They love him on the Lemon Islands. He and El Cinco started the worker-owner enterprise there, and from the beginning, it was a real rush."

"You mean they took to it like a fish to water?" smiled Carlos with feigned sweetness.

"Hmmph," grunted Fredrico, good-naturedly. "Why, yes, Carlos, unlike some folks I know who have to test a good thing forever!"

"Ooooh," smiled David, "I think he zinged ya there!"

"Yeah," smiled Carlos, "but I ain't the only tester in the valley. Before this is over, you're gonna have every damn attorney in South America on your buns."

"Interesting you should say that, Carlos. But let me get on with the three billionaires remaining. Gail O'Reilly is the chief of finance. She's set up a banking establishment similar to Mondragon's and she excelled in reaching millions of savers outside of the Cornerstone Constellation to deposit in the New Town Bank."

"What are the total assets of the New Town Bank?" asked Carlos.

"Only about fifty billion dollars. They're just getting started, you know."

"That's still a very respectable piece of change," David said.

"With good leverage, it's more than enough to launch a Constellation or two."

"Man, I could launch a million excellent deals with that kind of cash in hand," dreamed Carlos.

"Then, there is Anita Avilar from Argentina, the director of agriculture. She inherited a modest family enterprise in hydroponics and turned it into a multibillion dollar company. You'll soon get a chance to visit her estate. She's a dynamo and her house is a real piece of work. She loves to entertain and she lives in a cultured jungle outside of El Cedro."

"Hydroponics is the only way to go now," Carlos agreed. "The amount of farming land has dwindled dramatically in my own lifetime. It's hard to believe how fast the population has grown."

"Last, but by no means least, manufacturing is directed by Tom Brand, an American. He also works closely with Padre Parejo to establish new cooperatives. Padre Parejo, as you know, is a close confidant of all five and is in charge of education, modeled on the Mondragon system, at all levels of the cooperative structure."

"That's quite a group," David said.

"They certainly have the credentials," Carlos allowed.

The door opened and people entered the War Room for the meeting. David and Carlos sat next to Tom Brand, director of manufacturing.

David extended his hand and said, "It's a pleasure to meet you Mr. Brand. My name is David O'Laughlin and this is my colleague, Carlos Veda."

"Oh, yes. Fredrico told me about you. You're from Europa Development Corporation, right?"

"Yes, we're getting an education in Constellation Style economics. I've very much enjoyed reading your articles about corporate theories, especially the emphasis on human development as the key to a better corporate culture."

"Please call me Tom, and thank you. Actually those were early articles. I've come a long way since I wrote them."

"Have you written anything I could read to bring me up to date with your latest thinking?" David asked.

"Well, let's take inventory," Brand said. There was a short pause. "You see, I'm out of arts and letters and into action, fast moving action…the only things I've written lately are memos to my operations staff. And then, of course, Padre Parejo and I have a daily dialogue. Anyway, I'd like to tell you a story about how I made the quantum leap to join El Cinco. I was in a long range planning meeting with the Executive Committee at Hanover United Global Enterprises, or *HUGE* for short."

David chuckled at Brand's overly dramatic emphasis on huge.

"We were in our strategic planning session, scanning the economic environment, our competitors and problems…you know the scene. This led into new product ideas. One subsidiary brought up the idea of automatically inflated envelopes for cars, a surrogate for a garage. Another corporation was planning to introduce a new line of gourmet soups, including bouillabaisse, for God's sake!"

"French chefs would come after us with cleavers!" said David.

"Right. They had a new advertising gimmick to push everything from soap to chips. Suddenly, it all gelled in my mind: these were just middle-class toys raised a notch; little steps to improve this a bit or to sell more of that. It had nothing to do with advancing the real economic life of the average family. It was just another way to advance the life of the corporation! I realized then, what the world really needs are economic structures to advance human development, to move toward something real, something closer to authentic happiness."

"I know what you mean. That's why we're here."

"Does Europa Development have the capacity to start up new towns with a self-reliant cooperative structure?"

There was a long pause. "The chairman of the board and our CEO, Peter Erikson, wants to take a good, long look at Constellation Style. As for the rest of the organization…well, they're in for a total re-education if this turns out to be our new direction."

"And your job is to go back and bring everybody up to speed, and design the action plan."

"That's about it. Carlos and I need to collect many technical details, financing methods, organizational set-up…the works. We'll need at least a month instead of two weeks, just to get started. Then, we'll write a report to Erikson."

Brand said, "It's absolutely critical that the corporate world wakes up to realize that human development is the only way to feed people and avoid violence and all manner of cruelties. Over one hundred million people arrive on this planet earth each day, like babies from outer space, with millions of new mouths to feed and all the rest. Constellation Style is the only way I know of to deliver the goods. It's a new kind of self-reliant market which is built up by worker-owners, both for their own growth and for their sister cooperatives. It's not driven by greed or power…it's driven by an understanding that human life has a spiritual dimension. We can have all of the worldly possessions that are good for us in ample measure, and as a bonus, we can work just four-day weeks to earn it all. As the Constellations grow in an integrated fashion, they can produce much more for much less effort, as Bucky Fuller was fond of saying."

David's thoughts flashed back to the powerful creative surge he experienced after reading Bucky's work. Then he thought about his own drive to be creative and how Constellation planning held the promise of endless creativity.

"That's what I have yearned for all of my life—the time to be myself and do my own thing," Carlos said. "My jobs have drained out all of my time and energy. I've always felt that my job was stealing my life! The Constellation has given me some hope that I can break that cycle before I get too old to enjoy the spare time."

"Ultimately, we'll be working seven hour days, four days a week."

"That's a day I'll live for."

"I think they're about to begin the workshop now."

Brand then excused himself from the conversation and turned to the papers he had brought to the meeting. David looked around the room for Conchita Seguras. He saw her seated next to Fredrico. Fredrico was emanating his noble dignity and warmth. Conchita was dazzling with her charm. She wore a turquoise suit that framed her dark brown hair. Shortly, she rose and moved to the head of the huge table.

"I think we should have this family reunion more often." She paused for a long time and just smiled as she looked slowly around the room. With her "gracia," no one was impatient. It was a pleasure to pause and look at her, to take in her smile and her beauty. "I'm even more delighted to be present for Fredrico's presentation. He has shared some of it with me and I know you are in for a very special treat."

She paused again, and found David and Carlos in the room. "We are pleased to have with us this evening, two very talented men from Europa Development Corporation, David O'Laughlin and Carlos Veda." She held one arm up in the air for them to stand.

David and Carlos rose from their chairs, smiled and sat down.

"David and Carlos are what we might call 'advanced scouts' of the development world. They're here to learn everything they can about the Constellation Style of development. We hope they join forces with us to build future new towns."

There was more than polite applause for the newcomers as well as some sincerely interested looks from a few.

"And now, for the main event of the evening, I give you our own magician, a man with a dozen doves and rabbits in his hat…Fredrico!"

Fredrico approached the head of the table, full of brisk energy.

"Thank you, Conchita, I think we're *all* a bunch of magicians. I know sometimes I feel like I'm in the middle of a magic act. Padre Parejo's ethanol deal with the government was clearly a piece of magic."

There was a round of exuberant applause.

"Well, my friends, we have come a long way in This Holy House, as Padre Parejo says. We now have a very large family. As you know, the Cornerstone Constellation is established with Las Faldas at the heart of it all. We now proceed with a rapid buildout of sixty thousand population in each new town. To transform the nation of Rocadura will require one hundred new towns. It's an awesome task, but we've begun construction work on the Vizcaya Constellation and the third tier—appropriately named, the Trinity Constellation. We'll have twenty-one new towns strong, totaling a population of about one and a quarter million. It's a good start, considering that the total population of Rocadura is six million people. We've all worked very hard to make this come to fruition, and I'm joyful to be working with you all on what is rapidly becoming an historic event."

There were some strong, resonant feelings in the room. El Cinco remembered the early days, the struggles with the government, the Army, the rich land owners, and how easily those conflicts could return, except now they had the overwhelming success of the Cornerstone Constellation. They had established, at least, a foothold.

At that moment, Padre Parejo stepped forward to join Fredrico at the front of the room. In total synchronization with their thoughts, Padre Parejo said: "The Cornerstone is, today, a living challenge to the world. Fortunately, we've brought something into the world that most businesses and governments will welcome. We have opened new pathways for businesses to transition into the Third Way—Constellation Style. We are introducing globalization, family style. Enlightened corporations can join us in our cooperative enterprise by signing mutual agreements. Also, many corporations will be happy to provide the Constellations with their products. So rest in this: Let the corporations do as they will. For some, what we are doing is beyond their wildest dreams. We have taken economic freedom to higher ground. Many business leaders will be surprised, to say the least. Why? Because our economic system is *outside* of their domain, yet we can still do business with them. We've simply transcended the endless circle of economic deprivation. Of course, it will take many generations to bring the Constellations into full orbit. But, if God wills it, and I'm certain He does, nothing can stop its forward progress throughout the world. And God knows, there is no loving central guidance system, as powerful as ours, in any other economic structure today. That is the key difference between the Constellation and business as usual. In the Constellation, we know we're enjoying our realization of the union with the Divine. We have this special gift that gives the tone for all of our actions. Our work flows from our personal union with God. That realized union is what informs our every action. It is the wellspring of creative virtue in work, in play, in courtship and marriage. We know that God is our final end and we look forward to the wonders of being with our Father in Heaven. We experience a life of joy and inner peace in that union, here and now. In the end, we are faced with Eternal Reality and how close we have come to God in union or how far we have distanced ourselves. You are indeed blessed, because you know how to stay close in your union with God."

Padre Parejo paused. He looked above the heads of the gathering as if to collect his thoughts about what he would say next.

"My friends, you all know that the United States must strive to make peace with over one billion Muslims in the world. The Muslim dream will not be denied. Just like the dreams of our poor people in Central and South America, the dreams of Islam to have a decent living and to be united, as Muslims, in a peaceful world will not be denied. They have vowed not to become colonies of the United States or be ruled by corrupt Arab dictators. They demand, and deserve, the freedom to practice their religion. After all, they worship the same God that we do. The days are gone when Western powers could send their military forces to the Gulf to preserve a political order that has failed to deliver the national, emotional and material aspirations of millions of Muslim families."

Padre Parejo looked around the room and smiled.

"I am happy to say that the Constellation has begun to make a new bridge to the Islamic world. I have been in consultation with an Islamic peacemaker for the last week. He has expressed a profound desire for change. He sees the Constellation as a new pathway to fairness in economics, to a sense of community and solidarity. He sees the Constellation as a whole new way of Islamic expression in the village, in the region and in the world.

"This is just the beginning, but his vision is clear. We will hear from him again and he will want us to build Constellations in the Arab world because we have the way to produce more with less and the way to distribute wealth to the poor and middle classes with dignity and justice and dynamic creativity. The Constellation offers a new pathway to peace between Muslims and Christians."

El Cinco and the entire room rose as one in a standing ovation to what Padre Parejo had just said.

Padre Parejo smiled happily, stepped aside from the lectern after that point, and the room came alive with the buzzing of lively conversation. Padre Parejo could see farther into the future than anyone in the room. He had both spiritual vision and strategic options. These were highly prized talents in the work at hand, and El Cinco and company were showing their appreciation.

Padre Parejo beckoned to Fredrico to come forward.

"As you all know," Fredrico observed, "economic integration designed for human development is our creative solution. Padre Parejo has now discovered that it offers a new way of life to Islam that is consistent with their most cherished values. From this day forward, any economic system is not worth its salt unless it can create promising jobs and personal economic security for everyone—Constellation Style or better."

There was a grand applause of affirmation.

"While the formation of Constellations is not for mere profit alone, profits must be forthcoming in order to expand the internal wealth of the worker-entrepreneurs. Profit is also necessary to deliver superior technologies and future capital investment. So we come to the purpose of this meeting and the central problem is this: we can not create jobs fast enough to meet the incredible backlog of demand. Our resources are expanding rapidly. Our progress is admirable, but with one hundred million babies arriving on this planet *daily*, all nations are falling behind the curve. We need to invite the world's investment capital to join us."

The room buzzed again with affirmations. Fredrico paused until it had almost subsided.

"I must admit that a week ago, I was not happy with the options that we had prepared for your consideration. However, our newly found friends from Europa Development Corporation gave us an idea. David O'Laughlin recently asked me how many billionaires there were in the world. I estimated about twelve hundred. Then, David recalled a friend who used to say that it only takes about thirty-eight good souls to make a good town. And then, I remembered a conference I attended in Toronto where a very wise clergyman demonstrated that eighty-five percent of the boards of directors in that city were Christians, but none of them fully realized that they held a controlling spiritual interest among their board of directors."

Fredrico paused.

"Well, you have a hint at what I'm about to say. Padre Parejo and I call this proposal, for your consideration, 'The Global Billionaires Building Fund.' In essence, it's an invitation to invest in profitable human development, 'Constellation Style.' It will not be an easy proposal to sell. But we have designed a three-pronged attack: first, we are negotiating for capital from the World Bank and the Inter American Bank. And we do this with the full knowledge that we have 'banking certainty.' There is nothing closer to a banker's heart than to know that he's going to get his loan back with a tidy profit. Well…we're getting our investment back, aren't we?"

"Money and much more," Brand offered in an even voice.

"Twelve percent on the dollar and rising," said an accountant.

Fredrico smiled and softly added, "Capital is attracted to invest in a form of growth that is solid, self-sustaining, internally reinforced, externally secure, vertically and horizontally integrated. Bankers appreciate the gradual addition of mutually supporting modules. As my friend David O'Laughlin said, the Constellation is a finely woven cloth! It is designed to pay the bills! Revenues flow from exports and from internal transactions to pay for new growth. The maximization of human resources, cheap energy, appropriate technology, and the worker-entrepreneur structure combine to create built-in permanency. And built-in permanency gives financial backers a feeling of safety. They can go to sleep with this investment—even if it is in the developing countries. And now, we'll ask the staff to serve some wine and soft drinks."

The staff appeared with trays of glasses and wine bottles. When all were served, Tom Brand stood up and raised his glass for a toast.

"To banking certainty!"

The room rocked with echoes, "To banking certainty!"

After the uproar subsided, Fredrico resumed his speech.

"Secondly, we enlist the universities to accept our offers to establish a chair and a program that offers a master's degree in village building. Thirdly, we'll demonstrate to hundreds of corporations, throughout the world, that *their* future lies mainly in one place: supplying the thousands and thousands of villages in the world with the tools, equipment and processes of production. The world's corporations will be given a brand-new market that was never there before: supplying the villages through village builders. The more they supply this market, it is axiomatic that these markets will become more stable! And just how big is this market? Well, we all know that it is global and growing!"

El Cinco rose to their feet, instantly followed by the entire room, to give a second standing ovation.

Fredrico ticked off the advantages to the billionaires of the world. "With Constellation Style, corporations can forget about extreme economic instability brought about by the anxieties of poverty, mounting crime, violence, terrorism, military takeovers, and nationalization of their corporation's assets. They can simply concentrate on doing a good business in a stable political environment. Today, stable markets mean dramatically lower risk for your investment."

Fredrico turned to point to a large wall map mounted on a ceiling-to-floor track. It showed a graphic of the hundreds of villages identified in Central and South America alone that were ripe for harvest. Then, he moved to the Middle East and Africa. Then to Southeast Asia. By the time he was finished, it was a "no-brainer." "Who could refuse?" was the room's universal thought. The presentation was finished. The vote was recorded as unanimous to proceed with the whole plan for the "Global Billionaires Building Fund."

Arturo Estebar rose from his chair to address the group. "I know you don't need more encouragement for this new strategy, but I would like to say a few words in support of Fredrico's plan. I know you've all read about the incredible levels of local air pollution from automobiles in Italy, Mexico City and California. And you know that ethanol car fuel is one of the best options, if not *the* best, until solar cell electric cars or fuel cell driven cars become available. We've achieved a zero net gain in the emission of carbon dioxide with ethanol. We now have enough feed stock for ethanol growing in our fields—that takes in carbon dioxide—that it totally exceeds the amount of carbon dioxide emitted when our ethanol is burned as one hundred percent fuel. We do this just by using our vegetative waste and by giving certain plants an occasional haircut. As of today, through our research and development, the price of ethanol is down to sixty cents per gallon at the refinery gate!"

Applause.

Then Tom Brand rose to speak.

"Arturo has led the world to bring environmental ethanol forward as the logical replacement to burning gasoline. We need to encourage the leaders of oil companies to become ethanol distillers. They can use our expertise and planning, if they like. They have the capital to make the shift to ethanol production, and they can now make the shift of capital to something productive by investing in new towns, Constellation Style. They can make a profit, but they need to shift their investments gradually to ethanol and solar energy and village building. Oil can be used for other things than car fuel. Many corporations have already made the shift to products for a sustainable, ecologically sound economy. They have given us solar cells at nine cents a kilowatt hour, super efficient gas turbine generators, and vegetable burgers that are protein rich and tasty. Over the decades, corporations have brought huge gains in productivity and have raised the standard of living. They're proud of these accomplishments, as well they should be."

Applause and spirited conversation filled the room. Brand let the gathering go on talking for a minute or two, then began again.

"Many corporations will go on operating pretty much as they do today. They'll improve their products and create new ones, mostly aimed at the upper thirty percent income group and the luxury market. That's okay. Let it be so. But other corporations will see the enormous advantages and the potential for global growth of worker owned Constellations, and they'll compete to be the suppliers that drive that growth around the world."

Brand paused for a sip of water, and looked around the room at his friends.

"What a shame it would be if corporate leaders stopped these huge gains just when we have learned how to reach the next and highest level of human development: the reorganization of work so that we have productivity in distribution as well as in production! We've moved from the Post Industrial Revolution to the Self-Sufficiency Revolution."

Everyone applauded, as Tom Brand sat down. When the cheering died down, Anita Avilar addressed the gathering.

"My friends," she began, "this occasion calls for a special celebration. When Fredrico briefly described this afternoon's presentation to me, I knew we would want to share the moment. I'm so thrilled that you are all coming to my house this evening for dinner. Please bring a friend or two if you wish. We have the famous dance troupe that performed so magnificently at the Feria last year, 'El Barrio Triana.' I've brought in some choice items from our aquaculture farms and six chefs have been working since morning to provide you with some very special surprises."

The group surrounded Anita Avilar, gave her hugs, and there was little doubt this was going to be a very special party.

Conchita approached David with a glass of red wine in hand. "Well, David," she said, "in the hustle and bustle around here, did someone give you and Carlos an invitation to Anita's?"

"No," answered David ,feigning rejection, "we were lost and forgotten in Rocadura."

"You poor puppies," she smiled. "You and Carlos will be my guests—okay? Fredrico will pick you up at 7:30. I'll meet you there around 8:00."

Carlos flashed a wicked smile. "Thanks, but after Fredrico's speech I was going to crash it anyway!"

* * *

Conchita Seguras was getting dressed for Anita Avilar's party and had just taken a cool shower. She sat at her dressing table and combed her hair, singing an old Spanish song: "*No te puedo querer.* (I can't love you.) *Aparta de mis pensamientos.*" (Get out of my thoughts). All the while she thought fondly of David.

Just three months ago, she had untangled herself from a two-year relationship that had cut her deeply. She and Jorge had parted by mutual agreement. Their worlds had grown apart when she started traveling in South America to bring investments to the Constellations. He had grown jealous to the point of paranoia, constantly questioning her about who she saw and what she did as she traveled. Jorge's possessiveness caused arguments during every date. Finally, he secretly followed her to Bogotá, where he knew she had many male friends. When he found her in the hotel night club, dancing with a potential investor, he flew into a violent rage. She ended it quickly after that episode and it was an incredible relief to be free again. She wasn't sure if she wanted to start another relationship so soon. She needed time to heal. She knew one thing for sure, no man was going to own her like a piece of property. She *hated* possessiveness. Still, her strong attraction to David could not be denied. He would have to pass the possessive test, that much was certain in her mind.

She went to her briefcase and pulled out a photograph of David she had borrowed from the office file. She set it up on the dressing table while she finished combing her hair. *He's Irish, all right*, she thought, *right down to that mischievous twinkle in his eyes.*

She was deciding what to wear for Anita's party. *He's been to Sevilla and he likes gypsies.* She decided she would pull back her hair tight with a ponytail and wear a black evening gown with golden earrings.

She thought about how excited he was to work with on job creation for the Constellations. She and Fredrico knew they needed more planning talent to move this thing along. The least she could do was be charming to him and encourage him to join the team. She laughed at herself and spoke to the mirror.

Well rest easy! It's just all for the good of the organization! He must be charmed into joining the team. It's company orders to make myself irresistible!

What a team, she thought. Fredrico, Padre Parejo and El Cinco. If David joined, things could really get interesting, at a whole new level. Perhaps, she dreamed, a much sweeter level. Everyone had been working so hard, there was little time for the sweetness of life.

She remembered the days when life was not so sweet. The days of being ashamed of her clothes in middle class schools because her family was poor. She remembered graduation day from grade school and how some nasty girls laughed at her old, worn out shoes. Her family ate nothing but beans and rice for weeks on end. They were always moving from place to place so her father could find work to feed the family. Poverty had taught Conchita that she could survive on little. It had made her strong inside. She could endure real hardship and laugh at it if she had to because she already knew how bad it could be and it didn't scare her. She also knew she was gifted with intelligence and a good education and would probably make a very good living in promising jobs. She knew she was loved by God, so, even in the hardest, most bitter times, life was bearable and worth living. It could have been worse, she thought. At least she didn't have to live in the streets and run and hide to keep from being raped, to fight for life itself, like hundreds of abandoned street children in Bogotá.

Chapter 7
ANITA AVILAR'S PARTY

Fredrico picked up David and Carlos in the evening and drove to Anita Avilar's party.

"Anita's house was designed by a brilliant Brazilian architect," he explained. "It's a marvelous place to visit. She has huge gardens and hydroponic pilot projects covering three acres. She has perfected drip feed irrigation to produce abundant crops with the least requirement of water and energy."

They were stopped at a guard gate to have their identification checked before entering the estate. When the security guard recognized Fredrico he nodded and waved them through.

Anita Avilar's home was perched dramatically on a hill three hundred feet above the entry gate. It was a splendid sight. They caught glimpses of Spanish arches and bold overhangs done in modern style, with parts of the structure cantilevering precariously over the sheer face of a rock wall and a deep ravine.

The driveway was flanked by heavy plant growth on each side. As the road curved up the hill, a new vista would open at each turn to reveal yet another creation of beauty. They came upon groups of abundant flowering trees, climbing bougainvillea with bright purple and red flowers, brilliant white jasmine and magical groupings of rhododendron.

"You're actually looking at a huge organic garden that was purposely left untrimmed and wild," explained Fredrico as they were suddenly surrounded by cascades of white and pink flowers framed with palm fronds.

"It's a three-story house with split levels. It has an elevator with European style wrought iron doors," Fredrico exuded with obvious pleasure.

"There is an awesome view from virtually every room in the house which overlooks her gardens or the town below."

As they entered the inner courtyard leading to the house, they saw that Spanish tapas and drinks were being served. It was a bustling scene with chefs and waiters dressed in white delivering little dishes on huge trays to three buffet tables near a water fountain. The courtyard was enclosed by a stucco wall with Spanish tile trim and decorations.

Anita Avilar entered the courtyard from the house, elegantly dressed in a long red evening gown, cut with deep cleavage which was framed on each side by a golden baroque lame. She had a striking presence. When she sighted Fredrico, David and Carlos, she approached them with the self-assurance of a woman who never walked into a room apologetically in her life.

"I am delighted you could come tonight," she smiled graciously. "It is wonderful to see Americans coming to visit the Constellation."

David received her extended hand and suddenly felt very warm toward Anita.

"I really enjoyed the drive up the hill through your gardens."

"That's my beloved jungle," Anita smiled with self-satisfaction. "I learn about a new marvel every day in the Constellation, and as Conchita says, Fredrico always seems to have just one more rabbit in his hat."

"He's got bunnies hopping all over the place," David agreed.

"Isn't he a visionary? I just love Fredrico. She gave him a one-armed hug. "He has that special 'gracia' that few men possess."

"It's true," Carlos affirmed. "After the Fredrico and Padre Parejo speeches, I thought the room would literally burst if we didn't have a celebration."

"All right," Fredrico groaned, "enough of the extolling about my virtues. I think it was Abraham Lincoln who said, 'It has been my experience that folks who have no vices have very few virtues.'"

"Well, Fredrico!" exclaimed Anita with faked surprise. "I would love to hear more…can we play twenty questions about your vices?" Then, as she looked over his shoulder, she sighed, "Bad timing…I see the Brands have just arrived. But I'll be back to play twenty questions."

As she started off to welcome the latest guests, she called out softly over her shoulder, "Please enjoy the tapas, but save some room for dinner!"

"I'll take that as an order," said Fredrico, "Let's go get over-served on the amontillado and tapas."

"Pale dry sherry for me," said Carlos to the bartender, as they arrived at the outdoor bar. "It must be true that the older you get, the more your taste buds shift from sweet to tart, and to hot and spicy."

"Carlos, are you confusing your appetites, again? Tarts? Hot and spicy?" David teased.

"Yes, it's true, but I'm surprised a man of your supreme dignity would even *know* of such things."

They laughed together and David offered a toast, "To hot and spicy!"

They strolled over to the tapa table. David chose a bandillera skewer with pieces of green and red peppers, onions and marinated beef. Carlos selected a "Caballo," which was a small square of bread sandwiched between two pieces of thin-sliced roast beef.

When Conchita Seguras arrived David watched in fascination as she spoke with Anita. She wore a tight-fitting black gown and gypsy-style golden earrings. Her hair was pulled back tightly, Spanish style, with a full fourteen inches of ponytail. She was tall, just about five feet nine, and long-legged. *This lady has class*, David thought. Conchita glanced around as she talked, until her eyes caught David. She gave him a look that was concentrated directly on him—warm and inviting. He had a special feeling about her—the kind that said, You'd better hang on to the grass or you'll orbit out of control.

David strolled over to Conchita with two glasses of sherry. Extending a glass to her, he said, "You look very Spanish tonight. I'm afraid the Spanish dance troupe might try to steal you off to Sevilla."

"Well, if they do, you'll just have to come with me!"

"Now, that's a fantasy worth exploring. When do we leave?"

"Actually, when my work gets to a plateau, I would love to go back to visit Sevilla. But right now, it seems the Constellations are like growing children that just need more and more attention."

"Yes, I can feel the sense of urgency all around—'Our Lady of Perpetual Responsibility' as Garrison Keillor used to say."

"That's *so* on the mark. Painfully so. I don't know who Garrison Keillor is, but there is this spiritual consciousness around here that runs pretty deep in most of us."

"I like to remember that even Christ was playful," David said, with an Irish lilt in his voice. "For example, at the Wedding Feast of Cana, Christ was encouraged by His mother, against His will, to produce a miracle that would supply wine for the seven day long wedding party. Well, you would think maybe He could find a few cases of vino from a passing caravan. Or He could have put in a rush order to the local vineyard. But no, Christ had them fill six stone water vessels with water and transformed it into a hundred and twenty gallons of the really good stuff. Now, I think *that* was playful. Considering that one hundred and twenty gallons would amount to over five hundred bottles of wine. I mean, how big was this party? The whole town of Cana could get totally smashed."

Laughing, she tossed her head back and said, "So, you would like to introduce Our Lady of Perpetual Playfulness, right? Well, I'll drink to that." She lifted her glass for a toast.

"That's a good one. It has a ring to it, doesn't it? Here's to O.L.P.P.," David said as he raised his glass to hers.

They paused to look at each other. Conchita thought his eyes were really full of life. She saw fireworks in those eyes and he was much more attractive than she had remembered from their initial meeting.

David saw a woman he might want to live with for a long, long time, maybe, forever. That triggered feelings at such a deep level that he couldn't quite grasp them. He felt a movement at what he thought of as "the soul level." Things were starting to feel very comfortable.

David and Conchita were together for the rest of the evening. They enjoyed Anita's sit-down dinner which was presented in a casual way. The six chefs were stepping lively and keeping up a banter with the group of about forty people.

After dinner, they watched the flamenco show from a table at the edge of the dance floor. As the show cast its spell on the crowd, David joined in clapping "las palmas" and that encouraged the people at the adjacent table to do the same. Soon a local group of a dozen or so people followed David's lead and joined the clapping. Then the other side of the room erupted and the dancers demonstrated their appreciation. They made "ad lib" moves and suddenly came to life with a new force of artistry. Their eyes lit up and a whole new spirit took over the entire room. This was now an artistic event, because the dancers raised the level of their passion to please and perform.

"You really get into the flamenco, don't you?" said Conchita, loving the way David responded to the artistry of the dancers.

"It's like a bit of Heaven to me. Besides, I learned a long time ago that if you give spontaneous applause to a good performance early on, it gives the performer that needed boost. Before you can say 'Ole!' they've risen to a higher level."

"Yes, but, David," she said pointedly, "you *really* get into the heart of the flamenco."

"I already told you how I fell in love with Sevilla, and Spanish culture. Besides, getting into the flamenco is part of my Irish heritage."

"Well, I can understand that. I was at a wonderful Irish tavern in Washington, D.C., called the 'Dubliner' one night and I fell crazy in love with the music. I may have had a wee bit too much of the Harp and Guinness, but it was great fun!"

"Oh, you like the 'harf 'n harf,' do ya?"

"Yes," Conchita laid back her head and laughed, "that was where I learned how really good it was when you mixed 'em."

"Irish petrol," he said, with his most playful grin.

A new dance had begun. The troupe came out in a set of three couples. Anita Avilar had built a stage of wood on top of her marble floor especially for this event. The dramatic staccato of the heels biting into the wood gave that truly authentic sound to the flamenco. Short, clear-cut strokes of the heels connected with the wood. The steps started slowly, almost delicately. Then, gradually, the pace of the dance began to build. Suddenly, the rhumba flamenco rhythm broke out in full force. As the dancers swirled in motion, the staccato cadence—the regular rise and fall of light then heavy accent—pounded the highly receptive wood floor. The music of the guitars soared—reaching their peak of power and musical authority. The dancers had risen to the occasion: it was as if their feet and graceful body movements said, "Hear my passion! Feel my passion!"

Conchita and David watched in silence, until the music and the percussion on the wood floor needed to be joined by their souls. They began "las palmas" again, together this time.

The troupe finished their performance and left the dance floor. The orchestra played several numbers before they struck up a bolero.

"I can't resist a bolero," David smiled, offering his hand.

"Another good old Irish tradition, right?" Conchita teased.

"No, I had to take special dance lessons for this one."

David felt Conchita move to his hand pressure on her waist. They traveled backwards and forwards together and then slipped into half-time rhythm. It was a dance of tensions, counter-tensions and releases. He could sense her excitement. She was right with him, following closely with confidence. They danced together as if they were alone in the room. Conchita felt the sexual tension building between them. David pulled her in close to his body and released her by moving quickly beside her. Their hips brushed as they traveled. The orchestra was masterful and they were fully into their steps together, moving as one, well before "La Comparsa" ended.

"Would you like to see Anita's gardens?" asked David, still holding her by the hand as they walked off the dance floor.

"Oh, yes," she answered without hesitation. "I hear they are lovely."

They walked quickly along a path until they were alone in the garden. The music from the orchestra flowed strongly through the crisp night. The garden was filled with the fragrance of jasmine and they were virtually surrounded by exotic flowering plants which they barely saw because they were both immersed in the sensations of that most extraordinary flower: budding romance.

David turned to Conchita and assumed the dance position. They took a few steps to the music of the Foxtrot.

"Shall we stroll?"

They did the stroll step smoothly, breaking apart for a couple of steps then coming back together. At the end of the third stroll, David pulled Conchita close to him. He kissed her full on the mouth. They kissed again and again, caught in a delicious passion that they never wanted to end.

It was over an hour before David and Conchita returned to the party. Caught up in the moment, they had completely lost track of time.

"I need to slip into Anita's bathroom and make myself presentable," Conchita said as they approached the house.

"You look great to me."

"You don't count," she smiled as she entered the house, "you're biased, and try to wipe that idiot grin off your face."

When Conchita returned, she and David found a free table near the dance floor. He brought a glass of white wine for Conchita and he had a cognac in tow.

"Can we get together this weekend?"

"Only if you dance with me all night."

"Consider it done. How about dinner on Friday night?"

"Well, I have a better idea. I've been invited to a gigantic bonfire and cookout in the country."

"Sounds delightful."

"Oh, I know you'll love it. It's at Xavier Diego's ranch outside of El Cedro. I'll pick you up at your hotel at five."

"Wonderful."

They slow-danced while the orchestra played "Stardust" until Fredrico came to get David for the ride to his hotel. David kissed Conchita on the cheek, and felt a warm rush at her closeness. They squeezed hands before he turned and disappeared with Fredrico.

* * *

Conchita slept for four hours and woke before sunrise. She languished in bed with the incredible comfortableness that she felt with David. She was totally relaxed when he was with her. It was as if they had known each other for a long time. Her mind drifted in and out of each experience with David at Anita's party.

For an Irishman, he had a surprising Latin fire about him when he got into las palmas and dancing. He was playful and enjoying it to the hilt. She had not been able to laugh and play like that lately. David had freed up the "little girl" in her, which had been squelched, even oppressed by her last boyfriend. He had become a monster of criticism and jealousy. After each business trip, Jorge would question her in detail about where she stayed and who she met. She often had to make deals with businessmen over lunch or dinner. He would drill her on what clothes she wore, how old the men were, and how long the "supposed" business meetings lasted. He would ask, "Did she dance with them?" and always, "Did you go to bed with him?" Then, he'd say "I don't believe you" if she didn't confess to an infidelity that never happened. The pain was just not worth it, so she ended the relationship.

Then, she remembered dancing with David. How they meshed and flowed so easily together, on the first meeting. *It's just infatuation*, she thought. *It could be a flash of passion that will fade in the clear light of day. We know nothing of each other. Well, almost nothing, but he and I have something going here.*

She remembered looking in the mirror while she was freshening up after her stroll in the garden with David. In the mirror, she had seen a woman full of joy, full of life, truly alive for the first time in months! It was almost scary! Oh, yeah, it *was* scary. To feel so close to someone at that level so quickly? She felt a rush of falling in love and pulled back. She rolled over on her back and felt herself all over. She felt good. She rolled on her side and snuggled the pillow, imagining she was snuggling with David. She felt his body close to hers as they danced the Bolero.

She glanced at the glowing numbers of the clock, which told her it was 5:35. She knew she needed to sleep again, but her mind wouldn't let go of the night's memories. She wanted nothing more than to re-experience the sweet moments of her new romance.

Half asleep, half awake, Conchita remembered her lovers of the past and there were really only two that counted. Her first love, at eighteen, was a man of thirty-one. Roberto was experienced and charming. He took her to the theater, for long drives at night to the mountains, and to the finest restaurants.

After a year of being swept along in a flurry of social events and expensive gifts, she knew in her soul that Roberto was not the man she wanted to live with for the rest of her life. He was preoccupied with power and money. Then, came the shock. She found a card with a passionate note to another woman in his desk drawer.

So, from then on, she concentrated on her education and her independence. She decided to go to college in the United States. At the University of North Carolina, Chapel Hill, she was a serious student. The dates she allowed were few and far between. The men there seemed too shallow. They were boys trying to be men. If they had a spiritual dimension, it was imperceptible. They were too much in pursuit of pleasure and getting her in bed, not unlike Roberto.

Back in Bogotá, after graduation, Conchita enjoyed her family and friends. Parties were frequent enough to meet new people and have fun. It was a carefree life. No entanglements that could hurt. Then, along came Jorge. At first, she was very cautious about a serious relationship with Jorge because of her shocking experience with Roberto. Although she was strongly attracted to him, she always held a certain part of her heart in reserve. They loved to dance together. That was the romantic thing that held them together more than anything else.

Then, her mind drifted back to David and their dancing. Soon, she drifted off to sleep with a feeling that she was wrapped in love and peace.

Chapter 8
DIEGO'S BONFIRE

Conchita picked up David at his hotel at five o'clock. He wore black slacks, and a lobster-colored sweater flecked with hints of red and green, he bought in Maine. Conchita wore grey flannel slacks and a turquoise sweater which, as David observed, complemented her dark brown hair quite nicely.

"Lovely outfit," he said. "You look absolutely soft and huggable in that sweater."

She gave David her 200 watt smile as he sat down beside her, holding a tweed jacket in his hands.

Conchita took the jacket and laid it in the back seat. As she turned, David put his arms around her and they were immediately lost in light, sweet kisses. They both realized that passion was rising instantly and this wasn't the place. Conchita tossed her head slightly and wiggled her shoulders, as if to throw off the feeling, and started the car. They drove down the narrow streets of Old El Cedro with rows of buildings lining the very narrow sidewalks. The signs in the windows indicated that there were shops and apartments on the first floor and apartments above. Within 20 minutes, they were driving through stretches of forest which now and then succeeded in hiding the houses behind them.

"I've really been looking forward to this," she said. "A country cookout is so great in the fall."

"Yes," he smiled back, "that cool country air makes a body feel downright energized." He paused to take in her beauty. He paused some more. She was beautiful from the inside out. She radiated a kind of dignity and gracia that told him she was a very special person. She was delightful to behold and accessible. "You look very special this evening." It took an act of will not to kiss her again, at that moment.

Conchita gave him a "Thank you," with a smile and a little toss of her ponytail. "Do you think Europa will let you stay to work on Constellations?"

"Carlos and I will give a major report on the Constellation to Erikson after La Feria de Las Faldas. He won't waste any time getting down here. I have to be optimistic. It's my nature. But tonight, I want to know all about Conchita Seguras."

"I could tell you my life story in ten minutes. Or, I could remain a woman cloaked in mystery. I think I like the second choice best."

"That's a good plan. I like that," smiled David. "Except I already talked Fredrico into giving me your resume...along with several other folks just to cover up. I didn't fool Fredrico, but he didn't see any harm in showing me what you had written about yourself."

"Well, you may know a little then, but the real mysteries are still very much intact."

"And I'm thankful for that. I think everyone should be allowed to keep their authentic self a mystery, at least in part. I noticed that you were born and raised in a small town outside of Bogotá."

"Yes, it's true. I was raised in the country until I was eleven. Then, my family moved to Bogotá. My father became a manager in the coffee business. He helped me get through college. I worked in a restaurant called Club Rio which served the elite. At first, I couldn't believe what they spent on a dinner! They wanted to flaunt their money, they were so rich. Once in a while, they would call the chef out and tip him four hundred dollars! I was young and charming, so they gave me some very good tips as well."

"Then, you went to Chapel Hill for graduate school. It's a fine school. I visited a professor there once to talk shop."

"It's a beautiful campus. Except in the summer months. The heat and humidity is so intolerable that everyone leaves if they possibly can."

"So, you majored in communications and minored in economics. We have something in common. I majored in city planning and minored in economics."

"The communication courses were great, but as Hazel Henderson used to say, 'academic economics is a form of brain damage.' I took economics because I knew that everything was driven by bad economic theory. I was forced to study it in order to understand what's really happening. Free market economics just hasn't worked in Latin America."

"I know what you mean. Back in the fifties, most Americans had jobs that meant something. They were farmers growing food, they had jobs delivering important services that greatly improved people's lives. They built and sold things that were necessary for the good life, like cars and refrigerators. They felt that they were giving a service as well as collecting a paycheck. Their jobs had meaning because they knew they were delivering the necessities of life. Then, we shifted to a "service sector economy" where production of the basic necessities is highly automated so fewer workers can see the value of their work. Now, most jobs are sitting behind a computer processing paperwork, telling people what they need to live the good life and selling people things they don't need to live the good life. People are far removed from the value of delivering life's necessities. The work provides a paycheck but very little inner reward. So, people go out and shop until they drop in a pathetic attempt to fill the void left by meaningless work. People feel empty. Whether they know it or not, they are spiritually deprived of the meaning and fulfillment of good work that they know serves others."

"It's sad. Business leaders and politicians have no answers. They still ignore the best kept secret in economics…"

"Mondragon," said David with instant recognition. "Fredrico showed us the video. Very impressive. Politicians and economists just aren't asking the right questions."

"They never studied philosophy and human values. If they had, they would ask the right questions."

David was stunned with her insight because it was his as well.

"Conchita," he said with great warmth, you just astonish me. That was one of my biggest breakthroughs in understanding problem solving. Obviously, very easy for you. That's a hybrid of the Socratic method. You, me and Socrates. We just ask the right question at the right level of reality—and poof! There's the answer."

"And now, the right answer for both of us is the Constellation."

"Okay, Conchita, I'm going to ask you a really serious question. Are you ready for this?"

Looking nervously over his left shoulder, she said, "I think so," as she bit her lower lip.

"Do you sleep on the left side of the bed or the right?"

Conchita chuckled with relief. "Facing the bed?"

"Yes, facing the bed."

"Well, if I had a rich and handsome husband who was right-handed, I would sleep as I do now, on the left side of the bed."

"Oh well, I get one out of three. Thank God I'm right-handed!"

"Now it's *my* turn to play serious question with you. Are you ready for this?"

"I hope so. Fire away."

"Look, handsome, when are you going to become rich?"

"You mean I can't just get by on my looks?"

"Not if you want *me* on the left side of the bed."

"Okay, you can sleep on the right."

"Oh, you are smooth but not very bright. You forgot to ask me my definition of 'rich.'"

"All right, how rich must I be?"

"You must be *very* rich.

"You mean like two hundred thousand a year?"

"No, you must be very rich in true love."

"Oh, you drive a hard bargain, lady. That's the most precious thing in the world."

"I know."

"The development of true love requires a lot of closeness and giving. If I'm going to meet your criteria, you'll have to sleep on the left side of the bed."

"Okay, but you won't be in it until I sense you are making big progress in achieving true love."

"It's a deal. I'm highly motivated. But I'll need lots of close loving reinforcement to reach the awesome summit of true love."

"Good. Then, after you're rich in true love, you can start working on the money thing."

"Ah, we've come full circle now. The eternal quest of men and women: true love, great lovemaking and money grubbing."

"At least we have our priorities right: true love comes first."

"Tell me more about Xavier Diego," said David as they drove on toward the ranch.

"Well, I met the Diegos at the Feria de Las Faldas last year and we had a great time together. Last weekend, he invited me out to the ranch and said to bring a friend if I liked. I liked," she said, as she glanced at David.

David put his arm around her shoulder and kissed her neck, ear and cheek.

They came to a stop sign, where he kissed her fully but lightly on the lips. She kissed back with a delicately restrained passion.

"Are all of you Irishmen big cuddlers?" asked Conchita.

"Only the smart ones."

"Just be careful you don't distract the driver beyond her limits."

"Wouldn't think of it."

"Uh-uh, right," she said with total mock distrust.

"Okay, tell me the rest about Diego."

"He raises fast-breeding Asian quail, chickies and turkeys, for the Constellation, of course. He has a small five acre ranch and he just cleared about three acres of forest with a bulldozer to make room for more quail. According to Ramon, we'll see two huge piles of timber and shrubs to be set on fire. Each pile is about the size of four two-story houses."

"Whoa! That's going to be one helluva fire!"

"They have a permit to burn tonight if there's no breeze."

They drove down a valley for several miles along a creek bed. Then, as they approached the turn-off to Diego's ranch, they saw that the fires had already been lit. A flame plume rose about fifty feet above the top of the hill they were now climbing. It was an awesome sight. They were about three hundred feet below the top of the hill when it sparked into crimson and yellow with a rush of crackling sounds. The flames shot up to over one hundred feet with the rush of flames through pine needles. They wound up the gravel road, pounded solid by trucks hauling fowl to market. As they reached the summit of the hill, they could see the nearest roaring fire and the ranch house below. On a hill far beyond the ranch house, they could see the second pile of trees surrounded in a wall of flames. Conchita parked the car on top of the hill to look at the monster fire just below them. Flames shot into the air with awesome power and heat. It was a unique experience of friendly fire. There was a remarkable feeling of safety in the face of such a fiery furnace. The fire was well contained, and far from the Diegos' ranch house. They were entranced for several minutes. Then, a few cars pulled up behind them with their lights on. Nightfall was beginning to frame the huge hills of fire.

"We'd better move on," said Conchita.

They drove around the fire, down to the Diego ranch house and parked the car on the grass. About fifty cars had already arrived. As they stepped out of the car, they could feel the dry, cool, fall air with its invigorating freshness. David held Conchita's hand as they walked, swinging it back and forth, in child's play. Conchita laughed and swung with him.

Then, David sang: "We're off to see the Wizard, the wonderful Wizard of Oz," and they began to skip together. A soaring elation overwhelmed them as they smiled with joy and skipped down the imaginary Yellow Brick Road. After a vigorous trip, they broke up laughing and fell into each other's arms. They held each other tightly and kissed.

They entered Diego's house through the open door and found Ramon and his father pulling the caps off of beer bottles. These were quart bottles, obviously of home brew. Every time they popped a lid, one of two things would happen. Either the lid would hit the ceiling or blue smoke curled out and rose about six inches above the bottle. David approached Ramon to greet him.

"Thanks for inviting us, Ramon, it's a fantastic fire. I've never seen anything like it in my life."

"Conchita! So glad you could come!"

Ramon reached out to hold Conchita's hand in both of his.

"I see you on video and I know you are doing great things for our country."

"Thank you, Ramon. This is such a nice thing for you to do. I'm so glad I was invited. It's a magical night. Can we meet Xavier?"

"Of course. Dad, I want you to meet someone. This is Conchita Seguras...remember, with El Cinco?"

"Oh, yes!" said Xavier, swinging away from his cases of home brew. "I've always enjoyed seeing you tell us about what El Cinco are doing to help everyone. It's a real pleasure to have you with us tonight. And you're just as lovely in person as you are on the video!"

"You're too kind, Mr. Diego. Thank you." She squeezed his hand and kissed him on the cheek.

He hugged her like family.

"Would you like some home brew? I made it myself. It's about twenty percent alcohol, so don't say I didn't warn you," he said with a rascally Diego smile.

David took a bottle, poured two glasses, gave one to Conchita and drank.

"Marvelous. Aye, and it's as soft as an Irish day in the heather."

"And you'll be lyin' in the heather face down if you sample too much of that," allowed Conchita, with her best Irish accent.

"Well now, we wouldn't want that to happen, would we? No, no, nay never!" replied David in his best Irish brogue.

"Oh," said Conchita, laughing, "I remember that song. When I was in Washington a sweet lady from Ireland sang 'No, No Nay Never.' When she got to the part where you clap your hands three times, she'd sing 'Hike up your skirts,' because when the guys were singin' that they won't be Irish Rovers no more, a girl has got to do something!"

David tossed back his head and laughed. "Yeah, right. We all know how long those guys will resist those delightful female charms."

Señor Diego and Ramon carried a table and an old-fashioned tape player outside and set it up on the grass so people could hear some dance music and enjoy the night more. The music floated into the night like the smoke from the fire. The flames had gradually descended as the fire burned down. The flames had settled down to about forty feet above the ground. It was still a spectacular sight, but now, an even more friendly one. Around the edges, burning embers crackled, popped, hissed and sputtered. People gathered closer to the fire for warmth against the cooler night air as the temperature dropped a few degrees. Curious onlookers arrived in a continuous stream of cars.

Señor Diego had anticipated a sizable crowd and was able to offer several boxes of spiced turkey and quail sausages for roasting on the open fire. He provided long handled holders so people could find a niche where the fire was turning to embers and get close enough to roast the sausages. Back at the ranch, the Diegos were distributing cases of cold home brew, as if the supply was endless. As they ripped off the caps, there were appropriate "ooohs" and "arribas!" from those in close attendance, as the blue smoke curled or the cap hit the ceiling of the ranch house.

And still the cars came. They arrived at the top of the hill, surveyed the scene, and drove off. Dozens of these people reappeared, having gone to the local store for hot dogs, sausages and marshmallows. Soon it was rumored that the local grocery had been bought out completely. As the fire died down people moved their blankets closer and roasted their sausages. A crowd of a hundred and fifty people were gathered in small groups around the enormous bonfire. Another sixty people were dancing in front of the ranch house or just enjoying the incredible magic of fire, the night air and the music. Later, several couples took up their blankets and drifted off into the woods. Shortly, their flashlights disappeared. One could reach up and scrape the romance right out of the air.

"This is the most spontaneous party I've ever seen," said David, with Conchita resting on his chest as they watched the flickering bonfire together.

"I've been thinking the same thing. That's what makes it so special. Most of these folks had no idea they would find a great bonfire and a super-friendly party at the top of this hill."

"Where can we go to neck?"

"And what makes you think I want to neck with you?" she teased.

"I can't help it. I feel like Captain Kirk, with the *Enterprise* lost in the Mysterious Romantic Zone."

"And what's it like in this romantic zone?"

"Well, the crew is euphoric. Captain Kirk is euphoric. Everyone is suspended in a kind of delightful buoyancy. No one wants to leave the Mysterious Romantic Zone."

"Lost in romantic space, are you? I'm intimately familiar with that feeling."

"Well, the only problem is that Captain Kirk doesn't know what they'll find as this powerful tractor beam pulls the *Enterprise* deeper into the zone."

"So, what is Captain Kirk going to do?"

"Oh, he's going in all right. He's goin' in all the way."

"Boldly going in, hey?"

"The prospects are incredibly inviting—nay, compelling. He's optimistic."

"So, you're a storyteller, are you?"

"It's the happy privilege of the Irish to tell the most outlandish tales."

"Well, I too have a spaceship under the spell of the tractor beam...spirally deeper and deeper into the M.R.Z. Do you think our ships will stay side by side or will they crash and burn up together?"

"I think they'll fly together, brave the future and become inextricably intertwined."

"How exciting! The tractor beam is really growing stronger now."

Conchita stood up and David followed suit. She rolled up the blanket.

"As you said in Anita's garden," she giggled through her 200 watt smile. Then lilted her head to one side with provocative gaiety. "Would you like to take a stroll?"

* * *

The weeks passed quickly, as Conchita and David got to know each other. During that time, David and Carlos spent long hours in the sandbox with Fredrico planning energy technoparcs, manufacturing facilities, roads, transit systems and agricultural networks. They visited new sites all over the northwest quadrant of Rocadura. Then, they drew plans for the next Constellation and took their applications to the provincial government for approval.

Two months after Diego's bonfire, Conchita found herself in Caracas on a new assignment. She was on a trip with banker Gail O'Reilly to spread the word about the Constellation and to recruit new investors. Conchita went to the hotel swimming pool and moved a lounge chair into the shade of the hotel building. She lay back into the chair with a glass of dry sherry from Jerez and a little bowl of walnuts. Life is good. Life is sweet, she thought. She remembered the days when life was hard and painful. She was only sixteen when her mother had died. She died so young. Cancer took her away at the young age of fifty-one. How can you trust a God who takes your mother away so young, she howled! It was the toughest job of her life. How could she possibly trust in a God that would do that? But she discovered time and grace heal the most incredible wounds. She worked on it for months. There was no choice. It had to be faced. She was wounded to the core, and at times, she had felt totally decimated. Yet, there was something that she saw to hold onto. The love she shared with her mother was undeniable. At times, it alone sustained her. Where did that great love come from? She concluded God created love and is love. Now, when she spoke with God she understood she was speaking *to* Love. And that became her shield when the "fear lies" surrounded her soul and challenged her trust in God. She cried out with all of her heart: "Love is God's gift and love is my shield." As time passed, she realized her mother's death drew her mind and heart to her mother in Heaven. She was drawn to seek answers at the spiritual level, because that was the only place she could find the answers she had to own in her soul. She was drawn to contemplate her trust in God at an early age. When she passed through the gate of trust, she was given a gift of understanding, that God loves us absolutely, and unconditionally. That those who we think are lost to us are only stored up for us in Heaven. Conchita found her peace with God. She knew that every other gift in life that could come to her would be anticlimactic. Her joy was unbounded. She floated in the epiphany for weeks. She knew that she was loved. This understanding transcended all doubt and fear. Her life was changed forever and she knew that from now on, she could grow from strength to strength.

And here she was in Caracas, with a major kick-off conference tomorrow. She would make a presentation before a packed room of two hundred or more people. She thought about the steps she would take to communicate the richness of the Constellation to all of Latin America. Pretty heady stuff. But that was the assignment. It was time to raise more capital. It was also time to export know-how, planning and engineering services, financing infrastructure, cooperative organization, equipment, tools. It was time to lay the groundwork for new partnerships.

But she knew it was the heart of the Constellation that would win their minds and souls, so she rested in that good truth: that all she had to do was tell them about the heart of the Constellation, about banking certainty, the freedom of worker-entrepreneurs to create, Las Faldas celebrations, the economic security, the Home Plan, the incredible sense of community, and the joy of being within this way of life. It was second nature to her now. She drafted the notes for her speech and lay the notebook down on a table beside her chair.

Well, that was the work for the afternoon, because her thoughts had already turned to David.

She had known David for three months now and she had always been—well, mostly—in control of herself.

It was almost more than she could handle. Some gifts came in small packages, but this was oceanic.

And so the song started running through her mind: "*Me estoy volviendo loca, pero loca por amor.*" *Dios mio! I haven't had raging hormones like this since college. The man makes me feel so good.* A pang of conscience hit her. *Is this right? Is there danger here? Yes!* the answer came back quickly. She was loving and being totally out of control. But that is the essence of a great romance! Perhaps a once in a lifetime romance. She lifted her sherry in pure emotion and toasted the evening twilight. Then, she thought about the night at Diego's bonfire. What an incredibly romantic evening. Many couples had drifted off into the woods to make love. She wondered how many babies were conceived that night. She recalled David's story about Captain Kirk and their spaceships flying off together, intertwined. She knew David loved her. His warmth was undeniable. He was noble and constant in his honesty. That's what made her feel at home with him. He was just the opposite of Carlos, who was out with a different woman almost every weekend.

David had told her how he had lost his wife in an auto accident. Her car got into the blind spot of a tractor trailer. She was passing on the right and the driver never saw her coming as he switched into her lane. He said their marriage was a good one overall, but near the end, his wife had started to attack his every fault. She had been "gunny sacking," holding back her true feelings for years. She told him he was too dominating and he needed to be careful about the way he said things, more than what he said. She had taught him a lot about things he could not see in himself. He was making amends when she died. He said if she had not told him that she still loved him before she died, her loss would have been even more devastating.

Conchita thought he had learned his lessons well. He is gentle, and positively supports a woman to be herself. She loved the Irish rascal in his smile, the way he danced, the way he kissed and held her. She wiggled in her chair and reveled in the whole beautiful gift. Instantly, she had to be close to David. She would try to reach him on the phone. It took her all of four minutes to reach her room and start dialing David's hotel number in El Cedro.

"La Granada Hotel. Can I help you?"

"Hello, could you please connect me with Mr. O'Laughlin in room 214?"

"Certainly. Oh, just a minute. Mr. O'Laughlin is maintaining his room, but he will be out of town for a few days. He left this morning."

"Oh, dear. Thank you. Did he leave a forwarding number?"

"Yes, it's 700-642-1999."

Where could he be going? she asked herself. Then, she remembered that he and Carlos had gone with Fredrico to La Feria de Las Faldas. She would meet him there on Saturday night. *Ah,* she thought. *Saturday night at La Feria with David. That's going to be fine. Let's see, I'll take him to Nuestra Tapa bar. He'll love it. Wonderful.* Conchita took her last drink of sherry and dressed for dinner. She thought about David, Fredrico and Carlos driving to Las Faldas. Then, she remembered what Fredrico had told her about the spies who had uncovered Colonel Saldana's attack plan. She was immediately gripped by anxiety. Saldana gave her a cold shiver in her gut. She said a prayer for David's safety as she went down the elevator to dinner.

Chapter 9
ON THE ROAD TO LAS FALDAS

The next morning, Fredrico took David and Carlos by car on a trip through the central highlands to the new town of Las Faldas. They planned to arrive on the eve of the harvest celebration, the Feria de Las Faldas. As they left El Cedro, they followed an asphalt road up a long hill, which curved tightly through the trees. Through openings along the way, they looked down to see the city laid out below. The buildings were very close together and there were few trees, except for the large city parks. Spanish tile roofs filled the cityscape in the old part of the city. An occasional high rise hotel, hospital or public building rose above the relatively flat city. The surrounding hillsides were heavily forested, which gave visual relief from the stucco and pavement.

Fredrico drove along the ridge of the hill for a few minutes before the road plunged into a thick forest. The high elevation brought cool air and a heavy morning mist. The air was spring-like and fresh.

Fredrico turned off the air conditioner and rolled down the windows. "Isn't that a treat?" he asked, rhetorically.

"Oh yeah!" David responded instantly. "By the way, do you use drip-feed irrigation in greenhouses to grow truck garden crops? I know that's the way they do it in El Ejido, Spain. They have twenty thousand acres or more under plastic, and they grow enough to supply northern Europe with winter fruit and vegetables. But it's hot as hell for the workers. They're immigrants from Africa and the pay is very low."

"Yes, of course. There's not enough arable land or fresh water anymore, around the world. Everyone eventually has to go to drip-feed irrigation. But we don't bake our people in greenhouses. We install air conditioning," Fredrico allowed. "When we get to the Energy Technoparc in Las Faldas, I'll show how we can do that with cheap energy."

As they drove along, Fredrico pointed out several acres of soybean crops.

"Ya know, Fredrico, I tried those soyburgers and I used onions and garlic and I just couldn't do anything but throw 'em out."

"Well, we have a secret," smiled Fredrico broadly. "We mix 'em with turkey and Asian quail meat in small quantities—add the right spices—and that makes all the difference."

"Now, yer talkin'! I had a turkey-quail sausage at Diego's ranch. It was spicy and real tasty."

David drifted off for a minute thinking about Conchita. Her image seemed to form in his consciousness about every fifteen minutes.

They passed through seemingly endless forests of oaks and pines. In the upland valleys, the land was used for farming. The road from El Cedro to Las Faldas was a four lane limited access highway. A rapid transit railway ran down the center of the expressway with three tracks. The rail lines were elevated enough by grading and a four-foot wall so that cars couldn't hit the tracks.

"I notice there are separate rapid transit lanes down the center," said Carlos. "How does that work?"

"The center lane is switchable during rush hour traffic. You'll notice we've built large drainage canals along the foothills. Every year we have torrential downpours that can last a month. It used to destroy thousands of acres of crops and wreck the lives of millions of poor people. The canals take the storm water away quickly. They protect the croplands owned by the Constellation and everyone who lives near us."

"What's that low structure in the canal?"

"It's a fish farming operation."

"So, the canals serve a double purpose."

"It produces tons of fish," Fredrico said. "Just outside of Las Faldas there's a huge shanty town developing. They call it Camino Adelante, which means 'on one's way,' or 'on the road to something better.' They're people who have lost their jobs in the mines or were tenant farmers driven off their land by agribusiness. They come by the thousands looking for a better life in Las Faldas, but we can't absorb them that quickly. There are one hundred and twenty thousand people living in this shanty town. I'd like to take a side trip over there to show it to you."

"Sure," Carlos said.

"I'm game.

They drove up a long hill, winding their way along the hillside on a narrow dirt road. The terrain was rough, with pot holes and small rocks making passage difficult. After covering about three miles, they reached the summit of a large highlands plateau. Below them they saw the tin-roof huts of a huge shanty town that stretched out as far as the eye could see. There appeared to be one unpaved main street littered with garbage and sewage.

"The flash storms wash the garbage and sewage right up on the road and there are no street cleaning services," said Fredrico. "It's a cultural thing. They come from the country and think they can defecate in the ditches along the streets."

"Then," David said, "the kids play in the street, and get sick from contact with the feces and garbage. I've read about it, but I've never seen it before."

"Right. The town has grown from twenty thousand to one hundred and twenty thousand in five years. They have no infrastructure or city facilities. No sewer system. There are few jobs, little income, no tax base…so, no city services. They have no hospital, just a few clinics. It's a total disaster."

"My god! One hundred and twenty thousand is twice the size of your projected buildout for Las Faldas! They'll fill two new towns!"

"You got it. That's why we need you guys to join our team. We can't build 'em fast enough."

"But you can't stop them from growing larger," Carlos asserted. "They'll keep expanding until nature stops them."

"That's exactly right, Carlos. So, we build up with high density and we build in a huge outer green belt and dedicated farm land to stop the growth. If we didn't do that, the natural resources and arable land would vanish in ten years."

As they drove along the main street of Camino Adelante, dodging potholes, there was hardly a patch of green anywhere. People waved at them, holding up items for sale. Once in a while, a young man came aggressively close to the car to try to make it stop.

"And they come here hoping to get jobs in Las Faldas?" Carlos asked.

"That's right. To keep them from making the trip to Las Faldas and camping out with no food, we decided to set up an employment office here, to post the jobs and take applications."

"How do they survive?"

"The workers in the Constellation give ten percent of their surplus profits to charity and most of it winds up here in the soup kitchens and health clinics. We give them left over construction materials and we set up a furniture-making shop to employ about two hundred and fifty people. El Cinco even put in a hydroponics installation for growing food and hired about one thousand folks to harvest the crops and distribute them—free. But this is no place to build a new town. It can only be a holding station until we can employ them full time in the Constellation."

"And living in Camino Adelante is better than staying in the country?" David asked.

"One woman told me that in the country, if you have no food, you starve. At least in Camino Adelante there is a safety net provided primarily by the Constellation. Some of them work part-time in construction, building shanties and putting in water lines. But most of the new arrivals can't afford to pay the one hundred and ten dollars a year that the utility company charges for the water hook-up."

As they dodged the ruts in the street, they saw a dead dog lying in the ditch.

"You can't live without water. So what do they do?"

"They have no choice but to use the water from the ditches that flows through the shanty town. As you can see, it's filled with garbage, dead animals and raw sewage. They boil it and put in a bit of chlorine. That's what they use to drink, to wash clothes in and to bathe. It's a hard, bitter life when you have little or no income. El Cinco is building public water stations, at a cost of four million dollars to pay the utility company more than it can squeeze out of these poor folks. But again, it's just a holding action. I think you've seen about all there is to see in Camino Adelante. Let's drive on to Las Faldas."

"Amen," David said with a sigh of relief, shaking his head at the human misery all around them.

They drove out of the town and along several miles of highway in silence. The stench of Camino Adelante lingered, like the sight of the dead dog in the ditch.

They drove towards Las Faldas along a stretch of road that was heavily forested for several miles.

At that moment, Colonel Victor Saldana was flying down the same road with two helicopter gunships, fully armed for the attack on Las Faldas. Fredrico was totally unaware that Echeverria had convinced Saldana to attack two weeks earlier, in order to ruin the Feria and demoralize everyone in the Cornerstone Constellation.

As Saldana flew above the road to Las Faldas, he saw the LSI letters on the door of Fredrico's car.

"Turn the ship around!" he ordered excitedly. "We have a target of opportunity. That LSI car could be El Cinco on their way to La Feria. When we blow them away, it will blow everybody's mind in the whole damn Constellation!"

When Fredrico saw the black gunship rocketing down the road toward Las Faldas, he knew it was not a Constellation ship.

"My God!" shouted Fredrico. "Saldana is attacking early!"

"Attacking?" asked David and Carlos in unison.

"He's going to try to blow up the ethanol tanks in Las Faldas. I can only hope that our security forces know he's coming."

With that, Fredrico suddenly stopped the car, careening to the side of the road. Quickly, he dialed Constellation Security.

"Saldana is attacking—now! He's attacking!" Fredrico shouted. "His helicopter just flew by our car. He's five minutes away! You're ready? Thank God!"

The two gunships had swung around in a circle and came back up behind Fredrico's car.

"Jose!" shouted Saldana to the pilot of the other gunship. "Stand off behind me. This one is all mine! Garcia, give me the machine gun. We don't want to waste a missile on these lightweights. This is like shooting pigs in their pen," he smiled with hot revenge in his eyes.

Fredrico's conversation was cut short by a burst of machine gun fire. Bullets ripped through the hood of the car. Saldana's gunship was hovering beside them. Fredrico saw the silhouette of a man shooting at them from the open door of the gunship. It was about sixty yards away from the car, but to Fredrico it was right on top of him. He sensed he was trapped with death to soon follow.

He knew that the helicopter was armed with heat-seeking missiles.

"We're sitting ducks!" Carlos shouted.

They all knew the bullets would soon hit the gas tank and blow them away. Fredrico looked to his right and saw the dense forest.

"Bail out!"

The three men dove out of the car, away from the helicopter, and rolled down into the six-foot deep roadside drainage ditch. Saldana rained bullets on the car and a few bullets passed through the shredded vehicle, and tore up the turf beside them.

Fredrico felt a sting, like a knife blade across in his right shoulder and a hot shock in his right leg.

"I've been hit!"

David dragged him toward the entrance of a culvert pipe five feet away. They hoped this large culvert pipe would give them safe passage into the dense forest on the other side of the road. David lunged ahead with Fredrico toward the mouth of the culvert. He hunched over and carried Fredrico with his right arm around his waist and Fredrico's left arm around his neck. Fredrico was a large man, weighing two hundred pounds and David was using all of his strength to support him. Just inside the five-foot diameter pipe, David pulled up short at the mouth of the culvert. Carlos came crashing into his back and shoulders, almost knocking him down.

"Snakes!" David shouted. David handed the wounded Fredrico to Carlos and turned to face three large snakes lying in the culvert just six feet away. Suddenly alarmed, they coiled into strike position.

The machine gun fire continued to riddle the car, which partially blocked the line of fire. Occasionally a bullet ricocheted off the walls of the culvert.

David recognized the large diamond-shaped heads, and knew they were poisonous vipers. He had grown up killing Copperheads in the local creek and culverts. Instinctively, David ripped off his jacket and held it in front of the closest snake and shook it, in bullfighting style.

"Ha! Toro!" he shouted as he jerked the jacket, just in front of the nearest snake's head. "Ha! Toro!"

Two shakes of is jacket and the lead viper lunged a full three feet, and buried his fangs in the thick leather. David dropped his jacket and wrapped the snake inside. He hurled the whole package into the other two snakes. The jacket and viper slammed into the other two snakes at the far end of the culvert with full impact. The snakes quickly decided that it was time to leave this threatening scene. Filled with fear, they rapidly disappeared into the bush. The whole event took a matter ninety seconds, but to Fredrico and Carlos, it was like a slow-motion nightmare, a nightmare in real time, where their feet were cast in cement cubes and they could only move with agonized slowness, while the relentless death threat pounded mercilessly at their backs. Bullets continued to hit the mouth of the culvert as the three men hunched and struggled to make their way out into the woods.

Suddenly, there was a huge explosion that made the ground rumble.

"They hit the gas tank!" shouted Carlos.

Fredrico had passed out from shock. David had never experienced the incredible burden of someone who had passed out, putting all of their dead body weight on his arms. He couldn't believe how heavy Fredrico's body felt, but his adrenaline had kicked in with super human force. He threw Fredrico over his shoulder and plunged into the forest.

"Damn it! We're losing them!" shouted Saldana. "Get this ship up so we can see better!"

The gunship rose to hover above the three men as they staggered through the woods. The gunship crew could barely make out their path as they crashed into saplings as they went. Carlos looked back over his shoulder and saw the gunship was lined up directly on them.

"They've got a missile lock on us!" shouted Carlos.

"This way!" David shouted.

David released Fredrico and let him roll down into a twenty-foot deep ravine, knowing that it was the only way to save his life even if he suffered deeper wounds. Then, he dove head first down the hill. Carlos followed his lead and tumbled down the steep ravine. He felt the brush rip into his left arm, then the thigh, but Carlos was soon to find that the arm wound was not just a brush scratch. He had been hit by machine gun fire before he dove down the hill. The burning in his arm was intense now, like hot coals placed directly on his skin.

The pilot yelled to Saldano: "I've got them in my laser sights!"

"Fire!"

The gunship's rocket blasted through the trees twenty yards away. The forest fifteen feet away from them was an instant wall of fire, a moving crematorium, now just ten feet away. David was closest and his right shirtsleeve caught on fire. He rolled away from the flame and tried to suffocate his blazing sleeve.

David screamed as the back of his hair caught fire. Fredrico was between Carlos and David and Carlos could not reach him instantly. He ripped off his jacket and dove over Fredrico who was dazed and helpless. Carlos threw his jacket over David's head and flaming right side and patted out the fire.

"Oh, God. Thanks, man!"

"It's okay, David, it's okay. I got it all out."

Carlos and David pulled Fredrico away from the scorching heat, hoping the hill and the brushfire would hide them from the gunship.

"I think we got 'em!" shouted Saldana to his pilot. "Head to Las Faldas. We can't waste any more time."

The gunship rose fifty yards above the road and rocketed out of sight. The trio collapsed on their backs against the ravine. David and Carlos drug Fredrico away from the flames until they felt safe. They lay there quietly for a few minutes, recovering from the assault.

"Fredrico, are you all right?" David asked. "I mean, how do you feel?"

"I'm okay. They hit my shoulder and my right calf. They burn like hell."

David pulled Fredrico's shirt open and examined the shoulder wound. "You took a bullet. The good news is it's not bleeding much. David pulled a clean handkerchief from his hip pocket, covered the wound, and closed Fredrico's shirt.

Carlos examined the calf wound.

"You were just nicked. It's a two-inch slash. The paramedics can patch that up pretty good."

"I've got a beautiful wife and two wonderful kids waiting for me in Las Faldas. I'll make it now. I dropped my cell phone, but we'll find it and call for help."

"Good," said David. "Hang on, we're going to get some help soon."

"Carlos, are you okay?"

"The bastards nicked my arm. I'm just glad to be alive."

"Hey, buddy," smiled David, "just remember all of those skirts in Las Faldas who can't wait to be loved by you."

"You're good! You always did know how to get to me."

They rested against the hill, again watching the fire move away from them with the breeze.

It was Fredrico who broke the silence with a cackle, and then a belly laugh. "I've never seen a snake matador before," he chuckled. "I think you ought to take that act on the road. You'll make a fortune."

"I'll have to admit," smiled Carlos, "that bullfight thing was pretty damned comical. Where did you learn to scramble with snakes like that?"

"Look, guys, it was all raw instinct. When I was twelve, I lived in the country. There were always a few copperheads in the creek beds and culverts in the summertime. My pappy used to make 'em lunge at a stick. Then, he'd reach down and grab their tails and crack 'em like a whip. It broke their necks instantly. He taught me how to grab them just behind the head, with a forked stick around their necks. But I didn't have the heart to break their necks. I'd just throw them a few feet to let them know it was time to travel on. Snakes are secretive, you know. They really don't want to have anything to do with man."

"Yeah, but where did that 'Ha! Toro!' bit come from?" chided Fredrico, still burning with the pain from is bullet wound.

"I don't know. I guess I've seen too many bullfights. Anyway, that was no copperhead. That was a jumping pit viper. Did you see that big sucker? He struck from three and a half feet away!"

"Yeah, I saw it," said Fredrico with amazement. "I didn't know *any* snake could strike that far. It looked like a five-foot lunge to me. Okay, let's go back to the road and see if we can find the cell phone. I think I dropped it on the way into the culvert. Man, I hope Las Faldas survived! I'm counting on our security guys. They had advanced warning. They have three gunships against Saldana's two. I'll get someone to come out here to pick us up."

"Right," said David. "By the way, if Saldana was headed for Las Faldas why did he attack our car?"

"He probably thought he was attacking El Cinco," answered Fredrico. "He'd love to assassinate one of them. Look, guys, I owe you one giant apology. I just didn't expect the attack until well after the Feria. Security should've told me. I guess they were too busy trying to take on Saldana."

"I hold no grudges, Fredrico, but from now on I'm packin' a .357 Magnum."

"I'll fix us all up when we get back. This 'sitting duck' crap won't happen again!"

Fredrico found the cellular phone intact and called Security.

"What's happening?" asked Fredrico, in a calm voice. He listened intently and relayed the news to David and Carlos. "One of the gunships was knocked down about two miles outside of town. Saldana's gunship destroyed two ethanol tanks. He's being pursued by two of our ships. Las Faldas is safe. The fires are under control. One of our gunships has gone to destroy Saldana's base camp."

Fredrico rested against a tree and shouted with joy. "It's a total rout! Las Faldas is safe! OK, we need you to send a car to pick us up. Were on highway twenty-seven, about ten miles south of Las Faldas. Right." He put the phone in his jacket. "They're on the way."

Fifteen minutes later, the paramedics arrived. The driver was a Security sergeant. He greeted them with a big smile and shook their hands. Two paramedics went to work on their wounds.

"Hi, I'm Miguel. It's good to see you guys in one piece. We thought you were dead men before you called in the second time. Who's hurting the most?"

"Get Fredrico," said David.

They treated Fredrico's shoulder wound first. The paramedic cleansed the wound with alcohol and doused it with Mercurochrome.

"Haaaah!" Fredrico gasped.

"It'll only sting a second or two."

He cut a gauze patch to fit the shoulder wound and taped it firmly. Then, he took a knife and ripped Fredrico's pant leg open to expose the leg wound and followed the same procedure.

"Haah!"

"It won't burn long and it'll clean it out. This isn't that bad a wound. The bullet went straight through. You'll have a sore arm for three or four days. It'll take about four to six weeks to heal."

Then, they moved to take care of Carlos and David.

"Your wounds will be fine in two weeks or so. You'll all be feeling better in two or three days. I'm going to give you all a mild sedative to help you relax."

The paramedics helped them all into the emergency vehicle, where they sat along the seat on the side.

"You got any cognac in this rig?" Carlos queried.

"Gotcha," smiled Miguel, "that'll work just as well."

"That okay with you guys?"

"Oh, yeah!" David said with gusto.

Fredrico nodded his head appreciatively. He was sweating heavily.

"Here, drink some water first," Miguel said as he poured a cup for Fredrico.

Miguel poured three cognacs in plastic cups and handed them out. They all took a long draft and sunk back against the wall of the vehicle. Two more swigs went by in silence.

"A toast!" grunted Carlos. "To the matador!"

They raised their cups to David and took another deep swig.

Miguel said, "I'll be back in a second to take you into town." Then he hopped down from the back of the emergency vehicle and walked around the riddled remains of Fredrico's car, spread in pieces around the road.

"Damn." He took his hat off and scratched his head. When he got back to his wards he asked: "*That* was a car?"

"Yeah," said Fredrico. "If it we didn't have bulletproof glass and doors, Saldana's gunship would have nailed us instantly." Then, smiling at David, he said, "It was almost as bad as bullfighting with snakes."

The trio roared with laughter at their private joke. It was a full release of tension.

"Bullfighting with snakes? What are you guys talking about?" the sergeant asked.

They let Carlos tell Miguel about their viper adventure.

Miguel just shook his head in amazement.

"You guys must be livin' right!"

As they drove down the road to Las Faldas, David raised his cup and said, "A toast! To lousy shots!"

"To lousy shots!" Fredrico and Carlos said in unison, then they drained their cups.

"We'll check you into the hospital first," said Miguel. "Then I know that we all need a refresher after this incredible trip, so we'll drive you to Maria's guest house, where you'll be staying."

"Sounds good to me," David smiled, as the cognac began to take effect.

"I'll second that motion," Carlos added. "By the way, did they get Saldana?"

"I'll check it out."

"Pepe? Fredrico here. Did they get Saldana?"

"No. He landed in the jungle near his base camp. We think he had a car waiting there. He's probably long gone."

"Damn it! Saldana is still running loose. But he knows that we know who he is and we'll be on guard. We'll have an all-out search on for him."

"Yeah," Carlos said. "If the son of a bitch doesn't nail us first."

Chapter 10
RECOVERY

As they approached Las Faldas, David and Carlos wondered what impact Saldana's attack would have on the people in the village.

One mile from town they could see the column of smoke rising from the ethanol tank fires. It surged in billows, roiling and expanding at each higher level.

They drove past a residential neighborhood, mostly three-story town homes grouped closely together, each with a front porch for neighborly interaction.

Soon they entered the center of town.

"This looks real friendly," said Carlos.

"They have a strong sense of community. These Las Faldas families are close. People help each other."

The main streets were closed to traffic and filled with people dressed for an evening of celebration. The preparations for the Feria were complete. The street was grandly decked out for the major event of the season. People enjoyed a walk among the sidewalk cafes, where they met to chat about the Feria, people-watch and have a tapa and a drink.

When the emergency vehicle arrived at the hospital it was greeted with V.I.P. service. Two doctors examined the three men immediately and redressed their wounds. They were given prescriptions filled at an in-house pharmacy and delivered to them by orderlies. Then, they drove to the hotel were Carlos and David would be staying.

Miguel parked the emergency vehicle in front of a large two story mansion. "You guys should take it easy for a few days. You've been through some heavy violence. Take it from me, right now, you're living on the return to safety. Later on, you'll feel some shock and tiredness. Just go with the flow. Okay? Take it slow and easy."

"Right. Thanks, Miguel," David said, "you've been great, and we really appreciate it!"

"You can take your meals here in the dining room," said Fredrico. "This is a guest house with twenty bedrooms. We use it for out-of-town guests and travelers. I think you'll find it quite comfortable. My friends love the place because the hostess is a special person. Maria is a jewel. It's inexpensive and the food is very good here. I'm staying up the hill about a mile. Maria has my number. Just let me know when you've recuperated and we'll go to La Feria. Now, I'm going to spend some time with my family."

"That sounds fine to me," said Carlos.

"Perfect," said David.

"I know you'll enjoy the folks here and La Feria de Las Faldas. After that, I'll take you on a tour of the Energy Technoparc. That's the foundation of the whole operation, but you'll see for yourselves. If you need anything, just tell Señora Maria Leon. She'll be your hostess."

Fredrico introduced them to a short woman with black hair. *She is "muy Espanol" (very Spanish),* thought Carlos and he guessed she was about forty something years old. She smiled a warm and knowing smile, as if to imply, she carried a secret. Her brown eyes had a kind of wild look about them, accentuated by Spanish curls on her temples, but she countered her fiery appearance with a warm, courteous presentation. She gave the distinct impression that she was a woman of dignity and intelligence.

"Welcome to our house," she said with a smile. "We have been expecting you, and I've prepared some tapas and wine for the afternoon, *como se dice,* 'snacks'?"

"*Que maravillosa!*" Carlos smiled. "What a beautiful house. It looks like it was transported directly from Spain."

They entered through the inner courtyard adorned with a fountain and statuette. Orange trees lined the perimeter, and the blooms overwhelmed the air with their fragrance. Señora Leon led them to the front parlor where they found an abundance of palm fronds and exotic flowers. A young boy brought them the "little dishes of Spain" known as tapas.

"This is my son Jose Enrique. He will graduate from the eighth grade this year."

"Where do you go to school?" David asked.

"I go to Santiago. It's only a short walk from our house," replied Jose.

"It was built by El Cinco nine years ago," said Señora Leon. "It's a very fine school."

"What do you want to be when you finish college, Jose Enrique?"

"I want to be a Constellation builder," Jose said with a big smile. "I want to travel all over the world and help people build new towns. But I want to work in Rocadura first. Our country needs a lot of Constellation builders."

"That's why we're here. We are planners from America and we're visiting Las Faldas to learn how to build new towns like this one."

"Yes, I know, Fredrico told us."

Señora Leon interrupted, "Aren't you going to try your tapas while they are hot?"

The tapa delights included grilled garlic shrimp, Spanish olives, fresh baked Spanish bread and a fine sherry.

"These shrimp came in this morning from the Lemon Islands, thirty miles off the coast of Rocadura," said Señora Leon. "They also deliver a crop of shrimp developed in Asia that weigh one pound each. They can be raised in shellfish farms because they're not cannibalistic like some of the other ones. We use them like lobsters in our dishes."

David sampled a garlic shrimp.

"Señora, I didn't know shrimp could be this fresh! They are incredibly tender!"

"Oh, yes," said Maria. "That is one of the big joys of the Constellation. Everything is produced by us, for us, and delivered to the market with extraordinary freshness."

Suddenly, David felt the aftershock of the gunship attack.

"This is a great introduction to Las Faldas, Señora Leon," said David. "Thank you for your wonderful generosity. I'm really looking forward to talking with you more, but the day has been very intense, and I need some time alone to rest and absorb it all."

"It's hitting me too," said Carlos. "I'm just so drowzy."

"I was frankly astonished that you could be so calm after your experience with the attack. Let me show you to your rooms so you can rest."

It was six o'clock. Carlos and David went to their rooms and rested, with the thought that one of the greatest street parties in all of South America was about to unfold in the morning and they were exhausted. They soon fell asleep, like beaten, weary sailors after a long, violent storm at sea.

David woke after a little more than three hours of deep sleep. It was 9:30 p.m. The assault had taken its toll. He felt extremely lethargic. It was an effort to get up to eat dinner but he felt hunger pangs. He washed his face in cold water to revive himself. His thoughts were flooded with the bullets flying around the culvert, the snakes blocking their escape, the missile blast and the fire on his hair and clothes. Finally, he settled down inside. *Life will go on. Saldana is out of action, at least for a while.* He splashed his face with cold water again, trying to wash the strangeness away. Then, he realized it was no use. He knew he was not right inside. He was not his usual optimistic self. A mantle of heaviness covered his entire being. He tried to pull himself out of his strange feelings by thinking about Mondragon, the best kept secret in self-sufficient economics. What a trip. He realized how really dried up and stale his work had become before the Constellation. This is a real wake-up call. The bureaucracy, dealing with government "regs," had taken the joy out of planning. It had drained the creative juices out of him. *The Constellations do "up-sizing" instead of "downsizing"!* David exulted. He couldn't wait to tell Europa about this action! It was so damn much fun. He felt his energy level boosted somewhat by what lay ahead. *In a couple of days, Carlos and I are going to party our socks off. It's company orders.* David smiled to himself. *Actually, it will be our first chance to rub elbows with the people and find out how good these new town planners really are and how good the tapas and wine taste.* Then, the happy thoughts faded and the heaviness came back to weight down on his whole being. It was a truly strange experience.

David and Carlos were relieved to take the evening meal in the guest house dining room. They had not eaten since breakfast, but they were not quite sure why they were eating dinner. They ordered the special, consisting of gazpacho, baked fish with saffron rice and a salad.

"Helluva trip, hey, buddy?"

"Helluva trip."

"Well, we're both in one piece and that's what counts."

"I feel strangely sluggish," said Carlos, "like I'm in a slow motion world. I don't want to do anything. Ya know what I mean?"

"Yeah. I feel the same way. I just want to drift for a while. Just do nothing."

"We're in some kind of post-traumatic phase. I just need to rest a lot but I feel fine and relaxed."

"Of course, you're right. You can't go through something that life threatening without being wiped out afterwards. It just feels so strange, so unreal."

They finished their meals and crashed for the night. They slept ten hours and got up for breakfast. Then, they went back to their rooms and snoozed for another three hours. They watched TV and dozed on and off until 5:00 that evening.

"Come on," said Carlos. "Let's get out of these four walls and take a walk."

"Let's do it!"

They walked on Progresso Street in front of Maria's guest house, and they passed beautiful two- and three-story town homes with nice front porches. The sidewalk was wide and tree-lined, inviting a leisurely stroll. It was a warm afternoon, with a partly cloudy sky and a soft breeze. The town homes along Progresso Street were Mediterranean in design, with arches, stucco and wrought iron and finely detailed features against the plain walls painted in lemon, coral, white and rose. The street had two lanes and the cars were few and far between.

"They must all have parking in the back," said David.

"Yeah, it really makes a difference not to have all of that sheet metal in your face."

At the end of the block David and Carlos came to a large square which served as a small park. It was surrounded by five-story residential buildings.

"This reminds me of Savanah's squares," David remarked with surprise. "Hey, Carlos, I think these new town designers know what they're doin'."

They heard some traffic in the distance and walked two blocks south. There they entered onto a major tree-lined boulevard with a metro station. Cars moved briskly at forty miles an hour. After they had walked about five minutes on Por Venir Boulevard, they saw the surface metro bus with three cars pulling up to a loading platform. Three people got on and twenty-five people got off. They were well-dressed, mostly in business or work clothes.

"It must be the evening commute home for downtown workers," David surmised.

"No doubt. Didn't Fredrico say that seventy-five percent of the work force rides the surface metro system?"

"Yeah. Hard to believe, but we're getting some proof right now."

They walked down a local street until they were back on Progresso and started hiking back to Maria's.

"I'm starting to feel better already. This is energizing," David observed.

"Yeah! Let's pick up the pace. I need to get my energy up for those honeys at La Feria."

"Okay, Carlos, I'm not worried about you anymore. You're back!"

The breeze played with the leaves and swirled a few of them down the street. The air had cooled down and was powerfully invigorating.

"So, Carlos, what do you think about the Constellation new town planning so far?"

"The Constellation is impressive but there are some things I don't understand. For example, how do you reward the really intelligent and resourceful professionals who must be the core of the whole operation? I remember how it was in Sweden when the middle-upper class revolted. They complained the system wanted everyone to be poor, that you couldn't get ahead, or have the same professional recognition or luxuries as the upper classes in the U.S."

"Well, it's not uncommon to find expectations of more money among the brightest professionals. They naturally rise to the upper levels of their professions or they become administrators and they know they're involved in running things, and they do deserve to be appropriately compensated," allowed David. "That was the big issue in Ayn Rand's Atlas Shrugged. She raved on and on that the best and the brightest held up the world on their backs and they should be rewarded accordingly."

"Exactly," said Carlos. "Those who have the most talent to create wealth, invent and manage the world should be rewarded accordingly."

"Ayn Rand's solution was to have the elite inventors and professionals drop out entirely—leave the laggards who couldn't produce 'squat' to slowly die of their own incapacities. Let society go to hell in short order, and watch everyone get a taste of who really makes things work. So, Ayn Rand had no solution, except having this elite group go off by themselves to form their own secret society. For everyone else, she threw up her hands and said to hell with it! Do you think that's a solution to the problem of just compensation? I don't think so."

"Everyone wants what they feel is coming to them."

"I agree. But I don't think the CEO should get a hundred and forty times the pay of his average employee. Ten times $40,000 is $400,000. How do they even justify that huge increase in compensation?

"Hey, when the head is gone the place falls apart."

"Not if you're working Constellation-style. They replace general managers whenever required and just keep on truckin'!"

"How do they do that?"

"They are worker-owner entrepreneurs. They are trained to take on risks and assume management."

"But so few people can perform at that level."

"That's the big joke on corporation structuring versus Constellation-style. Corporations set it up that way. They don't know the other way. Again, Constellations are just a better way to run things."

"But who can get really rich and powerful and famous?"

"Hey, as Fredrico said, when you work a four-day week, you've got plenty of time to be creative and make a lot more money if that's what you treasure most. Fredrico keeps implying that average workers in the Constellation have more purchasing power than their counterparts in the U.S."

"Good points. I'm going to check it out."

"I think I'd have a lot of fun with Ayn Rand today, and she would have one helluva time dealing with the success of Mondragon and the Constellations. Now, the concept of 'self interest' has been extended into the spiritual realm and her great intellect didn't have a clue about that. I keep getting hints that these folks are seeing together in a new way. They can make things better for themselves and everyone else at the same time."

They arrived back at the guest house and found Maria in the kitchen helping with dinner preparations.

"Hello. How are you?" she enquired.

"We're feeling much better after a thirty minute stroll."

"Maria, didn't you say that the big procession and field Mass happens tomorrow tonight?"

"Yes, I'll take you if you want to go."

"Man, I've been so tired, but now I think my energy level might be up by then. I think I can make that," David answered, though he was still unsure of his capacities.

"I hope you can come with me. It's a really uplifting experience. You can dine anytime now. We're having a delicious pork roast tonight," she said temptingly.

"Sounds scrumptious! I'll get cleaned up," David said, with his appetite starting to rise from the smells in the kitchen as he spoke, but the strange, heaviness feeling persisted.

When they arrived in the dining room, all but two tables were full. The room was alive with robust conversation. It was mostly a young crowd and they were all talking excitedly about La Feria.

The pot roast special arrived and David and Carlos ate slowly, without conversation.

Señora Leon approached the table as the waiter brought the deserts and coffee. "Señora Leon," said David with a welcoming smile, "please join us for dessert."

"Thank you, I would enjoy that very much," she said. "Has Fredrico told you anything about the Misa de las Tierras Altas?"

"Yes," Carlos answered, "he told us that La Feria is always preceded by a huge outdoor field Mass to begin the holidays on a powerful spiritual note, but that's all I know."

"Good," said la señora, producing a small packet of photographs. "These are pictures of the Tierras Altas procession." She laid them out carefully on the table. "People form by the hundreds in the highlands and carry four-foot long candles down the mountainside paths. The procession represents the spiritual solidarity of the entire Constellation community. It's performed at all seven new towns at the same time each year."

"Can I see it from a place close by?" Carlos inquired hopefully.

"Oh yes. You can get a good view of it from our rooftop, at about ten o'clock tomorrow night," answered Señora Leon.

The next day, David and Carlos read some magazines and newspapers, but mostly they ate little and napped a lot. In the cool of the evening they took a longer three mile walk and felt much stronger for the exercise. That night, the residents of the house all went to the roof to see the procession. The candles began to descend the mountaintop from several trails which stretched across a mile or so of the highest ridge. Slowly, the candles, in pitch-black darkness, formed longer and longer lines as they curved and doubled back to make the steep descent. The candle lines now numbered seven and they began to converge, all abreast, near the base of the mountain. It was an awesome, mystical experience, both for the beholders and the participants. Then the candle lines formed behind the alter, forty deep on tiered seats, where the Mass was said for thousands of people.

"The Santa Misa de las Tierras Altas has a double meaning," said Señora Leon, "as you know, Tierras Altas means highlands and, on this occasion, it means 'the Highlands of the Spirit.' It is the celebration of the founding of the 'Solid Seven' new towns, which support each other."

Señora Leon left to attend the mass with David. Carlos opted to stay behind.

"Fredrico has arranged for us to sit near the celebrant, in a box reserved for special guests," smiled Señora Leon. Her eyes flashed with excitement. "The priest is Padre Parejo. As you know, he has been the spiritual leader of El Cinco from the beginning. It was his idea to use the Mondragon economic structure in the new towns. He also leads the educational effort throughout the worker-owned cooperatives."

The outdoor midnight Mass was especially powerful, thought David, as Padre Parejo began to address the people. The Mass was celebrated in Spanish. Even though it was a field Mass, Padre Parejo spoke frequently of "*Esta santa casa*"—meaning this holy house.

"He means the community of solidarity formed by the Constellation," explained Señora Leon.

David was entranced by the presence that Padre Parejo projected. He was a tall, stout man with black hair. He stood like a rock of determination, yet he conveyed a gentle message as he began his homily.

"We all know that we are blessed. The Lord has given us our little world of peace and joy. We have the strength to defend ourselves against the Saldanas of the world. We have a constant supply of our material needs. We have good work and the time and the opportunity to share the fruits of our work with each other. We have created our community with the fullness of our love and brotherhood and we have wonderful friendships. We are indeed blessed among men and women. May our work be a blessing to our children and our children's children. When you are troubled, remembered Christ's message: Be calm and have no fear. It has pleased your Father to give you the Kingdom. You have been given everlasting life."

At the moments preceding the consecration, David sensed a change in Padre Parejo's appearance. His spirituality projected itself without effort, David thought to himself, jolted by the realization. He watched entranced. David looked at Señora Leon to see if he could tell what she was thinking. She had the faintest of smiles.

"He's an extraordinary person, isn't he?" he remarked tentatively, trying to draw her out.

"Yes. He is known far and wide as a living saint," she said with a big smile of satisfaction, because she had intuited what David had seen. It was a common experience in the presence of Padre Parejo.

Chapter 11
LA FERIA DE LAS FALDAS

David woke on Saturday morning after a surprisingly restful sleep. The peace of the night lingered. He felt whole and refreshed again. Then, he remembered Saldana and the helicopter violently pressing their every move, the incessant machine gun fire, the blockade of vipers in the culvert, the rocket blast that nearly blew them all away, the fire on his head and arm, and the relief at being alive when the gunship finally flew away. For sure, he thought, *I'm livin' a charmed life. I'm kept here for a reason. I've got work to do. And it's good work! That's a charm to give life to a man.* He stretched the full length of his body and rolled on his side for a luxurious "snooze." When he woke again, he put his hands behind his head and thought about the day ahead. La Feria de Las Faldas. *No work—no demands,* he thought, *it's play time!* He imagined the streets of Las Faldas filled with people enjoying the music. *Beautiful ladies will be dancing in the streets.* He could imagine a thriving business at the tapa bars—around the clock. Coffee. Breakfast. Let's get out of bed!

Meanwhile, Carlos was moving his shoulders to salsa music on the radio while he shaved. Keeping time with the salsa felt good. Carlos danced into the living room, half-shaven, waving his razor in time to the music. He thought about the young maidens at the Feria. "Oouu-eeey baby!" he exclaimed to the walls.

The phone rang while David was putting on his socks.

"Hello."

"David?" asked Conchita with urgency. "Is that you?"

"Hello, sweetheart, I was just thinking about you."

"Oh, David, you're all right?"

"I'm fine now. The Saldana attack was a bit 'O hell,' but we all survived."

"No wounds?"

"Amazingly, just a few scratches from the underbrush, before the cannon blew it away...the underbrush, I mean. My shirt caught on fire briefly but Carlos helped put it out. Minor burn. Nothing to worry about."

"Oh! Thank God! I was in Argentina. They just told me this morning that you, Fredrico and Carlos were attacked. I thought I'd lost you! What a relief!"

"I want you with me. When can you come to Las Faldas?"

"I want to be with you so badly! It's been hectic here. The Saldana attack stirred us up pretty good. We've got lots of new priorities to take care of. I won't be able to get with you until evening. I have to play spokesperson at La Feria. I'll be working there all day."

"Fine, just tell me where to hang out and I'll wait for you."

"There's a great tapa bar on Calle Progreso. Let's see—Nuestra Tapa. I'll meet you there around six. I love you."

"I'm kinda fond of you too. I'll be there if I'm not swept away by some gypsy seductress."

"You rat! Now, I know you're well."

"Okay. I'm breaking out of my cage and comin' to nibble on you."

"Now *that's* what I like to hear! I'll see you tonight, love. Got to go get ready for La Feria. Bye, bye."

"Bye for now."

David met Carlos in the dining room. They ordered scrambled eggs with sautéed mushrooms, chorizo sausage, toast and coffee.

"This is one of those days you live for," said Carlos. "There's nothing quite like going to a party with a whole town!"

"After the procession of the Tierras Altas and the Mass last night, I think we're going to see a party with all *seven* new towns. The tone was set last night. It was a solidarity high. There was a lot of talk about Saldana's attack, but you could sense that these folks can ride out that kind of threat."

"Come on," said Carlos, rolling his eyes with impatience, "enough of new towns. Glug that coffee and let's get out there!"

As they entered the street, they saw small groups of people moving leisurely toward the center of town. They were dressed just like people dressed in any European city, on a special day of celebration.

"This is a cosmopolitan-looking bunch. I feel like I'm in Sevilla or Madrid. What happened to the wrenching poverty that we saw in El Cedro?"

"I saw a few poor folks on our way into Las Faldas. I'm sure they're still around somewhere, but most people in Las Faldas are making a decent living, from the looks of things."

"David, over there," said Carlos, pointing with a nod of his head.

There was a small plaza filled with twenty young men and women who were dressed in classical flamenco dance costumes. They were standing impatiently, adjusting their attire, and obviously waiting for something. About a hundred people had gathered to watch what was about to happen. As David and Carlos approached within yards of the group, the flamenco guitars began their fire-and-passion introduction. Suddenly, the dancers swung into action with tiered flamenco skirts flying in a rush of swirling colors—red, white, green. The women had black hair and blond hair tightly swept up with a bun in the back. As they took control of the dance, they smiled at their partners very briefly, then resumed the serious demeanor of the classic flamenco. They swirled their skirts out in a flowing parallel to the ground. The men, all in black, began a powerful performance, providing the rhumba flamenco and las palmas. Soon, the onlookers began to join in las palmas, and the excitement was building around the plaza, now drawing another hundred or more people.

When the dance was finished, a voice came from David's left, saying, "Very good. Very good. Keep your places for the next shot." Then, David saw the director's platform. "We're on a movie set!" As he glanced around the crowd his eyes were caught by a motion. It was Fredrico waving to them. David and Carlos worked their way through the crowd to join him.

Fredrico beamed and gave both men a hearty hug, Spanish style.

"So, how's my favorite snake matador today?"

David shook his head and looked sheepish.

"I'm going to make a killing as his agent," announced Carlos with a grand smile.

"I save your life and this is the thanks I get," said David. "Okay, next time I'll give you guys the cape and a little push into the arena."

At that moment, two black limousines pulled up and parked at the edge of the plaza. Conchita Seguras and four men dressed in suits emerged from the cars. The men were seriously surveying the crowd nearest to Conchita

Seguras. They were obviously bodyguards, thought David. David watched her constantly, as she moved briskly toward the director. *Enchanting lady, indeed,* thought David.

"She has an important announcement to make about the gunship attack," said Fredrico. "I think you'll enjoy her speech."

She picked up a microphone and the director gave the order to begin filming. "Hello," she said, "I am Conchita Seguras, and on behalf of El Cinco, we wish you the happiest Feria de Las Faldas ever! I am sure that many of you are concerned about the attack on the ethanol plants yesterday. Well, I am happy to announce that the leaders of the attack have been arrested and they will be deported from Rocadura by the federal government."

The crowd of two thousand people applauded and yelled out loudly with joy and tension release. Conchita Seguras let them have their way. Finally, after two minutes, she spoke again.

"El Cinco had an emergency meeting with President Bassencourt yesterday. The federal government will provide gunships, radar and intelligence services to protect all of the ethanol facilities in the Constellations we are building. President Bassencourt has declared that this action is in the national interest in order to maintain a positive trade balance and to protect the environment from the use of gasoline and oil."

The crowd exploded with another ovation.

She resumed: "And now, my friends, let's enjoy the Feria! This spectacular dance troupe, 'El Barrio Triana' comes to you directly from Sevilla. If you've been there, you'll know that it's one of the most romantic cities in Europe, and some say, in the world! And Triana is one of the most lively places in Sevilla. The streets are filled with people at all hours of the night, and the tapa bars are excellent. They tell me that they are as good as the ones here in Las Faldas—and so I have my work cut out for me—this will require hours and hours of dedicated research," she teased. One voice in the crowd yelled, "*Viva la investigacion!*"

The crowd applauded with vigor. She handed the microphone to a technician and waved to the crowd as she left center stage. She looked around until she found Fredrico and went to join him. They hugged each other as old friends do.

"Fredrico, I'm so glad to see that you're all right! That attack by Saldana must have been living hell!"

"Well, I survived it with a little help from my friends. David and Carlos helped save our lives yesterday."

Conchita took Carlos' hand but her eyes barely left David's. "Thank you, Carlos, for helping my Fredrico and David. They're very special."

She clasped David's hand in both of hers and whispered in his ear, "I'll see you later at Nuestra Tapa. Stay away from those gypsies."

"You're the *only* gypsy I want."

David watched her in the car as she was driving away. As the car left she glanced to see David. Their eyes made contact and David felt an attraction that he had not felt in years. He was lost in the magic of infatuation—and something much deeper. He watched the car until it was out of sight.

The guitars began again, with a rush of gypsy excitement. The gravel, "whiskey-voice" of the flamenco singer filled the mid-morning air. He was singing a gay and familiar song to David's ears: one of those "Tanguillos," which exclaims "that the life in Sevilla is the most beautiful in the whole world." After several more dances, the free show came to an end.

"Let's tango downtown!" shouted Carlos, eager to move on to the next happening. "We've seen the professionals, now I want to see how the natives party!"

"You go party," said Fredrico, "I'm going to rejoin my family. I'll see you Monday."

They said their goodbyes and worked their way through the streets, already swarming with people dressed for a day of leisure. *No "Banana Republic" here*, thought David.

"I see an open table at that sidewalk café!" shouted Carlos, as he sprinted over the cobblestone street to secure a table in the shade.

They ordered beer and a tapa of boiled squid in marinara sauce and sat back in their chairs to people-watch. Everyone was excited, joyful, laughing. They were immersed in an atmosphere of comfortable gaiety.

"Romance fills the air," said David.

"It's so thick you can grab it by the handful. And speaking of handfuls, do you see her?" as he nodded in the direction of a particularly striking young lady in a red flamenco dress.

"Hard to miss," but his mind flashed back immediately to the sight of Conchita Seguras. "But I can't think of anyone but Conchita."

"Why...David," Carlos beamed, "the lady has long hooks, doesn't she? She's a real charm boat, but she's way too serious for me. She's more your type."

"Did Humberto tell you anything about her past love life?"

He looked off into the crowd as if he had absolutely no intention of answering the question at hand. "Maybe."

"Okay, you 'Wisenheimer,' at the next bar, I'll buy your favorite tapa if you tell me."

"I could never resist a bribe like that. She's never been married, according to Humberto. She was going with a fellow for about a year, but they split. And I'll take a huge plate of garlic shrimp when we get there, thank you."

David smiled a very warm smile, inside.

A group of young men and women went by dancing to the salza music flowing from the restaurant's speakers. Another group followed their example and lingered to dance. When the next salza number began, half the street swayed to the beat and three couples stepped out in style. They danced with a special "gracia." The rest followed their lead and suddenly the whole street was moving to the intoxicating salza magic.

David struck up a conversation with a man who had lived in Las Faldas for seven years. He introduced himself as Atonio Gallardo. He wore a black beret, a white shirt, white trousers with a red sash and a red neckerchief. He explained that he had picked up the outfit in Pamplona at the annual running of the bulls.

"Did you actually run ahead of the bulls?"

"Yes, I did," replied Antonio, "it was a real thrill to be so close to the bulls. You see these threatening black powerhouses coming at you. You hear this thunderous sound and feel their sweaty presence as they close in on you. Fortunately, I sidestepped at the right time and it was over in seconds."

"That's exciting action. I never thought of trying a run with the bulls. Do you live here in the town?"

"Yes," answered Antonio, "I live on the edge of the town. I just moved into my own home a month ago. My wife and I bought a brand-new house together through a special savings plan at work."

"How does that plan work?"

"Well, instead of setting aside savings for retirement, our employer redirects that money into savings toward a house. After about five to seven years you buy your house. Then you can begin to save for retirement and still have twenty-five to thirty years to save. Everyone who works in the Constellation can own a home through this savings plan at the workplace, because the employer contributes what would ordinarily have gone into a retirement plan—about eight percent of gross salary. I saved $27,000 in six years, and my wife saved $21,000 in seven years. We merged our savings and bought a new house with $48,000 of equity."

"You must be making $40,000 per year, or more, to do that," said Carlos.

"I started at $24,000 and was earning $30,000 a year when I bought the house. But you have to remember that I was putting in eight percent of my salary to match my employer's eight percent. Sixteen percent at eight and a half percent interest adds up fast! Oh, I forgot to mention, these savings are tax exempt."

"You're kidding!" said Carlos, in disbelief. "That would be an incredible raid on the country's Treasury."

"Well, all I know is that they gave a presentation at work and demonstrated that the new tax revenues from building new houses would give the Treasury a big net gain. It was something like $10,000 per house for the average savings account. These homes would never have been built without the savings plan, and the Treasury would never have seen those tax revenue gains."

"I'll have to see the numbers on that one," mumbled Carlos, who was tired of being distracted from girl-watching.

"That's an impressive savings plan," said David, "We'll get the details from Fredrico."

"The best part is that my family has economic security early in life with all of that equity, and we have thirty percent more disposable income because we don't have to spend so much on a mortgage."

"Hey, Carlos," said David with a nudge of the elbow, "that gives the economy another big boost. All of that disposable income is going to translate into a lot of jobs."

"OK," said Carlos, with a note of testiness, "are we here to party or are you guys going to work all day to solve the world's problems?"

"Let me buy you a drink," said Antonio, in a conciliatory tone. "What would you like?"

"I'll have a six-pack of Cutty Sark," said Carlos, with a fake growl. David and Antonio broke out in laughter, while Carlos crossed his eyes and gave his best "go to hell" smile.

"But, Carlos," said David with a patronizing smile, "that Cutty Sark would violate your priorities: women, wine, food, and women—in that order!"

"That's right. Now let me get on with it, you bunch of workaholic jerks!"

"So, are you two just enjoying La Feria or do you work in Rocadura?" asked Antonio.

"Carlos and I are from the U.S. We work for a new town builder. We're getting paid to learn all about 'Constellation Style' new town building."

"Correction," Carlos interjected, "David is here to learn, *I'm* here to party!"

Before they parted company, Antonio gave David his address and telephone number, and said, "I'd like for you to meet my family. Tomorrow night we'll have a wonderful party at my father's ranch. We'll have music and a country cookout with paella and fine wine."

David said, "God, you certainly know how to hit an Irishman in the place that feels good. I'd *love* to do that."

Antonio drew a map to show David how to get to his father's ranch.

"It's only six miles out of town. Bring a date if you can. It'll be a very romantic evening."

"Well, I'll do my best," said David, with very fond memories of Conchita and Diego's bonfire.

They shook hands and parted with very warm feelings.

In the meantime, Carlos had struck up a lively conversation with two attractive young women. Soon, they were all dancing in the street. It was the last that David would see of Carlos until morning.

At 5:30, David set out for the Nuestra Tapa bar to meet Conchita. The streets were filled with happy people. You could feel the richness of romance in the night air. Joy was King. Joy was Queen and Princess. Joy had filled all hearts.

David thought of Conchita. He wondered when he could be alone with her again. He enjoyed his thoughts about "when" as he walked to the center of Las Faldas and Nuestra Tapa. He arrived at 5:45. By 6:20 there was no Conchita. He started to be concerned that her role as spokesperson would delay her arrival longer.

"I'll have a cognac, bartender," he said.

Then, he felt a tap on his shoulder. He turned to find that 200 watt smile.

"I'm sorry I'm late," Conchita said with strong sincerity. "The crowds were just unbelievable!"

"I know, I know," he said, clasping both of her hands in his. "Please have a rest," he said, as he offered his bar stool for her to join him. All other seats in the house were taken.

"Let's have some tapas," he said, as he waved the bartender over. "What's your pleasure?"

"The marinated monkfish," she said, without hesitation.

"Sounds good. And to drink?"

"Uuummm. Amontillado with walnuts."

"With walnuts?"

"Oh, yes, wait until you try that combination," she said with confidence. David canceled his cognac and ordered the amontillado.

The bartender took their orders. Then, in very fast Spanish that David couldn't comprehend, he queried Conchita. The bartender gave David a big smile and a strange knowing look.

"What was he asking about?"

"He just asked if you were Fredrico's friend."

Well, he thought, *I'll try any combination that this lady recommends.*

The bartender returned with the fried spicy monkfish, amontillado and walnuts in five minutes.

David sampled. "Oh, yes! I see what you mean. It's a match made in heavenly Spain."

"So, tell me, do you think Europa will join us?"

"They will if I have any influence on the decision."

"Do you?"

"Puuulenty!"

"Is Carlos sold on the Constellation?"

"No, not yet. He's a hard case."

"Well, who has the best chance of convincing Erikson? You or Carlos?"

"I'd like to think that I've got a very convincing report to give. But, Carlos can be persuasive. He always plays the devil's advocate. He asks the hard questions. But the Constellation answers the hardest questions that he has raised. Still, it's hard to say with all of the variables floating around."

"I only met Erikson once, but he seemed to be excited about what we're doing."

"Yes, we have a bit of an edge there."

"Here's to the Feria," she said, offering a toast.

"The Feria and the charming people you meet," said David, turning on his best 200 watt smile.

He exudes this Irish charm, thought Conchita. *His eyes laugh so wonderfully. He's so solid. I wonder if he knows how charming he is. Of course! He's probably a thief of hearts.*

"You know, David, you're getting famous around here."

"I don't understand. What do you mean?"

"Wait until Pancho, the bartender, gets back and you'll see," she said, with a totally teasing smile.

David was set back. He couldn't imagine what she meant.

Pancho came back and went straight to David.

"Señor, I hear that you killed the legendary jumping pit viper with a matador's cape!"

"Matador's cape? No, no, I just got lucky and the viper caught his teeth in my jacket."

"Of course! You improvised like the champion matador!"

David looked at Conchita. Then, he looked at the bartender.

"It was just a snake. I didn't kill him. He jumped under my boot and I tossed him into the other snakes. They don't like human beings, so they all left. How did you hear about that?" asked David.

"A friend of mine heard the story from the man on the scene, Miguel, the ambulance driver," answered the bartender. "Everybody in town knows that story."

"Did you hear that!" shouted Pancho, loud enough for half of the bar crowd to hear. And holding up David's hand over his head he shouted, "The jumping pit viper matador is here!"

There was a big uproar. People started moving closer to get a look at David.

"Oh, God no," David mumbled. "Can we get out of here?"

They finished their tapas and David made his thanks to the crowd for their unwanted attentions and swept Conchita out of Nuestra Bar.

As they strolled with is arm around her waist, she remembered the highlights of David's dossier which she obtained from Fredrico. Widowed. Age 39. Born in Cour d'lene, Idaho. Catholic by choice. Bachelor's degree from Loyola and master's degree in city planning from the University of Oregon. She definitely liked what she saw. He was solid from one end to the other. And best of all, they could work together to build Constellations. *He'll have a hard time getting out of my web*, she smiled to herself.

"Let's go get some dinner. What do you recommend?"

"The Barcelona. It's just around the corner," said Conchita as she pulled his arms behind her back, and kissed him softly on the mouth.

David and Conchita felt a warmth of soul that was at once totally natural and beautifully exotic. Their hearts grew bold at the same time. They stood in the middle of the crowd and held each other for a long, hot kiss. They lingered in the spell and held each other tight. The world had vanished. They were alone, together, totally as one.

Shortly, the world reappeared as a dancer bounced into David.

"Sorry," said the dancer, as he and his girl swirled down the street.

At the entrance to The Barcelona, a throng of forty couples were dancing to salza music. David and Conchita joined the group and felt the smooth intoxication of the salza beat and the cool evening air. They danced for five minutes, until the band finished and paused between numbers. They held each other around the waist until the next number began. During the dance, David and Conchita looked directly into each other's eyes. There was no doubt here. Life was very good.

They ate a dinner of Asian quail with rice and asparagus.

"It's late," said Conchita, holding his hand. "I'm going to need some rest tonight. I'll see you tomorrow for brunch at your hotel."

"And then?"

"And then, we'll see what happens."

David smiled with an Irish gleam in his eyes. "I think I know what will happen."

Conchita just smiled a confident smile. She was a lady who knew what she was doing.

"I like your style. And the truth is, I'll only be fully rested in the morning."

David walked Conchita to a taxi and they made their way back to their hotels in a heightened romantic elation. The night air was cool and fresh. The kisses were long and rich. They said their "good evenings." David retired immediately but could not sleep. He lay listening to the Feria noises as he daydreamed about Conchita's charms. A group of young revelers went by his open window at 3:00 a.m. They were singing a flamenco song, dancing and keeping time with las palmas. Their hands clapping gently floated into his window with the fresh night breeze. David went to sleep, filled with love.

Sunday morning, David rose with a warm glow of anticipation. "When" had arrived. He would be with Conchita for brunch at 10:00.

He went to 8:00 Mass at a church close to the hotel. He arrived late. There was standing room only. Most of the men wore suits with ties. He stood with the men in the back of the church, all with their arms crossed. It was like a challenge to the priest. Thirty men strong, standing in the back of the church as if to say, "We are the men who have to deliver for our wives and children. What good news can you tell us?" The older women were mostly dressed in black. The younger women were dressed to kill. On another day, they might have been a terrible distraction to David. Today, he was here for the Mass and Communion. Later, he would be with Conchita, who was, of course, the major distraction to his participation in this Mass. As the reading of the Old Testament progressed, David's thoughts kept flashing back to Conchita.

Conchita the Beautiful. Conchita the Inescapable. It was at that very moment that David knew he was quite ready to give up bachelorhood. As the priest began the reading of the Gospel, David realized that he was hearing and translating Spanish. It was the familiar story of Jesus and the Samaritan woman at Jacob's well. He saw then, that the Mass is said around the world, as the sun rises, and travels around the world. The Mass is said in nearly every language, every place, moving slowly across the planet with the sun. More than a billion people would hear Mass that day. Most of the very same words that he was hearing would be spoken to all.

Upon receiving Communion David sat in his pew and relaxed totally with his eyes closed. Instantly, he was awash with God's abundant love. His transcendent state lasted for several minutes. He could feel the peace in his soul stretching out into an enduring place of rest. His depth of feeling was finally broken by the words of the priest.

"Let us pray."

David always reacted the same way in this situation. *That's what I was doing at the deepest possible level!* he complained. *And now, I must go back to the surface.* But he realized quickly enough that people had to go to breakfast, read the Sunday paper and be on their way. *The only place this doesn't happen,* he thought, *is in the monastery.*

David walked back to his hotel under an overcast sky. *Sundays seem to be like that a lot,* he thought. Gray clouds. Stores closed. People indoors, almost in hiding. It leads to a kind of hibernation of the body. You instinctively want to just slow down, stay inside, rest, nap, read a bit and do next to nothing on a day like this. And so the morning passed. The telephone rang. David's heart picked up a few beats. He knew it had to be Conchita the Beautiful.

"Hello, you!" Conchita said in her perky, excited way.

"I'm sorry, miss," feigned David. "I'm just the bellboy. I'll see if Mr. O'Laughlin is available. Oh, here he is."

"So, you're a tease, are you?" queried Conchita.

"It's true. I'm a bit of a tease."

"Well, I like a friendly tease. I bet that I can tease your socks off."

"I can hardly wait."

"Wait until you see my new silk pajamas."

"You? In silk pajamas? I don't think I can stand it."

"I didn't say that I would be *in* them. I'll take them out of the package and show them to you."

"Oh. Darn. You are good. Okay. I concede. Have mercy. I've met my match. When are you coming for brunch?"

"On my way."

"I'll be the guy in the lobby with a big idiot smile plastered on his face."

"You're easy."

"Well, where you're concerned, I intend to stay that way."

"Good. See you soon."

"Hurry."

David met Conchita at the door to the hotel and escorted her quickly to the bar lounge area which was still unoccupied at 10:30 a.m. He swept her into a comfortable couch and kissed her several times on the neck and cheek and forehead and eyes before he allowed her to kiss him back on the mouth.

"Wipe that idiot smile off your mouth and kiss me again," she said softly.

And so the morning went. There was a monstrous and delightful brunch offering eggs and chorizo, ham, home style potatoes, fruit, pancakes, French toast, waffles with hazelnut butter cream, coffee and orange juice. After brunch, David escorted Conchita back to the lounge area where they necked brazenly until the bartender arrived. They read the Sunday paper together and he enjoyed a spicy Bloody Mary, while Conchita had a screwdriver, and then, another.

"I knew we were going to have fun in this hotel lounge," remarked Conchita.

"Well, truthfully, you have to tease your host unmercifully, prior to arriving, before you can have this much fun."

"I'll have to remember that."

"Come to my place, and I'll tease you some more."

"This is a proposal I can't refuse. Are my ears smoking?"

"I can't tell, but you can make the grill smoke on my deck and cook dinner for me."

In the morning, David woke earlier than Conchita. He got up and went to the bathroom, and dressed. Then, he looked out the sliding glass doors of her apartment and watched the sun rise as she slept. He looked at her often and fondly. She slept with peace on her face. She was totally comfortable, he thought. She stirred, stretched full length, and then rolled over on her side for a deeper snooze. He went to the kitchen and put coffee on. He set the table for breakfast and drank a glass of orange juice. On his return to Conchita, she was awake. He slid under the sheet beside her. They kissed and caressed each other for a long time.

"You said that your wife taught you some lessons. What were they?"

David rolled over on his back and thought a minute.

"She taught me that everyone comes with their own package. She taught me to accept others with all of their package, just as they are. You don't try to change them and make them like you. Your pleasure comes from seeing what a wonderful package they have. You accept them and give them space to be who they are. They can say anything they want in your presence. You follow one primary principle: love seeks the good of the beloved."

"Well, am I not doing that with you?"

"Oh, yeah!"

"Am I not doing that with you?"

"Oh, yes! Okay, I guess I'll keep you awhile longer," she teased.

"It takes time to work it all out," said David. "Actually, years. Most of all, there is one constant basis for true love. There is a word that expresses it all. In one word, it is comfortableness, having total ease with each other. Non-critical. Leave your quibbles behind. Don't express your prideful quibbles. Bury them. If you give space, one to the other, the rewards are great and extraordinarily comfortable."

"God, I love to hear you say those things. Kiss me."

Chapter 12
THE ENERGY TECHNOPARC

It was 9:00 a.m. on Monday morning when Fredrico arrived at the hotel to pick up David and Carlos to visit the Energy Technoparc.

David gave Fredrico a hearty handshake and then a manly hug.

"You look good. They patched you up okay? How do you feel?"

"I'm fine. My family treated me like a king. They loved me to death. My dog, bless his furry little hide, kept trying to lick my face off every chance he got."

"That's great. Carlos and I are up and at 'em again."

David gave Maria a warm hug, stepped back and held out his hands for her to take. "You've given us some wonderful hospitality and a new understanding about what life is like in Las Faldas. Thanks for everything."

"I enjoyed your visit very much. I'm glad you found our discussions worthwhile."

"More than worthwhile. It's all going into my report. I'm sure my boss will like what he reads."

"Gracias. Vaya con Dios."

"Bye for now."

As they walked to the car, David was still flooded with memories of the Feria. *La vida es sueno*—life is a dream, he thought, remembering the story from Spanish literature. *Today, life is suspended in a dream world of good feelings.*

"So, how did you like La Feria?" Fredrico asked with a confident smile.

"Truly, a unique experience, and I'll no doubt treasure it my entire life."

"The most fun I've had in years," Carlos exuded. "I could go on partying like that for days. These folks are *full* of life!"

"The people who live in the Constellation have so much to live for. We met a fellow named Antonio Gallardo, and he told us about your homeownership savings plan arrangement. It sounds like a great way for young people to get started off in life. Two working spouses can merge accounts and have forty to eighty thousand dollars worth of equity in their homes by age thirty-two!"

"That could save a lot of marriages because they all need a strong financial foundation."

"But it sounds like a huge raid on the Treasury," Carlos reasserted. "How much does this homeownership program cost the government in tax exemptions each year?"

"The latest figures show that the Treasury takes in a net gain of about ten to fifteen thousand dollars for each homeownership account. The program is eight years old. Nobody is arguing about the success of the program. In three Constellations, the Home Ownership Plan is on a path to create two hundred thousand permanent jobs in housing and related industries. The new construction, manufacturing, appliances, retail trade, all add up to a quite healthy increase in income taxes."

"Sounds like supply side economics at its best," Carlos offered.

"I'll drive you directly to the Energy Technoparc this morning. Today, you'll see the heart of our complex—because cheap energy drives a growing, sustainable economy. Solar cells and ethanol gas turbine generators provide electricity at six cents a kilowatt hour. Cheap energy is the equivalent of wealth, because it replaces manual labor. As you know, cheap energy drives equipment, computers and computer control systems, assembly lines, heating, lighting and cooling."

"So, cheap energy enables you to redistribute wealth from the rich to the poor," Carlos suggested.

"We're not redistributing wealth. We're building places for everyone to create new wealth for themselves, their children and their neighbors. Remember, Carlos, we've gone beyond global competition. In the Constellation, the production and distribution systems are joined together so that everyone gets more of almost everything. It's that way for the worker-owners from day one, when they walk through the doors. I'll show you some graphics when we get to the Technoparc."

"But how is the housing production linked to the distribution system? Do you build all of the housing yourselves?"

"Yes. The Constellation has three construction divisions. We build everything. Soon, we'll be manufacturing all of our own appliances, as well. We already make refrigerators, washers, dryers, toaster ovens and stoves. Microwaves, mix-masters and other gadgets are on the way."

They drove into the huge ethanol complex. They passed several large storage tanks and a loading station for tank trucks. Fredrico parked the car at a small office building at the edge of the complex.

"Come on in and I'll show you how 'Vodka Village' works."

They went inside and entered the conference room. Fredrico whipped off his coat, threw it over a chair and pointed to a large map that filled one whole wall.

"This is the entire Constellation network. It stretches ninety miles across the northwest quadrant of Rocadura. As you remember, each town is designed to build out at a population of sixty thousand. The towns will each contain about twelve square miles, plus a hinterland of another twenty square miles for agriculture, forestry and natural recreation space. The connecting lines are high speed transit corridors with two lanes dedicated to cars."

"It's a tightly knit configuration," David observed. "I see a set of three interlocking triangles. Now I see why you call it a constellation. It's like a group of stars."

"Why so few lanes for cars?"

"Well, when you arrive by car or rapid transit, you find you don't need a car to get around in these new towns. You can go anywhere you want to on the low-cost surface metro system because everything is built in high concentration on the transit lines or within a fifteen minute walk. We use rubber tire rolling stock for flexibility. Our transit stations are built just like subway platforms for fast loading. We use one hundred percent pure ethanol or solar cell electricity to drive the entire transit system."

"Is ethanol really the same as vodka?"

"It's high grade alcohol, the same kind that you find in vodka," Fredrico smiled. "It's very low technology. Once the engineers set up an ethanol distillery, it's simple to operate and maintain."

"So, you can fill your tank and as well as your jug for a dollar a gallon?" David speculated, while knowing there had to be a catch somewhere.

"Well, that's why the government requires us to put in a foul-tasting additive to make it undrinkable. But we're not fools. We're also starting to export high quality vodka made from potatoes. This map shows the ethanol production capacity of the seven new towns. As you can see, each town has ethanol plants producing fifty million gallons, or more, per year. The new town at Port Cortes has ten ethanol plants because it's our major export center."

"So, how much do you produce in all?"

"We produce over two and a half billion gallons a year. Enough to supply the nation and fifty percent for export. We'll double our exports in three more years. As you know, the future belongs to ethanol and solar cells for a long time."

"Especially since we can grow plants fifty percent faster and give them haircuts for ethanol feed stock," David agreed.

"Right. Fuel cells using hydrogen power and ethanol need some refinements to be economical. Battery driven cars are a bad joke when they're recharged by fossil fuel electric plants out in the country. They reduce local smog but they add carbon dioxide to the global warming account."

"I reached the same conclusions," David affirmed. "And since we can produce ethanol much more cheaply than gasoline, we can produce electricity using ethanol in our gas turbine generators. We use solar cells for electricity when the sun shines and ethanol-driven turbine generators when it doesn't shine. That way you don't have to worry about millions of batteries for storage. And we know only too well that batteries are really ugly to dispose of in the environment."

"Right. You don't want to deal with the disposal of all those acids, chemicals, lead, and plastics. One hundred percent environmental ethanol and solar cells—a marriage made by Mother Nature herself. In the developing nations, it's the best alternative, by far."

"In the industrialized countries, they have all of these special interests with long term investments in the wrong kinds of energy," David said.

"But that game has worn thin," Fredrico smiled. "A workout has to take place. It'll take decades, but it has to happen. We plan to speed up the process."

Fredrico turned to his video console and called up a program on the screen. "This is a series of charts that show it all. My wife calls these 'killer charts' because they say so much and 'kill' the devil's advocates."

The first chart flashed on the screen was titled:

"WEALTH GENERATION, CONSTELLATION STYLE."

"This is how a family builds wealth Constellation Style. The key here is purchasing power—what you can actually buy with

your earnings. This is the Home Ownership Plan that Atonio Gallardo told you about. By the seventh year of employment, the family shifts from renting and buys their home with forty to eighty thousand, or more, in equity. Immediately, their housing costs drop by thirty percent, about twenty-four hundred dollars per year. At this point, a worker-owner takes out a no interest loan of twenty-four thousand dollars, to provide equity capital to the Constellation. The loan is paid off at twenty-four hundred dollars per year for ten years. The money a family saves on housing costs pays for the buy-in as a worker-owner in the Constellation."

"So, this is how a person earns his or her way into worker- ownership?"

"Exactly. After they own their home and are well established, they begin to pay back into the system that gives them a wonderful livelihood. They were taking out eight percent of their salary for the Home Ownership Plan. Now, they take out eight percent to pay off their twenty-four hundred dollar loan in ten years. During this time, they contribute seven percent of their salary to retirement and the Constellation contributes eight percent. By the eighth year of employment, the young professional will earn about forty-three thousand dollars a year, not counting profit-sharing bonuses. With a fifteen year mortgage, they own their house outright by age fifty. Their disposable income increases again by thirty percent. They can travel and enjoy life in a very special way. By age sixty they can quit work with a very comfortable retirement, just as it should be."

"So, El Cinco can go on building new towns indefinitely from internalized savings by workers and outside capital from private investors?"

"Yes, once the original capital of El Cinco launched the first twenty-one new towns. But it's a slow process, when you look at the needs of the thousands of villages in the world."

"It's still pretty damned impressive," Carlos said. "It looks like a perpetual job creation machine."

"That's right, but there is more. A similar savings is gained in energy and transportation. When you spend less on cars, you have much more purchasing power. Rapid transit takes you to all major destinations. So, the family only needs one car and they will save as much as eight thousand dollars per year on transportation. They can take longer, more satisfying vacations throughout their lives."

"That would be hard to pull off in the U.S.," Carlos remarked. "Everything is so spread out, you simply must have a car."

"You could do it in new towns that are built from scratch," David ventured, "and in some measure, even when you build onto an existing town."

"Take a look at this transit layout," said Fredrico, as he displayed a large map of Las Faldas. "The only way to build a new town is to build the transit system first. Then, you build everything along those transit lines. Sure, we'll build a road system for cars, but the exclusive roadways for rapid transit is the primary movement system. Notice how all of the homes are within a fifteen minute walk of a rapid line."

"Is it a fixed rail system?" asked Carlos.

"No, you build paved transit lanes and use rubber tire rolling stock."

"Buses?"

"No, it's not a bus system as you know it. They're transit cars that have fast loading stations just like the subway in Washington, D.C. You build the system on paved roadways for maximum flexibility, and of course, for 1/50th of the cost of a fixed rail line. This rapid system was pioneered in Curitiba, Brazil, and it can be retrofitted on existing towns. Caracus has already started doing that. We'll go for a transit ride later this morning."

"I've always known this is the way to build new towns," said David, "but I could never get the developers in the U.S. off the stupid car system. They're totally brain washed and grid-locked because they think that's what people want. Curitiba tells a very different story. It's a national tragedy in terms of real city planning. Constellations will give a kick-start to developers in the future. Now, they'll have to consider building every thing on rapid transit systems lines."

"Let's get back to the wealth generation system," Fredrico continued. "Both the return on investment and wages rise annually in Constellations. Here is the big surprise: the productive power of the Constellation rises in terms of the internal production and distribution of wealth. As self-sufficiency grows, it takes fewer working hours to make products. Technology advances do the same thing. This translates directly into bonuses to the worker-owners. That gives a person a great deal of incentive to be productive. In the cutthroat capitalist system, the surplus wealth is usually creamed off by the top seven percent, the owners and managers, investors and the big stars: the entrepreneurs. Doesn't give a working person a lot of incentive, does it?"

Then, Fredrico showed a chart titled:

WORK TIME, PLAY TIME

"Here you see the standard work schedule: four days on and three days off. As time goes on, the vacation schedule increases substantially. Each worker-owner gets three weeks of vacation for the first five years. Then, it jumps to four weeks until the eighth year of employment. After that it goes up to six weeks, until retirement. In addition, people can take up to six months of personal leave with forty percent of pay. They can do this twice during their twenty-five to thirty years of employment."

"Amazing!" Carlos whispered.

"I love that free time the best," David hummed. "You can do all kinds of things with that much time to yourself. Whoa! You might even have a chance to be who you really are!"

The morning had flown by. It was 11:30 a.m.

"Let's take a ride on the rapid," Fredrico invited. "On the way out, I'll show you what Saldana did to our ethanol tanks."

They drove by two storage tanks that were spaced about a hundred yards apart to prevent fire from spreading. Then, they saw a construction crew already welding on the replacement tanks.

"Why do you think they did it?" David asked.

"The rich land owners want to continue living like kings. They'll fight to keep their game going. But, with the federal government on our side, we can buy them out and give the land back to the people as worker-entrepreneurs."

"These are lofty thoughts, my friends, and I find real merit in them," Carlos interjected. "But there remains the very worldly problem of greed. Americans are big believers in competition. They want to have all they can get."

"Competition?" Fredrico asked with a broad smile. "The corporations in the U.S. can't compete with the benefits of the Constellation. Not for the low income workers and the middle class. Not for seventy-five percent of the work force unless they become more like us. They simply can't deliver the quality of life I just described to you."

Carlos had no answer. He was stunned by what he was seeing, but he couldn't bring himself to embrace it. His mind set was too entrenched.

Fredrico led them down the street to a transit station.

"So, my friends, it's time to dispense with the car. We're about to enjoy a Curitiba-style metro."

They walked up a short ramp, bought their tickets and lined up for the next rapid. An articulated bus with three cars arrived. The doors opened just like a subway and within five minutes of buying a ticket they were seated.

"The metro will take us downtown within ten minutes."

They rode through downtown Las Faldas, which was now bustling with late morning activity. David could see how the transit stops were spaced so one could walk to any destination in a matter of minutes. The buildings around the transit stations were twenty to thirty stories high, with multi-leveled shops, restaurants, banks, and all manner of businesses built above and below the rapid station.

They transferred to another line and boarded a rapid that traveled through residential neighborhoods north of the downtown.

"How did El Cinco get the jump on Saldana?" Carlos asked. "You knew he was coming, but you didn't know when."

"The thief does not invade the strong man's house. We have security guards, electronic surveillance and scouting teams. We have heavily armed helicopters and the latest communications equipment. We can move men quite quickly to most any spot. But best of all, we have really good spies." Fredrico's eyes danced at that last comment and he was possessed by uncontrollable chuckling. Once he had regained most of his composure, he said, "And now I have a story for you, but you must keep it to yourselves. I'll consider it a breech of trust if you relay this information to anyone," he stated firmly.

His eyes began dancing again. "After the first surprise attack on the ethanol storage tanks we contracted some ex-CIA types to find out who and why. The Future's Way propaganda told us who they were and why they did it, at least on the surface. In a few days, these agents traced the location of their headquarters in the mountains northwest of El Cedro. They found out that their military leader was a retired colonel with a raving right-wing ideology. I mean, this guy is a real 'flamer.' Well, these clever agents found out that the colonel liked to play with toys."

"Toys?" asked David. "Like kids' toys?"

"Like gadgets. You know, expensive high-tech toys made for adults. Anyway, the agents found out that the colonel would be in this particular hotel for two days and they sold him a miniature blimp that was bugged. Saldana loved to have this thing flying around in his meetings."

David and Carlos laughed at the image of the colonel, bragging to his cohorts about how much fun they were going to have with these blimps at briefings on the attack.

"So, in a matter of days, we were wired right into their headquarters. We learned that they were really a front organization for several rich landowners in Rocadura. The colonel and his men were mercenaries hired to stop the growth of Constellation Style new towns. Their raving right-wing ideology had us painted as the destroyers of capitalism and the freedom of landowners to use their land as they wished."

"Poor babies," David mocked. "Their rights to exploit the poor at fifty cents an hour were threatened."

"You've got it. Anyway, we found out that they were planning a second attack on our ethanol plants in Las Faldas. This time they were coming in with two helicopters to wipe out the whole Energy Technoparc. They put the 'copters' in trucks and reassembled them within forty miles of Las Faldas. We let them get that close and then we planned to take them on the ground with superior force. You know the rest. Saldana attacked early but we knocked him out. He may have survived but we've captured most of his bosses. It's not likely that they'll strike again."

"Slick move. Those spies of yours must be real characters."

"Yeah," Fredrico smiled a satisfied smile, "and they never found out how we trapped them. Our chief of security is Pepe Gonzalez. He lives by a book called *The Art of War*, written by Sun Tzu, two and a half thousand years ago."

"You mean they had official spies way back then?" David asked.

"Oh, yes."

Fredrico, David and Carlos arrived at their restaurant of choice in suburban transit stop.

"The main point of *The Art of War* is this: the goal is to disarm the enemy's aggression without fighting. Spies are used to gain inside information that can be used to prevent a war."

"So, your spies could not stop a battle, but they were good enough to stop a war," David allowed.

"Right."

"That's very interesting," Carlos observed. "But will other landowners regroup and attack again."

"It makes me uneasy that Colonel Saldana is out there on the loose. He's dangerous and he's crafty. He may team up with other landowners."

"The Constellations have the potential to stop future wars," David allowed, "by putting food on everyone's table."

"Yes. We need to shift the nation's focus from the art of war to the art of human development."

"So, Fredrico, tell us more about the energy system."

"Well, now that you've seen the Energy Technoparc, you know how cheap energy drives most of the work and creates wealth. Food production and processing, apparel, manufacturing, housing production, and modular industrial and commercial construction."

"The basic necessities sector of the economy," Carlos offered.

"Exactly."

"And now, I have another new town story to tell you. It's about the seventh new town."

David immediately got the feeling that Fredrico was very fond of this story. Fredrico looked around the metro car with a relaxed expression, a quiet little smile curling at the corners of his mouth.

"In the beginning, we were just building new towns and trying to create thousands of jobs the Mondragon way. We weren't even thinking about self-sufficiency. All of the economists had given up on the idea of self-sufficiency a long time ago. We built the first three new towns and planned it so they were naturally supporting each other with different varieties of food, raw materials, and services. Almost automatically, it seemed, we found that things were falling into place effortlessly. Without much serious thinking, the first four new towns were providing each other with a wide variety of goods."

"So, it just evolved that way?"

"That's right. It was as if the combination of the first four new towns raised them exponentially to a higher level. Self-reliance, self-sufficiency, confidence and economic permanence were being built-in. Everybody saw it happening. It was off-the-chart exhilarating! Well, we just threw away our existing plans for the next three new towns and started over."

"The lights went on, eh?" offered Carlos.

"Big time. We were like little kids building castles on the beach…and someone had just given us superior technology and art supplies for the job! What a fun trip! LSI was in total delicious chaos for months! Everybody had ideas. The juices were flowing. We started playing with economic integration—vertically and horizontally. Work had turned into play entirely. Even on the site plans, we could see that the whole was greater than the sum of the parts. With each new town we added, we raised self-reliance exponentially. When we raised the system to the sixth power, we were frankly awed. It was like a God-given symphony unfolding on our computer screens. But then, we made the mistake of taking our planning too seriously. The ascent to the seventh power became difficult. We thought we had to fill in as many of the missing gaps as we could."

"But why did you have to stop at seven new towns?" David asked. "Why couldn't you simply add numbers eight and nine to complete the job?"

"Well, that could be the case for the next Constellation. For openers, we knew we were close to a masterpiece and we started straining vainly to achieve some purposes. The more we strained, the more the synthesis evaded us. Then, one day, we fell back into the playful mode. We started from scratch and things started to click and hum again. We worked and played like crazy nuts, going from calm control, to a frenzy of mixed joy and exhilaration, then to raw, unrestrained passion, then back to intuitive calm. We added manufacturing facilities and aquaculture operations outside of the new towns themselves, yet they were worker-owned and inside the Constellation economy. Again, the whole Constellation was emerging perfectly in so many newfound ways."

"Sounds like creative heaven," David said.

"A real sandbox," Carlos allowed.

"When you are playful with God in the world like we were, the symphony writes itself."

"That reminds me of Mozart. He and God were playing together at age six when he heard his first composition in his head and wrote it down," said David.

"Does the success of adding the seventh new town come mostly from integrated technology or some kind of synergy?" Carlos inquired.

"Both and more. I think it's superior and appropriate technology plus human development and integrated economics, the sharing of wealth by the producers of wealth among themselves. As you know, the seven new towns work first to build for themselves—for their own family of friends—then, they share it with the whole Constellation."

"So, one of the really new ingredients is how people create and share together," said David.

"That's what makes it so exciting, because that caring, playful process is infinite—it has no end. We learned that when we designed Constellations, the path is playfulness. When we work like that, it's only 'work' in the sense that something concrete gets done. We experienced a little of that in our Sandbox, remember?"

"Oh, yeah," David smiled with a warm memory, "I felt the child in me having fun again."

Chapter 13
A GENTLEMAN'S DISAGREEMENT

David and Carlos had gathered enough information to send a final report to Europa Development Corporation. They also planned to send a copy to Alfredo Humberto at the State Department, as promised. David and Carlos finished a technical planning report including several pages of financial data supplied by Fredrico. David wrote a cover letter to the CEO, Peter Erikson. Carlos read the cover letter carefully twice. He was clearly disturbed by its contents.

"David, I just can't agree with this analysis," Carlos challenged. "To me, Constellation Style economics raises many problems…too many unresolved questions. I've been going along with you and Fredrico as far as I can. I've listened and held my tongue for a long time."

"What is it, specifically, that bothers you about the Constellation?"

"Well, to start with, I see major land wars. Fredrico went through that issue too easily. There are many Colonel Saldanas in the world and plenty of landowners that will pay them. There have been wars over lands in Latin America since the beginning and they will continue until the end of the world."

"Okay," David said amiably, "since Saldana almost took us out of the picture entirely, I can't deny it all. It's a significant problem. Let's beef it up in the report. What else?"

"Another big one: I don't see enough profit for the investors. Ten to fifteen percent is just not inviting. The real action guys want *big* buck returns—twenty to thirty percent at least."

"Well, there are five billionaires who are happy with their return on investment. I take that as a good sign. And don't forget, they have a bank that is drawing huge assets from all over Latin America, based on the Cornerstone Constellation. They'll have tens of billions of dollars that will roll in when people really find out what they can do."

"Fine. You've got five very exceptional people who probably bought into this thing for very personal and spiritual reasons. Most billionaires I've read about have very strong egos, the whole world serves their interests very well and they are quite accustomed to having their own way. The Global Billionaires Fund idea may fall on its face."

"Not if Conchita and Gail O'Reilly keep reeling in investors. You've got to give credit where it's due. They're doing one helluva job."

"Granted. Time will tell. I'll have to give you that one but you've overlooked the biggest problem of all."

"What's that?"

"Constellations work fine in Rocadura and Mondragon because they're all Spanish-speaking and mostly Roman Catholics with a common heritage and cultural background. In the U.S., we've got this diversity thing to deal with. Do you think you can convince whites, Afro-Americans, Latinos, Asians, Indians, Muslims, Jews, Atheists, Protestants and Catholics to play nicely together in the 'sandbox'?"

"That's the tough one all right and I don't pretend to have a solution. I've been working on it for a long time. There is one thing they all have in common: their children and their children's children. They all want the best for their kids. They want them to have it better than they did. We've got kids growing up in wretched families, violent hellholes, and unsafe schools. What those kids need is a strong economic ladder in their community. Their parents need to have a way to show them how they can get an education, get a promising job and have a good family life. You have to get them on board in grade school and show them a better way to earn a living than pushing drugs.

"Man, I really agree with that. I like your economic ladder concept. Have you fleshed it out?"

"Well, yes, a bit. I've written an article on it, which I plan to publish in the U.S. It's based on the Allecoop model in Mondragon, which sets up a worker-owner cooperative that serves local businesses. Allecoop gets orders from industrial cooperatives to assemble electrical components for refrigerators, stoves, dish washers and cars. The kids work on simple but important tasks. They can work their way through vocational school or college in what I call The Ladder Cooperative. Parents are strongly encouraged to join the Ladder Lodge, which is empowered to make darn sure that all local, state and federal officials deliver the goods to build and maintain The Ladder. Those in power who wave the 'family values flag' have to see that those economic ladders get set up for very young people and are funded to thrive and grow. Eventually they can be self-supporting from the products they produce for businesses."

"I can see how that might work. Afro-Americans can have Ladders in their communities for their kids. Latinos and Asians can do the same. They send kids with good character and working habits to the Ladder cooperative. It's a start."

"Thanks. I believe that people should be judged by their character and nothing else. They need to send their kids up the economic ladder into a Constellation that accepts everyone because, they're good people who just want to make a promising living. I've been to the Bahamas. I was astonished that I sensed no racial tension there and maybe, just maybe, it was because they control the economic system. Whites have to get a work permit! My experience with Bahamians suggests that it is possible to have a healthy racial mix in a Constellation, but it's not for everyone."

"No, you'll never please everyone."

"Let's take it one step further. These young people are going to receive some high caliber Constellation training. They'll know how to mix socially and culturally. They'll know their trade or profession pretty well. So, who is going to want their talents?"

"Corporations and businesses all over the world."

"Exactly, and the Constellation graduates will be totally free to make their choice."

"Man, I never thought I'd hear that comin' from you."

"Hey, contrary to popular belief, I'm not anti-corporation, I'm anti-bad corporation. I'm very pro good corporation and there is one helluva difference. My hope is that Constellations, working alongside of corporations will show them how to do it better. That's all."

"All right. I think we've covered some territory but we still haven't come together totally."

Okay, let's take your major concerns and we can change our letter, and add in those specifics."

Carlos paused for a long time, looking out of the window. He folded his arms across his chest and stared at the palm fronds blowing in the wind.

Finally, with his back to David he spoke.

"No. It goes right to the heart of the matter. Fredrico is talking about a new kind of economic structure. It's not capitalism, so it must be opposed to capitalism. If it is opposed, then it can't work! Look at the oil companies. Are El Cinco going to take on Big Oil and the Arabs? Just think about those interlocking boards of directors. Just ask yourself whose ox is going to get gored? Then prepare to see them fight to protect their interests. Capitalism is based on self-interest and if those interests aren't being served, well, that will be the end of the Constellations. They will dry up and vanish. They'll be forgotten," and then he turned to look David fully in the face, "just like Mondragon."

This was a bit more than David could bear. Mondragon held a special place in his heart.

"Damn it! Mondragon is clearly the most successful economic system in the world. And now the Constellations will be far more advanced by following their lead. Mondragon has only been forgotten by people with no vision and by greedy bastards who don't care about anyone but themselves. Hell, most people have never heard of it because the American media hasn't shown that it exists!"

The term "greedy bastards" brought the heat up on Carlos' collar.

"The world operates on self-interest. At first, people want *enough* money. But as soon as they get enough, they want *more* money and what it will buy. And that isn't enough either, then they want even more! You can't change the world, David."

"That's true with a some people, but many people will accept more than enough, lots of vacation time to play and a few luxuries, as long as they can live in a kind and fair economic structure. They also hunger for anxiety reduction and peace of soul. The way the Constellation is organized, people only need to work four days a week. Like Fredrico said, people who want to earn more can do it! They can create a second job in the luxury sector of the economy, if they have the drive and the talent. With the Constellations, working people can earn more luxuries than they can under capitalism. Most people will be satisfied with good food, and parties with plenty of friends who are all living a comfortable life. Just look at Las Faldas!"

"Las Faldas is beautiful," Carlos agreed. "But how can you change the minds of the rich?"

"Oh, you're right about that. You can't change the so-called 'human nature' of the rich and powerful easily. But that's where it stops. Because I'm talking about working people—the seventy percent of the world that wakes up every morning knowing that, short of a small miracle, they *aren't* going to get rich. The economic structure needs to be reinvented for the seventy percent. The Constellation is a unique alternative that offers working people a very rich life."

"Okay, but what are you going to do with the lazy people that don't want to work? The ones that think everyone should hand them a living without lifting a damn finger?"

"There are some of those types on both ends of the scale, aren't there? I mean, you've got people born with silver spoons in their mouths, like George Sands, who left a suicide note saying that he had played and consumed himself into total satiation and because he was so bored, the only thing left to do was commit suicide."

"You're proving my point. Human nature is corruptible."

"Ah, now we're getting to the *real* underlying issue that separates us. You choose to focus on the fact that human nature is corruptible, which it is. I choose to focus on the fact that human nature is worthy of the mercy and love that God gives us, and we all have free will to turn toward the good and grow."

"I see feet of clay everywhere I look."

"Have you taken a good look at Fredrico and Padre Parejo lately?"

"There are a few exceptions."

"Yes, and they make all of the difference, because they know God loves them, they have the capacity to love others."

"What about the laggards, David? Who is going to give those lazy do-nothings a living?"

"Nobody in the Constellations, because when you're a worker-owner, you've got peer group pressure to carry your own weight. The people you work with determine who earns a raise. That's the way it works."

"That's good. I like that part."

"But we've always got the planner's nightmare: the mentally ill, the sociopaths, the physically ill, the disabled and undernourished, the folks with the very low IQs, the abused, who are prone to violence, and the angry young men and women who are mad as hell at injustice and won't take it anymore."

"Right, and how do you deal with that?"

"You tell me. How do *you* deal with that?"

"I let them take care of themselves and I take care of myself," Carlos answered.

"The Constellation has a better idea. They give ten percent of their salaries to try to deal with those problems and they employ as many as they can. They give them an economic ladder into a better future."

"That's fine, but the best and the brightest win, David. A lot of people have a shot at being at the top—if they get off their duffs."

"The best and the brightest? I'd say the people at the top are the quickest to take an opportunity when it opens up. The brightest? Bright people maybe, but they have no wisdom, no concern for the men and women who work for a living. There is no correlation between intelligence and human values. Look at Al "Chainsaw" Dunlap, the CEO who fired thousands. Look at Enron, and Delphi and GM. You call them the *best?* No way in Hell. They're smart at making money for themselves while the economic system falls apart for their employees and the rest of the nation."

"But you see my points, don't you, David?"

"Yes, I see some of your points," he answered evenly. "I think human nature is redeemable and you think it's not worth the effort. Christ told us we're all worthwhile, and I'll take His word over anyone in the world. He even told us to love our enemies. Maybe you should write your own cover letter and I'll write mine."

"Fine. That's exactly what we should do."

"I think people are happy in Las Faldas, and that's the real test," David asserted.

"So you really think being middle-class like everyone else will satisfy most people? Well, I've got news for you. I think that most folks are just waiting for the 'big hit' so they can quit working and live like kings. Hell, that's why everyone plays the lottery."

"And how many people make the 'big hit' in the lottery at fourteen million to one odds? Not very damn many. In the business world, a small number make it to a nice fortune…which is built on the backs of their employees who did all of the work." Looking Carlos directly in the eyes, he said, "Yeah, Carlos, don't be so damned brainwashed. If you're in the top thirty percent you can sit around asking yourself, 'How can it get any better?'"

With that, Carlos stormed out the door, slamming it with a blow that brought Maria Leon upstairs to see what had happened. Carlos passed her at the foot of the stairs and went straight out of the door into the night. Maria caught a glimpse of his fiery eyes and went up the stairs to see what had caused the anger. Jose Enrique was right behind her.

"Is everything okay?" she asked, with a note of alarm.

"Yeah. Carlos and I just had a gentlemen's disagreement about the meaning of the Constellation."

"He doesn't like it?" she asked in amazement.

"Let's just say he has a few unanswered questions," he said, in an attempt to bring the situation back to semi-normal. "We're both still learning a lot. Give him time."

"The Constellation isn't Utopia, but it's really nice. We work hard, but we have strong financial security, like we've never had before. There is plenty of really good food, enough of the basics and many luxuries. We still suffer with pride, you know, and a few have a grumble about this and that. You know how people are. They reach a certain level, then they want more. People get credit for what they do, but some want to have more power and influence."

"The political animals," David smiled. "They're always around. So, would you say some folks in Las Faldas grumble because they want more power or money? More things?"

"Just a small number do, but all of my friends are very happy or at least content. Everyone knows they have a tremendously good thing compared to working outside. Being a worker-owner is so much better than being in the boss-slave system. Everyone in the Constellation is optimistic about the future. We know we're making a better life for ourselves, our children and grandchildren. That means a lot. Many are trying to help those who are outside to survive until more new towns can be built."

"I know, we saw it all in Camino Adelante," he said with a cold shiver, as he remembered the stench and the dead dog in the gutter.

"We see their miserable suffering every day. That's why Jose Enrique wants to become a new town builder."

"You're saying some people feel they have enough to help others who are less fortunate?"

"Yes. Hundreds of thousands of people are standing in line to join the next set of new towns. Getting into a Constellation is all they talk about. It makes some of us feel guilty when we know how much we have and how desperate others are, just trying to survive every single day. There's a debate going on right now about how much to give to charity. In Mondragon, they give ten percent of earnings. Some people think it should be lowered to eight percent. But, my God, compared to what we had before, the Constellation is the best way of life this side of Heaven."

"Thanks, Maria. You've given me a lot of answers to Carlos' questions."

"I just know how I feel and how my friends feel," she said. "You saw for yourself how happy people were at La Feria."

"Well, that says it all where I come from."

"Would you like to join me for a nightcap? I have some cognac from Jerez."

"I thought you'd never ask," David responded with a most sincere and large smile.

David had a pleasant chat with Maria and a very fine cognac.

The next day David telephoned Fredrico and had a long conversation, discussing all of the issues that Carlos had cited. David took careful notes and redrafted his letter to Erikson, as follows:

Mr. Peter Erikson
President and CEO
Europa Development Corporation
478 Plaza de Espana, Suite 214
Washington, D.C. 20537

Dear Peter,

As you will see from the attached report, we have found something extraordinary here in the new town complex called the Constellation. We have been introduced to what could be the next evolution in economic structures, moving well beyond the stagnant and ineffective marketplace system. Discovering the Constellation is like exploring a new life form!

I can only touch on the highlights in this cover letter, to key you into what I think are just some of the most important features of this fascinating new town complex.

First, the Constellation is a unique kind of, desperately needed, "life support system" that can be built alongside of the corporations and the marketplace system. I believe they can co-exist nicely. Carlos still has some concerns about that. However, there is the most extraordinary thing about the Constellations that gives them assurance of political survival: they can provide millions of jobs for the unemployed and underemployed in the developing countries—and they can do it by providing an astonishing new market for corporations in terms of tools, equipment and a myriad of other products and services.

Secondly, it's a boon to financial institutions. I believe that bankers have rarely seen such a fine example of the thing they love most dearly: "banking certainty." The Constellation has been built to be self-reliant, to make its own way, and to pay its bills with ever-increasing economic solidity. The entire economic structure is designed to enable people to earn the basic necessities of life and some luxuries. These new towns have the whole array of bankable physical assets in place.

What kind of return on investment can a banker expect? El Cinco provided the equity investment for the seven new towns at market rates. International banks have also supplied several very large long term loans at market rates. Additional capital is added to the system for growth by the worker-owners themselves, mostly from pension savings.

So how do the people feel about this new town complex?

People are wonderfully optimistic in Las Faldas, the new town where they held the big harvest fair this year. Employees are enrolled in two savings plans: first to buy a house and second to save for retirement. They can own their home in about 7 years, with about $30,000 to $80,000 worth of equity. They have lower monthly payments because of the equity, so they increase their disposable income by 30% at that stage of their lives. Then they save for retirement and they pay $2,400 for 10 years to provide capital investment in the Constellation, which makes them an owner. After that, they work to advance the forward days of each family and their children. All technological breakthroughs and innovations are shared among the seven new towns.

This kind of promise for the future can really increase a person's loyalty to the mission of the organization—and after all, the organization is serving the worker-owners. This is not an ESOP. These workers have all of the seats on the Board of Directors.

There is no security for the majority of employees in the United States. Cynicism is the order of the day and as a result, loyalty is in the trash can. Such is not the case in this new town complex. I don't think the "Constellation Style" of job creation can be stopped now by anything. This means corporations will be treated to a new kind of "corporate culture" in a new world that delivers on the promise of human development.

Most all of the technology is "off the shelf" and all of it is environmentally sound. El Cinco did some added research and development with solar cells, and by the way, they have their own research centers. They use the Lonnie Ingrams process to turn vegetative waste into fuel ethanol. The magic is in how the technology is used to increase wealth and in how that wealth is distributed. Ethanol at $1.30 per gallon is used to drive super efficient gas turbine generators to produce electricity. Ethanol power drives assembly lines to produce solar cells. Computer driven mechanical assembly lines are used extensively. By using know-how and very inexpensive energy to great advantage, the Constellation builds production arrangements which require very little human time and energy. These production lines are designed to last a very long time with minimal retooling. They produce energy, housing, food, clothing, furniture, appliances, cars, transit systems and computers: all of the basic necessities, and primarily for local consumption. Ethanol is a major export item. They are among the lowest cost producers of ethanol in the world and they export 50% of it to buy luxuries they can not yet produce.

In the words of Fredrico de la Chica: "Once these production lines are in place, we reduce the amount of time it takes to earn a living. We will have created wealth together that will advance our forward days, as Bucky Fuller was fond of saying."

As you can see from our report, we have gotten down to some real substance… and what substance! As we discussed on the telvid, we need more time to gather enough data and to build our relationship with El Cinco to make this expedition a full success. We'll keep you fully abreast and we look forward to your reaction to the enclosed analysis.

I'm excited to know that our team at Europa is in on the ground floor to develop new towns "Constellation Style." I'm thinking we will find the highest level of acceptance in Latin America, rather than in Europe or the U.S. initially, primarily because they are more eager for social justice in the economic system. Once we build a complex of new towns we can look at our options. It is certainly too early to make a call on where to expand at this point. I therefore recommend that we continue to

stay close to El Cinco and let them indicate some logical options.
Give a "Big Happy Hello!" to everybody.
With warm regards,

David O'Laughlin
Advanced Planning Team

Carlos wrote his letter to Erikson, stating the same concerns he'd laid out to David. They discussed the package they were sending to Europa Development over breakfast.

"I'm glad we got our views out in the open," Carlos said. "I was feeling a lot of strain until we laid it out." Carlos knew the gap between them was large, yet he felt something still held them together.

"I just love those no-holds-barred fights. It keeps a man healthy and well-grounded," said David, who was not really concerned about their friendship holding up.

"Yeah, it's Latino," said Carlos. The Italians excel at it."

"Maybe we should buy some cheap dishes to throw at the walls," suggested David with a toothy grin.

"So, once again, we have agreed to disagree."

"Yes, but it's very invigorating. And it probably is a microcosm of what will happen when the Constellation is played out on the larger stage of life."

David thought that Carlos would eventually change his mind about the Constellation's chances of success, maybe with more proof. As for himself, he had all of the proof he needed.

Carlos thought capitalism would rule for more than his lifetime, but he was beginning to believe the Constellations could eventually replace the market economy.

David was convinced Constellation Style economics would take about ten years to spread, but in the long term, truth will rise to the top and no human being will stop its inevitable arrival. The thought of building new Constellations gave him a rich spiritual satisfaction, the kind that caresses you with a great night's sleep and a feeling of wholeness of spirit in the morning. David had found home.

"Well, Carlos, there's one thing we have in common that will never die. I mean, how many men get attacked by a monster gunship and vipers on the same day?"

"Oh, man," groaned Carlos. "I thought for sure we'd bought the farm."

Shortly after receiving the report from David and Carlos, Peter Erikson fired back a quick telvid. They were out to dinner when it was sent, so they played the tape when they returned to their hotel room, as follows:

"I understand you need more time to collect needed information. I'm intrigued by your diversity of perspective. Sounds to me like you are having *way* too much fun. So, we're coming down on the twentieth of this month to join the party. It'll be a working vacation for the staff. Please let LSI know we are coming en masse...plus Humberto. We've made reservations at La Granada Hotel in El Cedro."

The remainder of the message was a video splice taken from a recent musical, titled *Gypsies, 2000*. It was one of those classic hits that everyone loved. It had charm, vitality, romance, playfulness and music that matched. The piece that Erikson broadcast was an entrancing dance number— "Prelude to the Prelude."

"Well, David, it sounds like our report really lit a fire in old Erikson's belly."

"Yeah. Not to mention the staff and Humberto," David smiled mischievously. "How many do you think 'en masse' means?'"

"Hell, knowing Erikson, it'll probably be all of the line directors, and the seniors in research."

"Let's see. That's nine...plus three, plus Humberto equals thirteen."

"Well, you better add in about three executive assistants, because they run the place and Erikson will want their services down here, for sure!"

"Okay, that's Carolyn, Vicki and Ricardo...it's sweet sixteen and they've *all* been kissed! Man, it's going to be wild around here. Just like Erikson to use the dramatic entrance with the telvid."

"You got that right. You know he was down here for five days before he sent us. He knows a lot about what's goin' on at LSI. I get a kick out of the old man when he has his juices flowing. He takes strong action and it's usually pretty damned good."

"Well, I'll call Vicki to get the total number," said Carlos, "then we'll make arrangements for this Europa invasion of the southern hemisphere. Which reminds me, let's see Fredrico about getting a case of Gran Sangre de Toro."

"Come on! A case will last that bunch about two dinners...after the tequila, vodka and scotch."

"Oh, man! You're right. We're in full field combat! The logistics got away from me." Carlos lay back on the couch and jokingly groaned, "Stretcher bearers! Stretcher bearers!"

"Two cases and they'll have to fend for themselves."

"Damned right."

"Hell, two cases of Gran Sangre is a *really* nice gift."

"Yeah," Carlos agreed, putting his hands behind his head. "It's a classic gift. And…you could greet them with your own paella delight!"

Chapter 14
THE EUROPA INVASION

Colonel Victor Saldana was not looking forward to his next meeting with Echeverria. He barely escaped his surprise attack, because they knew he was coming. He thought that in the eyes of Echeverria, he botched the attack on Las Faldas. Saldana felt strongly that this was an unfair assessment of his military prowess. He was accustomed to living up to his name. Someone had leaked the information to El Cinco, but who? He had called in all of his men to grill them and cause them to show their guilt. He found nothing, since they all appeared to be loyal beyond doubt. He had wracked his brains for weeks and could not find an answer. Now, he must face the man who financed the attack with no answers except the security leak for his perceived failure. He had a strong stomach but this was causing him to have high anxiety.

Raul Echeverria was forced to leave his mansion in El Cedro and go into exile. He had settled in the second largest city in Rocadura, Santa Rosa.

The same security guard let Saldana in to meet with Echeverria.

"Hey, Tomas, how are you doing? Did you have a good weekend?"

"It was okay, but too short. Come this way," said Tomas, with a cool and guarded look in his eyes.

Saldana's heart skipped a beat, because he felt this cold greeting was not a good omen. Tomas opened the door to the study and Saldana saw Echeverria with another man he didn't recognize.

"Welcome, my friend. I want you to meet an old buddy of mine from way

156

back," and he whispered his name softly in Saldana's ear, "Jose Calaveras. He has a job for you." Echeverria put his finger to his lips, and indicated that the room could be tapped.

"A pleasure to meet you," said Saldana with some relief, "I've heard many good things about your family over the years."

"Raul has told me good things about you as well."

"Let's get some fresh air and take a stroll in my garden," said Raul Echeverria, as he handed a scotch on the rocks to both Saldana and Calaveras. The three men walked out of Echeverria's mansion into a carefully manicured garden lined with six-foot high hedges and royal palms.

Five hundred yards away, on a small hill, Tom Foley and Steve Rankin lay on their bellies looking through a telephoto lens. They had been camped out there since morning and excited that their two week stake out might pay off. They had been extremely cautious about being seen because they knew the equipment they were using could be in the hands of their prey, looking right back at them.

"Get the boom mike on them! They just came out of the house!" whispered Tom.

"Mike is on."

The three men strolled slowly through the garden.

"We know you walked into a trap at Las Faldas," said Calaveras, "but you still managed to knock out two of their ethanol tanks and escape alive to fight again. I respect you for that. Was there a double agent?"

Saldana felt the grip of anxiety fall to nothing in that instant. "I am convinced it was not a security leak from inside my organization. I know my men, and I've grilled them. Somehow, our communications was tapped."

"I reached the same conclusion. My men found phone taps at my house in El Cedro, that's why we're not taking any chances. No one knows I'm back in Rocadura but you and close members of my family. By the way, people know me as Enrique Franco here."

"It's great to see you back in action, Señor...Franco."

Saldana gave Echeverria a robust Spanish hug, and spilled some scotch on his hand in the process. He licked it off with his tongue and observed with a mischievous smile, "I'd rather lick it off a nipple."

That brought some knowing laughter and the mood shifted to a more light-hearted mode among the three men.

"Well, if we're going to play games with the ladies, we need to keep making the big bucks, guys," suggested Calaveras.

"How well I know. *All* my chicks are high maintenance. By the way, didn't Raul say you had a little job for me?"

"Yeah. Let me give you some background. The bastards are trying to steal our land in Vizcaya Province with eminent domain, then they'll turn around and sell it to the Constellations! Governor Francisco is the pig who is about to screw us and I want him to disappear. Once he's taken out, we'll get our own man in power and no one will have the guts to try it again."

"So, that's the job?"

"It needs to happen within the next two weeks. We need to take him out before they go public with this eminent domain thing, otherwise, we'll be prime suspects."

"Does he have bodyguards?"

"Yes, they guard him, but..."

At that moment three crows flew between Calaveras and the boom mike, squawking loudly.

"Damn it!" said Steve softly, as they missed the next words from Calaveras.

"I want it to look like an accident. They don't always stay with the car."

The crows passed and the squawking faded in the distance.

"Can you get me his schedule for the next few weeks?"

Calaveras handed a piece of paper to Saldana. "We have an inside source."

The note gave Saldana the time, place and method of attack.

"That's good intelligence. It makes everything so much easier."

"Can you handle it alone? We can't afford any leaks this time."

"That's the *only* way I'd take the job. What's it worth to you?"

"Give me a price."

"What is your land worth?"

"It's worth a hundred and fifty million."

"How much will they pay you if they take it with eminent domain?"

"The bastards are trying to steal it for a hundred and seventy."

"I think it's worth two percent of the one hundred and fifty million. I'm risking my life here."

"That's a lot of money for one job."

"I'll have to leave the country and move around the rest of my life. I'm already on the prime suspect list."

"I'll give you two million if you kill him and make it look like an accident."

"Okay, it's a deal."

Calaveras and Saldana looked each other sternly in the eyes and shook hands.

"Good!" said Echeverria with vigor. "Let's go in the house and seal the deal with some more Chevas."

Steve looked at Tom and whispered, "Here we go again. We've got the time frame and the target but we don't know when or how!"

"Let's get to the van and talk it over, my legs are cramping and man, am I dry!"

The two men carefully made their way back to the van and stretched their muscles.

"I hate stakeouts," Steve remarked as he bent over and rubbed his aching calves, "but when they pay off like this, they're hard to beat."

"Right now, Jack and Seven will be hard to beat," Tom smiled as he poured two glasses and handed one to Steve.

"Whoa! That tastes good!"

"Yeah, it's been a long day. Now, let's review what we've got. Saldana is going after Governor Jaime Francisco."

"Uh-uh, and it's going to be done in the next few weeks."

"Well then, it's triple bodyguard time. Do you think Fredrico will want our services?"

"Does the crow squawk in the woods?"

* * *

Meanwhile, David and Carlos checked into La Granada Hotel and began preparing for the "Europa Invasion."

A large party of twenty from Europa Development Corporation arrived in El Cedro on Sunday evening. David and Carlos provisioned a party room where everyone gathered for drinks and appetizers before dinner. There was much handshaking, hugs and kisses for David and Carlos, who were perceived as the catalysts of this much-needed working vacation for the staff. Then, David brought out three large paella pans filled with shrimp, chicken, scallops and twelve other essential ingredients. The ladies in the group sampled his gourmet delight and conspired to thank David. Three of them went into the ladies restroom, painted their lips extravagantly with vermillion lip stick. The ring leader announced, "David, we want to thank you for your wonderful paella." Then, they surrounded David and proceeded to paint his face, neck, forehead, arms and nose with the naughtiest kisses they could sexily deliver. The staff gave them a standing ovation.

When Carlos finally had a private moment with David he said, "Okay, man, that does it. You're going to teach me how to make your paella! Just name your price."

"After what we've been through together, I'll do it. Buy the $150 dollars worth of ingredients, bring a bottle of Gran Sangre de Toro, and a bottle of Jameson. We'll need chef's helpers. Bring your girlfriend and I'll bring Conchita."

"Damn I love to take advantage of your generosity!"

"That's okay, one day I'll make you so guilty you'll think you've been worked over by a Jewish mother and then, I'll get what I really want."

Carlos looked suspiciously out of the corner of his eye and asked, "What's that? What do you really want?"

"I want you to be my buddy in building Constellations. Sometimes I think your heart is elsewhere."

"Hey, all I can say is that while I'm with you I'm with you."

Eventually, Erikson joined the two of them in a quiet corner to discuss the report on El Cinco and the Constellation. Erikson was a tall man, about six feet two inches, in a slender frame. He was wearing a "go to hell" tropical shirt with palm trees, pink flamingos and parrots. He had on white slacks and Italian loafers with no socks. Strictly South Florida, thought David.

"Well, I enjoyed your report," said Erikson. "This Livelihood Systems group is probably the most fascinating outfit on the planet today. I couldn't wait to get down here and see it again for myself."

"They're quantum leaps ahead all right," David noted, "and it's damned exciting."

"It was a fine report, fellows. The levels of economic integration are extraordinary," said Erikson, while interlocking his fingers to graphically describe the meshing of the system.

"I'm especially fond of their financial structure," David allowed. "They gather money from all over Latin America and pay one-half a percentage point more than most banks. El Cinco are making their capital go far by using that money as leverage."

"Yes!" said Erikson excitedly. "How much do you think El Cinco can raise to keep this thing rolling?"

"After talking with Gail O'Reilly, president of the LSI bank, I think El Cinco can raise, worldwide…oh, only about two hundred to three hundred billion in the two or three years, we'll have to see after that!"

"That's a nice start," said Carlos. "These fellows *are* impressive, but they still have three big hurdles to clear. The way I see the scenario: first you've got major land wars. Then you've got bureaucratic delay problems. And thirdly, you've got to attract professional talent at high paying salaries or it just won't work. In the U.S., you've got to deal with the old melting pot of races."

"I agree with you, Carlos," David said quickly. "Those are the major concerns I can identify, but I think, in the long term, they all have solutions."

"You can make three hundred billion dollars go a long way with the right kind of investment strategy," said Carlos, "but eventually, your cash runs out and you have to wait for capital accumulation."

"Maybe not," said Erikson. "El Cinco can also borrow plenty of money on those fixed assets in place, and keep on rolling. And as David points out, they have a perpetual revenue generating machine from worker-entrepreneur investment. David, how many new towns do you think they can build with their financial structure?"

"They've built seven new towns and have twenty-eight more new towns under development in Rocadura. They'll need to build about fifty new towns there if the country is going to employ most all of the unemployed."

"Okay," said Erikson, "Fredrico has invited us to design and build two Constellations. That's about fourteen new towns. But it's clear they also plan to move strongly in Latin America, and they're reaching out to us to bring in more capital and talent to continue to build Constellations."

"The big question is: are they about to leap into the frying pan or can they co-exist with global capitalism?" Carlos asked.

"Yes, Carlos, your letter made those concerns abundantly clear. David's letter seemed to answer some of your issues, but it looks like you guys are still worlds apart. That's why I like to team you two up—it adds spice to my life."

"Carlos and I have agreed to disagree on the future impact of the Constellation," David observed, "but we agree on the facts in the report. It's undeniably a highly successful self-sufficiency system."

"That much I'll grant you," smiled Carlos. "Now, we'll see if it can survive in the global arena where capitalism is king."

"Capitalism is a dying king," said Erikson, "unless it transforms itself into a Constellation Style corporate culture. Why? Because Constellations enable people to care about each other in a community with real freedom again and they provide health care and retirement benefits. Today, young people are rebelling because sixty percent of them are not receiving those essential benefits. Oh, by the way, David, I really liked the economic ladder you described. That will be absolutely necessary to make Constellations work in the U.S."

"Thanks, I put in a few years of thought on that one."

"Well, in my opinion, that was time well spent. But the big question remains. How will capitalism provide promising futures for eight billion or nine billion people on this planet? Corporations have no plans to provide economic self-sufficiency. The Constellation provides self-sufficiency *and* new ways to increase wealth for its members."

"If capitalism is so dead why does it continue to control the whole world?" Carlos asserted. "It will be a long, long time before Constellations can be built around the world."

"Of course, it will take time. I'm speaking of the death of the old dream and the birth of the new dream. It's that simple. Rich people can now line up to invest in the new dream—globally. That is where their fortune can grow handsomely, as well. When the king is dying, the court looks around to see who and what will replace him. There may be a better replacement than the Constellation, just waiting in the wings, but if there is, it hasn't come on stage yet."

Erikson paused to sip his drink, looking directly at Carlos. Carlos had no reply. The thought of capitalism dying was too new to him. He needed time to absorb it and reflect on the implications.

"David, you indicated we shouldn't try to build a Constellation in the U.S. at this time, that we should stay close to El Cinco and cut a deal to build jointly with them in Latin America. Well, I agree for now. But every politician in the world is desperate to create jobs and the Third Way International Conferences always focus on economic efficiency and social justice. Your economic ladder concept will be key in convincing politicians to create quality of life for the young. Didn't you say it would cost about fifty million to set up a local Ladder cooperative?"

"That's a high estimate. It may be much less, depending on local resources and support. But remember, the goal is to make The Ladder self-supporting by providing services to businesses."

"Now, that's what I call a worthwhile investment. Hell, to the Pentagon, fifty million is a penny. Get the kids on The Ladder. We'll save billions on crime and social disasters and have 'puleeenty' left over for military waste."

"The *Times* had a huge article on the worker protests, strikes, and student demonstrations," said David. "It's happening big time in Europe, as well."

"What's the latest in Washington?" asked Carlos.

"They brought out the National Guard again, for the third time. But the Guard just stands around and applauds the demonstrators! The joke around Washington is that they'll have to call in the Marines to defend Congress from the Army!" Erikson laughed.

"Sounds like things are really comin' to a head," smiled David.

"Guys, you've been away too long. Now, some senators are jaw-boning corporations to create more jobs with a promising future! They are talking sustainable economics and full employment."

"That's amazing!" said Carlos.

"Then, we have the Totally New Party, and their only goal is to have a national referendum on the corporate charter. They know that a corporation has to have a state charter to operate at all! So, their idea is to guarantee that people's livelihoods come first in corporate policy—and the shareholders and corporate 'execs' second and third."

"That's extremely radical!" shouted Carlos with a scornful growl.

"So, people *are* ready for the Constellation alternative!" said David, excitedly.

"Believe me, before long, the Constellation will be good news in America! In the last twenty years, corporations have fired thirty-eight percent of the work force! Fully half of the nation has a family member holding down two jobs to make ends meet. The corporate elite have swung the cutting blade too deep and too long."

"It's flaming brutal," said David. "People endure it only because they don't see an alternative."

"But Carlos has laid out the difficulties very well in his letter. American corporations want to keep playing the game with them on top, naturally. For the working man and woman, fifty years of brain-washing is hard to overcome. It can't be done overnight."

"You got that right," said Carlos. "The Constellation might work here, but it's not going to work in the U.S.A., until it's a proven model in Latin America, and maybe, not even then."

"Maybe not quite yet," smiled Erikson. "But the time is not far off. At the moment, the politics are so ugly, I don't even want to *think* about it. But we're in on the ground floor with El Cinco and we'll learn how to do it right in Latin America. Then, we'll look at the U.S. Every country is ripe for this kind of action! China and Islam are desperate for this kind of economics."

"We've got a whole world crying out for secure, promising paying jobs," said David. "The Constellation surpasses that dream by several miles. There are a lot of rich people worldwide looking for a stable investment with banking certainty."

"Oh, yeah, David, I *loved* that part of your report."

"Thanks."

Erikson sat back in his chair with his hands behind his head, "Okay, guys, here's what I'd like to do while I'm down here. First, our staff has been working their buns off for eighteen months straight and they really deserve this vacation. We've got to play before we go back to work. Everyone wants to party, hit the beach and loaf for a while."

"Well, the Lemon Islands are a great place for that. I snorkeled there for a week once, and it was damn fine. Lots of fish on the reefs," Carlos recalled.

"Perfect! We'll set 'em up there for a full week."

David opted to be with Conchita, semi-separately from the group, so they could celebrate Erikson's decision to build Constellations in Rocadura. After the meeting with Erikson, David telephoned Conchita with the news.

"Hi there!"

"David! What did Erikson decide?"

"It's really good news, sweetheart. Europa is going to accept El Cinco's offer to build two Constellations! Let's party!"

"Oh, David. I'm so happy."

"Let's go to the Lemon Islands for three days."

"Oooou. Sounds delicious. My suitcase is packed. I'm going to need a vacation before all hell breaks loose around here."

"What's comin' down?"

"Oh, just a court trial over eminent domain that will have an impact on all of Latin America."

"Sounds like big stuff all right."

"I'll have to spend a lot of very personal time with you. Your job is to keep me in a state of romantic euphoria. Okay?"

"Well, I'll just be my usual self falling all over you. Will that work?"

"I like your style."

"The Europa gang is there, but they're all going to snorkel on the leeward side of the island. We can have more privacy on the windward side."

"Smart move."

"Don't forget to pack your silks."

"You rogue."

"You gypsy savage."

"It's true."

"I'll set a course for the Lemon Islands. Would you like to have our initial rendezvous at twelve thirty for lunch? I should have the plane tickets by then."

"El Alcazar, then at twelve thirty?"

"Great choice. See you there!"

Chapter 15
UNEXPECTED VISITORS

Fredrico called the LSI staff together for a briefing on fast-breaking events. Carlos and David were invited to join the group in the conference room at LSI headquarters.

Fredrico was sharply dressed in a tan suit with a red and white striped tie. He was sitting casually on the edge of a long conference room table as David and Conchita entered the room. Gradually, the LSI staff found their way to seats at the table. Carlos was the last of twelve people to join the gathering.

"Well, it's show time once again, folks," began Fredrico. "We're about to enter a landmark court trial as friends of Vizcaya Province against the Calaveras family. Carlos and David, for your benefit, the Calaveras family is one of the most powerful families in Rocadura. They own thousands of acres of land. They have a reputation for paying low wages and playing hardball politics."

"They're the ones who burn their sugar cane stalks to fire that electric power plant out east of town, right?" asked David.

"Right," answered Conchita. "I've probably got some of their soot on my car right now, as we speak."

Fredrico continued. "This trial is critical to all future constellations—it will determine whether or not government can use the powers of eminent domain in Rocadura to provide more jobs and sustainable livelihoods as a public purpose. As you know, we're able to negotiate land purchases with almost everyone, because we pay cash at or above the appraised market value. The Calaveras family is comprised of nineteen households, and together, they own fourteen thousand acres. They wouldn't negotiate a sales price or a lease agreement on any of their land. As you know, all land owners can enter into a partnership agreement to lease their land to LSI if they don't want to sell it outright. We would like to buy ten thousand acres for our next set of new towns—the Vizcaya Constellation."

David leaned over toward Conchita and whispered, "I read somewhere that Vizcaya means 'an elevated place' in the Basque language."

"How beautiful," she whispered. "I didn't know that."

"What do they want to do with all of that land?" asked Tomas Xavier, an associate planner. He was a young man, in his mid-twenties. He had a lively and engaging manner, a sense of humor and quick smile. He was blond, with a small mustache. David had seen him working with Fredrico from time to time.

"They want to continue using thousands of acres to raise beef cattle and grow sugar cane. They're all millionaires from gouging the poor with poverty wages. After abusing them for decades, they kicked three thousand tenant farmers off their land, so they could start an agribusiness operation. They're growing expensive red peppers and beef for export and nothing for the local market."

"And of course, the farmers they kicked off the land can't find jobs or can't grow enough food to survive," Fredrico asserted.

"Right. It really provoked the provincial governor. He had those three thousand peasants and their families dumped on his doorstep for days. It was one of the biggest mistakes the Calaveras family ever made. So, when we showed up with a new town plan, Governor Francisco was enthusiastic to say the least. Well, you may know that it takes sixteen pounds of feed to produce one pound of beef and only three pounds of feed to produce one pound of chicken. The government knows that nine thousand acres of this land is being underutilized with cattle grazing or nothing and they've taken strong action to correct the situation. Vizcaya Province drafted an ordinance which would enable the province to use eminent domain to buy ten thousand acres of the land for public purposes. The ordinance declares that building new towns and creating thousands of jobs is a valid public purpose. Vizcaya Province intends to buy the land and then sell it to us at the same closing table."

Fredrico paused and looked around the room.

"Now it's very important that everybody understands that you can't 'take' land with eminent domain without a true public purpose, and, of course, just compensation must be given to the landowner."

"Who determines what is just compensation?" asked Carlos.

"Three independent state certified appraisers will determine their estimate of the market value of the property. A jury will make the decision on the final dollar amount. We estimate that the ten thousand acres is worth about a hundred and twenty million."

"Well," said Tomas, "that means the Calaveras family will find out who the appraisers are and bribe them to make the price so high as to be uneconomical for us to make the purchase."

"Good point, Tomas! We'll have to make a plan to deal with that. See me after the meeting, okay?"

"My pleasure, I assure you," said Tomas with an absolutely mischievous grin.

Fredrico passed around a handout. "Calaveras has sued to stop the eminent domain procedure. Vizcaya Province and LSI have counter sued to allow economic development and the creation of employment. This handout is a summary of the legal points that Calaveras is making against Vizcaya Province and LSI. They charge that their property rights are being grossly violated by the unjust and unnecessary taking of their land. They argue that the principle cause of the taking is to pass the land on to another developer, namely us. You'll also find our lawyer's case for the use of eminent domain. The key issue here is the expanded definition of public purpose to include the construction of new towns and a Constellation—including the construction of roads, water and sewer treatment, waste disposal systems, rapid transit, parks, affordable housing and workplaces in the new town. The land would be immediately sold to LSI to manage the development under a strict agreement with Vizcaya Province. However, judging from the arguments in the Calaveras brief, this will be no cake walk. If we lose, it means years of agonizingly slow development. If we win, it will be a landmark opinion that will rock all of Latin America!"

"Well, I hate to bring the downside into this," Carlos ventured, "but the inverse is true. The people with money, power and large land holdings all over Latin America are going to be brought into this on the Calaveras side—big time!"

"It's the sad truth, and we damned well intend to be ready for them."

Fredrico flashed a confident smile.

"Okay, with that thought in mind, let's go get our jobs done to win this case! If you've got any more of those great ideas, please come and see me anytime."

The trial date was set and the news media began to investigate the Constellation and El Cinco in earnest, and word of the Constellation's success quickly whirled around the world. Electrons were flashing from point to point on the globe, twenty-four hours a day. The Internet was alive. Newspaper articles were followed by magazine coverage, followed by more magazine spreads. LSI was deluged with requests for interviews. Fredrico searched his files to find full descriptions of the Constellation to give to the media, but most of his information was obsolete. He tossed aside several reports as incomplete. Until the answer came to him in a flash of certainty. He telephoned David immediately.

"David, we need to address the media surge. Right now, they're like a school of starved piranhas."

"This is our big chance to get the word out. We'll have to organize some responses and feed those fish."

"You read my mind. And I think I've found the best answer. It's your report to Erikson and the Europa Development Corporation."

"No, kidding? You think that's good enough?"

"It's by far the best and most current. Can we release it for public consumption?"

"I'll call Erikson right now and get back with you."

David was deeply gratified that Fredrico thought his report was the best analysis to send around the world. He called Erikson.

"Hello, Comandante! Things are really on fire down here at LSI. As you may imagine, we're under full scale media assault. They're all digging for more information."

"Ah, yes. Shark feeding time," smiled Erikson knowingly. "At first, it goes to your head. Then you realize they'll consume every minute of your day, if you let them. And they always have to find something to criticize."

"We need to throw out the real meat. Fredrico thinks it's to our advantage now. He asked if you could release my report to you—the final report."

"Well, let's see. It's an in-house document. It'll need some minor editing. I want you to take out the paragraphs on Europa's future actions. Eliminate any red flags you see that might make really nasty political waves." There was a brief pause. "Sure. Go ahead."

"Great!"

"So, who is calling you these days? All of South America?"

"Higher."

"The European Block?"

"Higher."

"The United Nations?"

"All of the above and higher: The U.N. is sending down a team for a few weeks. The Vatican is sending three cardinals next week."

"Three of 'em? They're following the star. Right?" laughed Erikson.

"Cute. And it's not even Christmastime."

"Sounds like you really have your hands full."

"Thank God we've got Padre Parejo."

"Perfect," smiled Erikson. "The man's a living saint!"

"That's not all," said David. "The Padre and I are going to Washington to meet with a group representing Big Oil, the State Department and a surprise visitor: an Islamic peacemaker."

"Whoa! That *is* high stuff! Let me know how everything goes. We're definitely on the leading edge here."

"I'll call next week. Bye for now."

"Bye. And send me a copy of the revised-for-sharks report. Okay?"

"Consider it done."

David called back Fredrico to give him the news. Then, he told the receptionist to hold his calls and went to work on revising his report. He finished it by late afternoon, faxed it to Erikson, who signed off on it, and then he took a copy to Fredrico.

Fredrico was on the phone when David entered his office. He waved and smiled enthusiastically when he saw the report in David's hand. David sat on the edge of his desk and listened to Fredrico's telephone conversation. LSI staffers rushed by the office in an effort to keep up with the pace. "Yes, ethanol is our biggest export product," Fredrico was saying. "I agree. There has to be a way to transition from oil to ethanol. We'll put our minds to work." Fredrico covered the receiver with his hand and said, "It's Sheik Omar Ammad. The Saudis want to go to solar and ethanol in the long run."

David nodded with no surprise.

"Fine. We'll have a complete report on the Constellation concept for Friday's meeting," Fredrico said. "David O'Laughlin and Padre Parejo will see you at five p.m. That's right. Okay, until then."

"It's crazy around here."

"And it's getting worse."

169

"Tomas!" yelled Fredrico, as Tomas scurried by his door and then made a U-turn. "Did you find out what Padre Parejo needs for our meeting with the Vatican?"

"Yes. He can't find his copy of the last Papal Encyclical on work and human development."

"I've got it in my files," offered David.

"Fantastic! I won't have to download it from the Web." It takes over an hour to get things like that off the system these days," sighed Tomas.

"Okay!" said Fredrico. "That's a wrap. I think we're ready for them. Let's shut down the phones and get out of here where we can think."

David picked up his phone and called Conchita. He knew it was a long shot. They had not been able to match schedules for five days. *That's way too long when you're in love,* thought David.

"Livelihood Systems, Offices of El Cinco, can I help you?"

"Hello, Elena, this is David. Is Conchita there?"

"I'm sorry, David, she's giving a presentation to about three hundred economic wizards."

"Oh, man! Where's the presentation?"

"It's at the Universidad del Futuro. It started at four, if you take off now, you can just catch the end and see her on the way out."

"Thank you, Elena. You saved my life. Remind me to kiss your ankles the next time I see you."

"You are too much, David. But few men make such gallant offers these days. Go, wild man. Good luck with Conchita."

"Smooch, smooch," sounded David, with exaggeration, before hanging up.

David caught the next metro bus to the university. He ran up the stairs, asked the information desk where to go, and entered the lecture hall. He found a full room with standing room only in the back. There she was—tall, stately, always a class act, dressed in a brilliant blue business suit with a white neck sash. She wore those slightly understated golden earrings he had given her for being a gypsy. Standing boldly before three hundred and fifty elite economists, financiers and potential investors, Conchita held her own like the pro she was. *She's a wonder woman,* thought David.

"I would like to close with a brief summary of the advantages to investors who join the Constellation enterprise," said Conchita. "Most of the financing comes from the worker-entrepreneurs over the long haul. Investors play a major role in providing the research and development resources to advance the productivity, expansion and banking certainty of the whole enterprise. Once the Constellation of seven new towns are built, we have a basic structure with bankable assets that are a perpetual profit machine. When fourteen more new towns are added to the original seven, we'll have a regional trading block of over a million and strong investor protection from any downside risk, as well as a trading block free of global competition. You have banking certainty with virtually no downside risk."

A man rose to ask a question. "I'm an investor who seeks a return of twenty percent or more. What can you offer me?"

"I can offer you between ten to fifteen percent return on your investment in the Constellations and banking certainty, based on our bankable assets in place and our economic arrangements. If you want twenty percent or more, you will have to gamble with what we call the 'boom and bust' economy, which can reduce your gains to zero percent in the twinkling of an eye on the global stock market."

"Then I'll go elsewhere," said the investor.

"Well, perhaps that's what you should do," replied Conchita. "We are here to offer a new alternative. With the Constellations you invest in families, in employment for your children and your grandchildren, your community, and your nation. You'll have a stable investment for yourselves and for millions of people as the Constellations grow. It is entirely possible that your return could grow to fifteen percent interest in some years, based on productivity gains within the Constellations, which are creative dynamos."

There was a strong round of applause that lasted a full twenty seconds.

Another man rose to his feet to ask a question.

"Miss Seguras, I am representing a Central African country that has fallen on very hard times. I am concerned about financing. At the very beginning of the Constellation enterprise, it seems there is a gap. Without the incredible wealth of El Cinco leading the project, where does the initial capital to start up the whole operation come from?"

Conchita responded with confidence: "There are several potential sources. As I indicated earlier, some of the start-up capital for the new Constellation generally comes from the banking system of existing Constellations. A Sister Constellation can also adopt the new Constellation and bring some of its own cash reserves to the project. But the primary source is capital raised from investors globally who seek to earn ten to fifteen percent interest while advancing the Constellation enterprise as sustainable development."

"Very good," said the man from Africa. "Let's say we are starting from a recently bankrupt nation with no capital reserves for infrastructure. How can the Constellation possibly be built under those circumstances?"

David winced and wondered how Conchita would field that question.

Conchita answered, "In general, local government provides sixty percent of the infrastructure costs and the Constellation provides about forty percent. The World Bank and foreign aid can be targeted to add part of the needed infrastructure. We all know that hundreds of billions of dollars can be shifted from the War Departments of the world to the Constellation solution. We have been facing these challenges for ten years. And again, I assure you, that you and our planning team can solve this problem by design. If we can design and build Constellations in Rocadura free of global competition, then we can design, finance and create liveable cities and stable economic systems in Africa. I invite you to join our planning group to solve your specific problems, anytime in the next thirty days, schedules permitting. It's really not as hard as many would like to make us believe. Will you join me?"

"Yes, yes, of course," said the man from Africa.

About fifty people rose to give Conchita a standing applause. Others quickly followed their lead, applauding with vigor. She had expressed the very heart and rising power of the Constellation enterprise, and the assembly loved her response.

David rushed to the back of the lecture hall and intercepted Conchita as she was leaving out the back door. "Conchita! Conchita!"

When she turned and saw him she smiled with delight. "David!" she said as she dropped her umbrella on the floor and rushed back to him. "Tell me tonight is ours!"

He picked her up in his arms and swung around with a strength that gave her a rush.

"Yes, sweetheart," shouted David. "This night is ours! I love you. I've missed you. You were brilliant out there!"

"I felt good. Those Devil's advocates need to feel the fire now and then."

"We'll you roasted their chestnuts that time. I love it!"

"Let's pick up some takeout and go to my place and get acquainted again."

"Damn I love your style. How long has it been?"

"Never mind. We're together now. Be here now, remember?"

"That's Mr. Now to you, young lady."

"You've arrived in that *now* place already?"

"Oh, yeah," smiled David, "as soon as I felt my hands around your waist."

They decided on Greek takeout and a bottle of Chianti.

Once inside her apartment, Conchita kissed David full on the lips and lingered in his arms awhile. Then slipped out of his tight embrace, and waved as she drifted off to her bedroom.

"I'm going to defrock and freshen up. See you in something very shortly."

"Something very shortly?" said David, fluttering his eyebrows like Groucho Marx.

"Will you warm things up 'til I get back?"

"Oh, yeah!"

David proceeded to heat up the dinners and dish out the Greek salad in bowls. He poured two glasses of wine and took a candelabra from her cupboard, set it in the center of the table and lit four candles. He dimmed the lights and selected a romantic piano album on the player. *Conchita is sure taking her time*, thought David. He sipped some wine and waited for Miss Inescapable.

She returned in a rose colored satin robe and did a little spin around like a model on the runway.

"It's lovely," said David, "but it's not very shortly."

"Very shortly," she smiled teasingly, "is under Ms. Longly. But you won't see that unless you're a good boy, clean your plate and promise to love me forever."

"Ah! I see how it is. Let's eat, I'm famished forever."

* * *

The next day, David and Padre Parejo left for their business meeting with envoys from the Middle East and the State Department. David had looked forward to the flight to Washington with Padre Parejo. Just to be in his presence gave a person a very comfortable feeling.

"You seem happy planning Constellations," said Padre Parejo. "We're all very glad to have you aboard. You and Europa have given us a real boost at the right time."

"I feel like my whole life's work pointed to this. Except for Saldana's attack, everything falls into place like it was meant to be. I keep looking over my shoulder for the bad guys or the next political blockade, but things keep rolling along."

"Life doesn't have to be just one darn thing after another if you follow the right path. Many people look at what they don't have and waste their lives struggling for more and more. They forget that all good things come from God. Christ said, 'Seek first the Kingdom of God and all of these things will be added unto you.' You and I have suffered like everyone else, but we know that God can give anything to anyone at His pleasure and sometimes it's incredibly good. When he healed people, Christ said, 'You have been saved by your faith.' The Constellation happened when a small group of people took down their umbrellas and just let God's grace rain upon them. We're in tune with reality, so things flow easier. If it looks like a miracle, walks on water and *smiles directly at you*, relax and enjoy it!"

David tossed back his head and laughed out loud. He just looked at the good padre and smiled, nodding his head in instant understanding and affirmation.

They flew along in silence for a while. David thought about Conchita and how she looked like a miracle and smiled directly at his soul. *When things get this good, it is scary*, he thought. *Oh, well, the padre is right. Just relax and enjoy the gift.*

"David, you know how many people are waiting in the world for economic security. Fredrico told me you saw Camino Adelante, with a hundred and twenty thousand souls desperately pleading for a life in the Constellations."

"Yes, he put my soul in guilty pain and I'm not even Jewish!"

The padre broke into laughter. "You know, we're very close, Jewish people and Catholics. When it comes down to the bottom line we can count on each other to deliver together."

"I know what you're saying. I've had a few Jewish associates who were right with me in the endeavor. They're good-hearted and they know what the economic system needs to deliver better than most. They're the best!"

"Well, you're about to find out that the Muslims are also drawn to Constellation Style. We are making a lot of very good friends, David."

"Father, you are incredible."

"No, David, I have little to do with what's happening. It's divine providence expressing itself through us, as it should be, that's all."

"It blows my mind."

"I know. I've had the same feelings. We're experiencing the only source of creative virtue, which is the ever-deepening realization of our union with God, the indwelling and fellowship of the Holy Spirit. The Spirit gives us the power to rid ourselves of the vicious circle of bad consciousness, the endless voices that invite us to gain our lives through pride and vain pursuits. We can move forward and reach what you Irishmen love to call 'the high ground.'"

"It's the realization of our union with God that gives us creativity—makes us co-authors."

"Yes, creativity and much more. It gives us the will to act and the courage for the long haul."

"I'm thinking of Mozart. I wonder if he had a realization of his union with God at such a young age."

"I think God and Mozart played together like children. Mozart had to know God laid the gift of music on his very soul. The question is, did Mozart realize the dimensions of that union beyond his musical gifts? That's his secret."

"He died young, but he had a wonderful, fun-loving wife who stood beside him all the way. You know, Padre, I've always wondered how priests can have so much love for people and deny themselves the love of a wonderful, spiritual woman."

"Well, I can only speak from my own experience. I once loved a woman in a beautiful relationship before I became a priest."

There was a long pause.

"We were attracted to each other so strongly because we found we were spiritual beings, on kindred soul paths—very much like you and Conchita are today. You and Conchita have something we didn't have—you have similar vocations. Not only are you kindred souls but you have the same God-given mission in life. This was not the case with my love. She was an artist. She needed to love in her own way, following the muse wherever it took her. I found that I needed to love in my way as a priest. We adored each other, but our vocations separated us. She went to paint in Vermont and I went into the seminary."

"Do you still have a friendship with this lady?"

"Oh, yes. We write letters at Christmas time to keep abreast of what's happening with each other."

"But what about intimate, personal love?" asked David.

"Well, at first, it was a great sacrifice in my mind. The loss of close spiritual and physical love seemed overwhelming to me. But I prayed, and God gave me the grace to find a new solidity in my heart—centered on being a priest. I was given an abundance of grace and a wonderful, deep, inner peace. It can only be understood by personal experience. And over the years, I've heard a lot of confessions by married men and women. It seems that everyone has what I like to call 'the usual troubles,' no matter how much they love each other. Married people find many trials and in some cases, torment of the soul. Many of them can't rest in the deep inner peace that I've found."

"I think I understand what you mean," David said. "It's something that couples have to work through."

"I gradually realized that, as a priest, I could love *all* women with a pure, spiritual love that would be most dear to their hearts and souls. Knowing that is soul-satisfying and that adds to my inner peace."

Suddenly, Padre Parejo fell into silence. He closed his eyes and began meditating. David thought he might be tired and needed a nap but he sensed the good Padre was experiencing that deep inner peace that he had just described.

David had also experienced that deep inner peace. When he lost it, it was usually because some people or events around him were playing some nasty games and threatening him with direct harm. His standard answer to inner turmoil was to go to Mass, receive Holy Communion and deepen his capacity to love those people who were giving him trouble. Then, he went about getting the creative job done and watched his troubled relationships fade into nothingness. This had worked incredibly well for him repeatedly and he thought, as Woody Hayes, the famous Ohio State football coach, used to say: "Never change a winning game."

Being in the physical presence of Padre Parejo had moved him deeply, beyond words, beyond thought, he was now floating in grace. He was floating in his love with God and with Conchita. He floated on and on and did not want it to end. But it gradually started to fade.

Then, once again, he found himself back in the world of the ordinary sense of things. He heard the engine of the plane droning on and the voices of a few chatting passengers. A man coughed. A baby cried out because of the pain in its ears from the change in air pressure. He could see the mother rocking the baby, trying to console her. But it wasn't the same. It could never be the same old worldly world for David.

The stewardess moved her refreshment cart beside him.

"Would you like something to drink?" she asked.

"No, I'm fine, just fine, thank you."

He glanced at Padre Parejo, who had now drifted into sleep.

He decided not to wake him.

David and Padre Parejo arrived in Washington at 1:00 p.m. They refreshed themselves for the meeting with a stop at David's favorite restaurant in Alexandria, and had the "Catch of the Day." Then they drove to the designated address, a town house, just eight blocks away. David parked the rented car and looked around the complex. It was quiet. He was met at the door by a husky man dressed in a dark brown suit.

Security, thought David, *and obviously Muslim.*

"Welcome. Everyone has arrived for the meeting. Could I see your I.D. please?" He spoke with an Indian accent, in what David fondly called "high camel driver" intonation.

David showed him his Europa Development Corporation photo I.D. "I'm not carrying, if that's your next question."

"Ah, thank you, it's always a pleasure to meet someone who understands the trade," he said as he ran a scanner over David and Padre Parejo from neck to heel.

With the preliminaries taken care of, they were ushered to the library on the second floor. The floors were covered with Persian rugs, the walls were laden with Arabic art and the ceilings were painted with Muslim religious symbols. David especially enjoyed the detailed Arabic arches forming the doorways into each room. As they entered the library, they were immediately greeted by Humberto.

There were three men seated at an oval conference table.

"This is Padre Parejo and David O'Laughlin, my friends," said Humberto. "This is Robert Warner, chief executive of Petroleum United Resources. To his right is Sheik Omar Ammad. You already know Stephan Alcott."

David shook hands with Alcott first, an economic analyst with the State Department. "Hello, Stephan. It's been a long time."

"Good to see you again. You're certainly in the heart of the action right now. The Constellation is on every magazine cover."

"It's an enjoyable event to be at this table with so many of my friends from around the world," said Humberto, from behind his familiar, well-manicured handle bar mustache. "As you know, we are gathered here to discuss the recent developments in the Middle East regarding oil, the rise in prominence of the Constellation enterprise and the latest Carbon Tax proposal by the World Trade Organization. The key question here is what can we do about the global oil situation and the growing potential for instability as the standard of living declines in the Middle East. I am especially delighted that Sheik Omar Ammad has joined us as our quest to understand the import of these fast-breaking events. Without the spiritual and cultural perspective of the Islamic world, I fear we could not fully grasp the situation."

The sheik nodded with a pleasant smile at Humberto's diplomatic gesture.

Then, Humberto turned to David. "David, please bring us up to date on the Constellation's impact around the world."

"As you are aware, from yesterday's *Business Street Journal,* the Constellation Style of new town building has become quite popular in Latin America. If we win the eminent domain case in Vizcaya Province it will set the stage for a major overhaul of Latin American economics, but that's a big 'if.' LSI and Europa Development Corporation have been besieged by Latin American governments which want us to plan and build new towns onto their existing villages. We can't meet the demand at this point. We have to use some of our key staff to educate and train thousands of engineers, planners, architects and financial analysts. We have received inquiries from France, Italy, Spain, Saudi Arabia, Iran, Africa, India and China. We have a meeting with representatives from the Vatican next week in Rocadura. Building Constellations requires trained professionals, contracts with landowners and businesses, and, of course, billions in financing."

"Stephan, would you tell us all about the proposed new Carbon Tax on fossil fuels?" asked Humberto.

"Certainly. The United Nations has prevailed in influencing the World Trade Organization to reduce global warming. As you know, over the last decade, the price of gasoline has risen in the U.S. Americans pay three dollars and seventy-five cents per gallon. Europe is paying five dollars or more, per gallon. The proposal is to gradually bring U.S. prices up to the European and global price level of five dollars per gallon, since the U.S. consumes so much. The Constellations have shown us how to shift from oil to ethanol and solar energy."

"I didn't believe it when I first heard it and I don't believe it now," said Robert Warner. "The American people won't tolerate such an outrageous increase again."

"I'm afraid it's a done deal," said Stephan Alcott. "Global warming has caused so much bad weather, droughts, hurricanes and lost crops that according to the latest World Watch report, annual grain harvest has plummeted. There is no surplus grain in the world. Millions of people are threatened with hunger and starvation. Billions of dollars have been lost, and most people can't afford insurance on the coasts, as the oceans rise. We need bread and cereal more than gasoline."

"I want to see that Global Warming Report. There are always a bunch of soft spots in the data."

"Not this time," said Alcott. "They predicted the cost of the last four droughts and the seven devastating hurricane floods. They even successfully predicted U.S. hurricane destruction at forty billion dollars last year. That was just three hundred million off target. Global warming has screwed up the Earth's weather patterns big time and everyone is being hit with the economic impacts."

"The American people will rebel," said Warner. "They won't pay five dollars a gallon for gasoline. The WTO is nuts. The U.S. won't let it happen."

"The United Nations has tremendous influence on the WTO. Ever since the U.N. moved to Geneva, the U.S. has lost influence on certain issues. There are a hundred and twenty nations versus the U.S. on this vote."

"It's not as bad as it sounds, Mr. Warner," said David. "The Constellation produces ethanol at $1.30 cents out of the refinery gate. Since there is no carbon tax on one hundred percent ethanol, Americans can buy it at $1.75 per gallon when state and federal taxes are added. The only problem is availability. We must build ethanol production and distribution facilities."

"If that's the way it's going to be, I'll be damned if I'll be a caretaker for a dying dinosaur. I'm a fighter. I want to be on the cutting edge...all of the time. Let's talk ethanol. Omar, old friend, how can we do a workout and get into ethanol?"

"Well, Padre Parejo and I have been discussing this with David's associates. There may be a way to make the transition from oil to ethanol. I need to set the stage with a little background in Islamic beliefs and culture. For decades, we have been searching for a new economic way of life. Our people have a strong sense of social justice. We know the rich value of a good family life. We long for a sense of community, for Islamic unity, what we call Ummah, that comes from having spiritual values built into our economic structure. That is why we have been seeking a third way: a way beyond capitalism and socialism. Making money merely for money's sake is not the Islamic way. Therefore, we find the Constellation most appealing to our core beliefs."

"That's fine, old friend, but how does the Constellation fit into a transition out of oil?"

"Padre Parejo," said Sheik Omar Ammad, "you can explain it much better than I. Would you honor us with your wisdom?"

"The wisdom you have just spoken will outshine what I have to say," Padre Parejo replied. Then, he leaned back in his chair and smiled softly. As he did this, Warner, Alcott and Humberto leaned forward in their chairs to hear what he was about to say.

"In much of the world of Islam, there is plenty of oil, but a scarcity of fertile land on which to grow plants for the production of ethanol. However, there are abundant plants in central Africa, where we have been invited to build Constellations. The Arab states have the capital from oil to build Constellations. We can build Constellations in Arabia and several in Africa as one democratic entity. They can share from each other's resources as cooperators in one enterprise."

"So, the Constellations can overcome resource problems like that without difficulty?" asked Warner.

"That's right," said Sheik Ammad. "It's all done by contract between equal worker-owners. We don't have to pay for imported ethanol when we can trade goods and services within the Constellation's economic system."

"I can see how Constellations in Arabia can switch from oil to ethanol, but I don't see how my corporation will do a workout," said Warner. "As the price of gasoline goes up, demand will fall. People just won't be able to afford to buy as much."

"The large capital reserves of your oil corporation can be shifted to the production of ethanol. As more ethanol is produced, it is blended with gasoline, first by fifty percent, then by eighty-five percent, and so on, until ethanol replaces gasoline entirely."

"Ah! Now, you're talking!" said Warner.

"Gentlemen," said Humberto enthusiastically, "this is truly a wonderful workout. Since the Carbon Tax is not placed on ethanol, the tax will be reduced by eighty-five percent when ethanol and gasoline are mixed at E85. Even with the Carbon Tax, the cost of E85 fuel at the pump will be $3.70 per gallon. What is needed is a rapid acceleration in the production of ethanol."

"To do that," said David, "your board of directors can agree to a buyout by the employees in your firm and you can establish a new Arabian Constellation. In other words, your corporation would become a cooperative within the Arabian Constellation. The stockholders would be bought out over time. You would stay on as general manager."

"It makes sense, by damn, that makes sense," said Warner. "Especially, since there are no other visible options. I'll look forward to working up the details with you and Omar."

"Allah be praised, my friend," sighed Omar. "To avoid a full catastrophe, it is simply necessary to have cooperation in the region."

Padre Parejo and Sheik Omar Ammad rose and clasped hands. They reached to their nearest partner and clasped their hands as well. The circle was closed in a spirit of union and solidarity in the decision.

"Gentlemen," announced Sheik Ammad, "refreshments and dinner will be served in the dining room."

David walked with Padre Parejo to the dining room and said softly, "If it walks on water and smiles directly at you…"

"Just relax and enjoy it," smiled Padre Parejo.

As the evening progressed David had one gnawing thought: *the only enemy is time.* He had to learn how to deal with that. Maybe if I had a son or daughter to carry on the work. His mind drifted off into thoughts of Conchita and her delightful manner of being.

* * *

One week later, El Cinco, Padre Parejo, Fredrico and Conchita were seated at the conference table in the LSI War Room, waiting for three Cardinals to appear on behalf of the Vatican. And to everyone's surprise, Sheik Omar Ammad had spoken with the Pope. Padre Parejo had invited the Sheik as well to the gathering.

Everyone was assembled when David arrived. As he glanced around, his eyes fell on Conchita. They glanced knowingly at each other. The room was full of Cardinal Red robes and black suits, contrasted only by the dazzling white robe of Sheik Ammad. Padre Parejo made the introductions.

"This is David O'Laughlin, who comes to us from the Europa Development Corporation. David is a senior planner and we find that he brings new ideas to enhance the Constellation concept."

"Senior planner. That means I'm older."

That brought a few chuckles.

"This is Cardinal Franco Rosellini, the Pope's diplomatic envoy, and this is Cardinal Guillermo Ruiz of Sao Paulo. He told me he had the pleasure of working with Archbishop Paulo Evaristo Arns, who was one of the most effective leaders for human development in all of South America."

"Oh, yes," smiled David broadly, "I'll never forget a *Firing Line* show where Archbishop Arns completely charmed William F. Buckley into becoming an ordinary human being. Every time Buckley would make a point about the superiority of the market economy, Archbishop Arns would meekly bring him back to the goals of human development and economic justice."

"Yes, I remember that. Archbishop Arns totally disarmed Buckley."

"This is Cardinal Francisco Palacios representing Argentina. He has just been assigned to Cordoba Nueva, where we are planning a new Constellation."

"It's a great pleasure to meet all of you," said David.

"And, of course, you know our new friend, representing the Islamic world, Sheik Omar Ammad."

"You seem to be in two places at one time," remarked David to Sheik Ammad. "Has Islam achieved a new mode of spiritual travel?"

"Ah!" laughed the Sheik. "That would have been a very welcome ability over the last five days. But, I assure you, Allah has only given me the wings of urgency."

The ice was broken. Hearty laughter filled the room.

"The Holy Father sends his blessings to all," said Cardinal Rossellini. "He told me to tell you he is deeply impressed with Constellation Style economics. His prayer for years has been to find a way to create enduring good work for the world's millions who suffer from hunger and economic oppression. Your report, Mr. O'Laughlin, was very well received by His Holiness."

"Thank you. I'm deeply honored. But as you know, I merely reported on the work of El Cinco, Padre Parejo, Fredrico, Conchita here, and the rest of the LSI team."

"Yes, I understand. We've been following the emergence of the Constellation since its first baby steps. The Holy See has received ten reports from Padre Parejo over the last five years. Your report added several new insights."

"As you may recall, Pope John Paul II made a ten day tour of Brazil in nineteen ninety-one," said Cardinal Rosellini. "At the time, he challenged government authorities regarding the fact that two percent of Brazilians owned fifty-seven percent of the land and he also pointed out that much of it was underutilized. I am here today, with Cardinal Ruiz and Cardinal Palacios to formalize our support of your endeavors. The Holy Father would like for us to provide you with a team of working priests from Spain, who could serve the dual role of assisting you with administrative duties. As Constellations grow in number, they can also act as liaisons with the Vatican."

"On behalf of LSI and El Cinco, I have been authorized to accept your generous offer," said Padre Parejo. "I might add, this is a decisive historic event in the unfolding of the Constellation, which now is blessed by the Holy See."

"As you know, Pope John Paul II strongly encouraged investment in a new vision that embraces human dignity and the value of the human person."

David took a deep breath. His mind raced to understand the potential meaning of this interchange which was obviously pre-arranged by "Saint" Padre Parejo.

Sheik Omar Ammad spoke. "As you know, I can not represent the whole of Islam. We are many nations and tribes within nations. But we have one God and we all hear and see when a new phenomena offers hope and a future to a very troubled world."

The sheik paused, and his eyes smiled as he looked at the positive reaction around the table.

"I represent only those in Islam who have been searching for a Third Way beyond the market economy," he continued. "A Third Way that combines social justice, a sense of community, and a more secure economic future for families. Clearly, in my mind, the Constellation provides a path to achieve all of these things. We're living in a world full of sand, with our oil income declining. We need to establish an entirely new livelihood system for the region."

"I never met an Islamic peacemaker I could refuse," Padre Parejo said with a wry smile. "Of course, you're the first, so I can only count to one."

A chuckle rolled around the room.

"Ah, yes," Sheik Amad replied, "but if you add the millions of Muslims to the millions of Christians in the world and find that they have chosen the same dynamic path, well then, the world would have a real spiritual force to reckon with."

"How true," Padre Parejo said. "Of the seven billion people in the world, twenty-three percent are Muslims and thirty-two percent are Christians. That's a fifty-five percent majority! God is clearly playful, and He likes to see his children play together on the world stage."

Cardinal Rosselli reached over the table to shake hands with Sheik Amad. "The Pope will be powerfully energized when I tell him of your vision. When Muslims and Christians build Constellations together it will be an awesome sight to the world. World leaders will have to consider our mutual understanding and reexamine their own thinking."

When the meeting was adjourned, David knew he was part of something much larger than he had ever expected.

Walking through the streets of El Cedro David felt as if he were a ghost. The path to his hotel was well-trod, requiring no conscious exertion. He saw nothing around him. His mind was so powerfully focused on the meeting and what it meant. Christianity and Islam finding a common path! He reached his hotel room, unlocked the door and sat down in a comfortable chair.

Paradoxically, he felt a sense of elevation and apprehension. He could not quite believe the effects of the Constellation were going to be global. For some reason he was a part of that action. All that he could see was that he had written a report about what others had done. Well, he had participated in a meeting about what he and others were going to do. Big deal! For such a small thing he is given such a big reward. He was always left to wonder why God poured out His love on him. *Capax Dei*, thought David. *We're capable of being filled by God. An Irishman is not drunk as long as he can hang on to a blade of grass, they say. Well, you open up to Him, and you better hang on to the grass!* thought David.

Chapter 16
THE CONSTELLATION VERSUS
THE CALAVERAS EMPIRE

It was late Saturday morning in El Cedro. Conchita was in her bathrobe, reading the morning paper when the phone rang. It was Fredrico.

"Sorry to bother you on your day off, but the Calaveras court date has been set. I need to brief you a bit before the press starts crawling all over the office."

"You mean slithering, don't you?" Conchita asked, sitting in her big easy chair while tucking one leg under her. "Actually, I don't mean that, some of my very best friends are in the media."

"Well, since you're our one and only snake charmer, we need to chat about it as soon as possible. Can you come in after lunch?"

"After lunch will be just fine."

"Okay, I'll see you at my office at one thirty."

"Will do."

Conchita arrived at Fredrico's office after lunch with David. Fredrico extended his hand in greeting.

"Well, Conchita, we're about to embark on this big adventure."

"Yes, I know how much it means to us, but I'm not uneasy about it because the truth will come out. Once we lay out the facts, a lot of people will have their eyes opened...for the first time."

"I feel the same way. All we have to do is put our truth up against the selfishness of the Calaveras family and pray to God our message gets through. So, I'd like to go over some points we should make to the press from the beginning. Oh, by the way, no change of venue request was filed. What can that mean?"

"Ummm, it probably means they have some trick up their sleeve that needs them to stay local. Sounds scary to me."

Conchita and Fredrico spent the next two hours developing their case to take to the media and the courtroom. They went over the legal briefs and developed their own points, based on their knowledge of the Calaveras family and the way they were doing business. When they were finished, they were both drained of energy.

"Well, Fredrico, I think we've covered the territory pretty well, and I'm exhausted. I feel really good about our case. We have every chance of winning."

"I know we can win," smiled Fredrico. "There's someone bigger than Calaveras!"

* * *

JUDGE MARCOS INSTRUCTS THE JURY

"In the judgment of this court, there are two principal issues in this case," Judge Marcos began. "The first issue is centered on what constitutes a valid public purpose for the taking of land by eminent domain. Secondly, the jury is advised that if valid public purposes are established for the taking of land by Vizcaya Province, over the traditional property rights of the Calaveras family, the jury will decide on the amount of just compensation to be paid to the Calaveras family by the Province."

Judge Marcos looked directly at the jury.

"Are these points clear to the jury? If so, please signify by raising your hand."

All of the jurors raised their hands.

Looking at the Calaveras table, Judge Marcos said, "Then both the counsel for the plaintiff and the counsel for the defense may proceed with their opening statements. The counsel for the plaintiff may begin."

THE OPENING STATEMENT FOR CALAVERAS

Counselor Jorge Martinez rose to approach the jury box, and looking directly at Judge Marcos, and said, "Thank you, Your Honor, for this privilege."

He buttoned his dark blue pinstriped suit coat as he walked, attracting attention to the fact that he was immaculately dressed.

He was a tall and lean man, measuring six feet four inches, a virtual giant among men. His hair was black, with striking white temples and he had a neatly trimmed black mustache. It was perfectly manifest that he had long been one of the elite of the elite. Jorge Martinez, in a phrase, was a strikingly handsome Latin man. As he moved, one could almost hear the sighs of the women in the courtroom. They would be watching him for days. He clearly represented all of the pride, honor and wealth of Latin tradition. He was famous for his victories in court and especially for his manner of expression. He was well known for his ability to speak to the heart of the Rocaduran, be they man, woman or child.

"Judge Marcos has advised the jury well," began Martinez, "the central issues involve the just or unjust taking of land." He paused for emphasis.

"This proposed taking of land by the provincial government is unparalleled in the history of our country. It is unheard of in several ways. The worst way…and the most unjust so-called 'public purpose' I will save for last. First, these land holdings represent the source of livelihood for the Calveras family. To take their land would be the same as taking their livelihood, the livelihood of their children, grandchildren and all future generations to come. Therefore, we will contend that this is an unjust attempt to take a family's land for selfish government gain."

Martinez surveyed the jury and decided his first point had indeed struck home.

"Secondly, the Calaveras family has created many jobs over the last twenty years. Over fifteen thousand people have worked on Calaveras land in the last two decades. Is it just to penalize the Calaveras family for creating jobs for you and your children? Thirdly, the Calaveras family pays enormous taxes to the government. This has amounted to millions of dollars that have gone to benefit not just those in this province, but the entire country. Is it just to penalize businesses who create employment and pay the lion's share of taxes? I think not."

Martinez was now in his element. He strode up and down before the jury box like a man who was in total command of the situation. He sensed his positive resonance with the jury.

"And while we are speaking of businesses. The Calaveras family went to great trouble to build an electric power plant using its sugar cane stalks as fuel. This power plant provides the electricity for forty-one businesses in Vizcaya. Many of your families or friends work in these businesses that are blessed with a reliable and inexpensive supply of electric power, so that two thousand five hundred people can have jobs. Is this not a wonderful public purpose? I think it is. It is a generous action that deserves credit for providing a great public service."

There was a noticeable stirring of the courtroom. Glances of recognition were exchanged by the jurors.

"And now, we must ask ourselves the question of the day. For what greater public purpose does Vizcaya Province want to use this land? The answer is simply this: they want to take this Rocaduran land—this livelihood, this property that gives thousands of jobs to you and your friends—and give it to a foreign business known as LSI. That's right. They want to take this family owned land and hand it over to a group of billionaires. Now, my friends, we must look carefully at this so-called grand public purpose. They are wolves in sheep's clothing. This is a pass-through maneuver to give the land cheaply to a developer. The developers will make a huge profit, perhaps an obscene profit, because they got the land so cheaply. There are very few places where you can find ten thousand acres of land owned by one family in Rocadura. This is a very precious thing. It can scarcely be measured in dollars and cents. This land, this ten thousand acres, all in one piece, is nearly priceless! And yet, the Vizcaya Province wants to take this land and sell it to billionaires for a song and dance. It can be compared to the tax man robbing the poor people to pay the richest men in the world! And what will they do with the land? They will crowd it with concrete and steel, destroying the natural environment. There will not be even twenty acres of natural pasture land by the time they are finished. I urge you to reject this travesty of justice. This proposal is clearly unjust, both in terms of the taking, and in terms of the attempt by billionaires to steal the land."

After that powerful fusillade, Jorge Martinez strode to his seat, with great dignity and with the eyes of a man who believed he deserved to win.

Judge Marcos nodded toward Alan Sierra. "The counsel for the defense may now proceed with an opening statement."

Alan Sierra was also a tall man. His leanness suggested a self-disciplined, spiritual mode of life. He possessed a graceful manner and his face was intensely serious. As the jury would soon observe, there was never a question about Alan Sierra's integrity, he emanated honesty. He walked in front of the jury box with guarded confidence.

"You will spend many hours hearing testimony, so I'll make my opening comments brief. I will prove to the jury that the people of Vizcaya Province will have far more sustainable employment and permanent livelihoods with basic economic security with the Constellation as opposed to employment by the Calaveras family. The Constellations are owned by the workers themselves, and worker-owners in a cooperative do not fire each other and throw each other out into the street, as the Calaveras businesses have done."

Sierra scanned the jury and allowed time for that major point to be assimilated in the minds of his audience.

"I will prove that the Constellation is a higher and better use of the land than cattle raising and agribusiness style farming for foreign export. I will bring witnesses forth to demonstrate that the Constellations offer a strong public purpose in the form of sustainable livelihoods, and by that I mean sustainable, secure and happy employment. And what higher use of the land is there than providing thousands of permanent and promising jobs with ample material rewards and security for families? The Viscaya Constellation will provide sixty thousand households with jobs compared to the four thousand or so that the Calaveras family will offer. The Constellation is a cooperative with worker-owners who will establish economic stability, wonderful housing, safe drinking water, sewer systems and a rapid transit system that will take you anywhere you want to go, so you will only need to buy one car in your family, if that. Constellations have their own banks, their own supermarkets and their own schools. You can buy more with your money. Children grow up in a new world where they know that they are worth something—that they are valued members of a large, happy family. And once you are a member of such a large, self-sufficient culture, no greedy employer can ever kick you off the land because, together, you *own* the land."

Alan Sierra looked at the jury and decided he had made his points. Then, turning to Judge Marcos, he said, "Your Honor, that is all I want to say at this time."

"Very well," said Judge Marcos. "Mr. Martinez, you may proceed."

"Your Honor," said Martinez, "I would like to call Ernesto Pax Santana to the witness stand."

There was an immediate buzz of excitement in the courtroom as Santana was sworn in.

Conchita leaned over toward David. "Santana is the president of Motores de Cordoba," she explained, "the biggest carmaker in Latin America. I don't like the looks of this. Carlos was right. They're calling in the big guns."

"Señor Santana," began Martinez, "ordinarily, I would ask you to tell the court who you are, but I think everyone knows you are the president of Motores de Cordoba. Would you tell the court about your plans for the use of the Calaveras property?"

"Of course," said Santana with a large smile, "it will be my pleasure. Tomorrow, I will hold a press conference to announce my intention to build a new auto-assembly plant on the Calaveras' property. We intend to lease seven thousand acres for fifty years. This plant will employ twenty-five hundred workers and will create employment for suppliers and others in Vizcaya Province for an additional five thousand workers as suppliers."

The courtroom exploded with excited conversation.

Judge Marcos waited for a minute then brought the gavel down. "Order…order in the court!" he said repeatedly.

Finally, the people in the gallery settled down to hear what Santana would say next.

"Of course, this agreement between Motores de Cordoba and the Calaveras family depends on the successful outcome of this suit," Jorge Martinez said. "However, I am sure the jury will see that the new auto plant will bring a whole new era of economic stability and permanent jobs to Vizcaya Province. I am convinced there can be no higher and better use for the land than to build such a magnificent facility."

"Objection," Sierra interrupted. "The counsel is leading the witness and counsel is drawing unsubstantiated conclusions in terms of the actual numbers of people to be employed."

"Objection sustained. Strike that last remark from the record."

"I'm sorry, Your Honor," Martinez answered, "I was carried away by my excitement. Señor Santana, you have said the new plant will create about seven thousand five hundred jobs, counting suppliers and others. What others would be employed?"

"For every manufacturing worker, at least one more job will be created in the area for those who provide goods and services," Santana answered. "When an autoworker spends his paycheck, he buys many things. People have to open new stores and shops to supply his needs. It's what economists call the multiplier effect."

"So, when you employ twenty-five hundred workers at the auto plant, another twenty-five hundred jobs are created in Vizcaya Province, correct?"

"That's right. Also, the plant will have contracts with local suppliers of materials, and for outsourcing work. This will employ an additional two thousand, or more people, locally."

"And the grand total is about seven thousand five hundred jobs?"

"That's our best estimate at this time."

"And of course, there would be room for future growth and plant expansion?"

"Of course. We intend to build cars here to supply Rocadura and her five closest trading partners."

"Thank you, Señor Santana, for this wonderful news. I have no further questions, Your Honor."

"Would you like to cross examine the witness, Mr. Sierra?"

"Not at this time, Your Honor, but I would like to reserve the right to call the witness to the stand at a later time."

"Granted. You may step down, Mr. Santana, and you may proceed, Señor Martinez."

"I have no further witnesses at this time, Your Honor," Martinez advised. He then sat down with a winning smile on his face as he talked confidently with the Calaveras family.

Judge Marcos said, "Very well. Mr. Sierra, you may call a witness at this time."

Sierra stepped forward. "Your Honor," he began, "I would like to call Juan Gonzalez to the witness stand."

Juan Gonzalez was sworn in to testify.

"Mr. Gonzalez, is it true that you worked for Señor Calaveras as a tenant farm worker?"

"Si, señor."

"And how many years did you work for Señor Calaveras?"

"About ten years."

"Señor Gonzalez, how much were you paid for a day's work?"

"I started working at three dollars a day. When I was laid off, I was paid three dollars and eighty cents a day."

"That's less than fifty cents an hour," Sierra said. "The minimum wage is four dollars per day. Are you telling me that Calaveras would not even pay you the minimum wage?"

"Si, señor. Last year we had a strike. They laid off sixty workers who demanded the minimum wage. Calaveras brought in the police and his security guards. They attacked us with clubs and guns and killed three men. They hit me in the head with the butt of a rifle and they wounded eleven of my friends. The government did nothing."

"So, you worked under oppressive conditions...under threat of armed force. You and three thousand tenant farm workers were virtual slaves for the Calaveras family."

Jorge Martinez rose to his feet. "I object! Your Honor, the counsel is leading the witness. He is putting words in his mouth that are not true."

"Sustained. You know the rules of the court, Mr. Sierra."

"Yes, Your Honor. What did you think about your situation after the attack, Mr. Gonzalez?"

"We felt helpless. There was no place to turn for help."

"And then, Calaveras evicted you and a total of three thousand tenant farmers from the land so he could start an agribusiness, growing sweet red peppers for export. Is that correct?"

"Señor, I don't know what he is growing. I just know that now, I can not find steady work. Sometimes I get to work in construction for a month or two. Before, when I was a tenant farmer, we had a little garden to give us vegetables. Now, we go to the soup kitchen."

"Where do you live now, Señor Gonzalez?"

"Camino Adelante. We are waiting for jobs to open up in Las Faldas."

"Las Faldas is a new town in the Cornerstone Constellation built by LSI Corporation. Are you aware of that, Mr. Gonzalez?"

"Si, señor. They're the village builders. They're our only hope for a good life now."

"I have visited Camino Adelante, Señor Gonzalez. You have no water system and no sewer system. I saw feces and garbage in the streets. Children die of diseases daily because they play in these conditions. But I understand that El Cinco are now building new water and sewer systems and have given you free meat, vegetables and soup kitchens. Is that correct?"

"Si, señor. They give ten percent of their pay to help us survive while we wait for good jobs."

"Thank you, Señor Gonzalez. I have no further questions."

"Does the counsel for the plaintiff wish to cross-examine the witness?" Judge Marcos enquired.

"No, Your Honor," Martinez responded.

"Your Honor, I would like to call Governor Jaime Francisco the stand," Sierra said.

Governor Francisco was sworn in to testify.

"Governor Francisco," Sierra began, "you have just heard the testimony of Juan Gonzalez, formerly a tenant farm worker for the Calaveras family. Why didn't the government take action to stop the oppression of the workers on strike, and prevent them from being slaughtered by Calaveras?"

"I object!" Martinez said loudly. "Counsel is using emotional language and leading the witness to false conclusions."

"Sustained. Please rephrase the question."

"When the police and security guards killed three men and wounded twelve during the strike against the oppression of the Calaveras enterprise, why did the provincial government not take action to investigate the situation on the Calaveras ranch?"

"You will have to ask former Governor Heron that question, Mr. Sierra. I was elected after the strike. Had I been in office, I assure you I would have taken action. In my first six months in office, I have been enforcing the legal rights of all workers in Vizcaya Province to receive the minimum wage of four dollars per day. I am preparing a bill for Congress that will raise the minimum wage to ten dollars per day. They will probably not pass the bill. But if the Vizcaya Constellation is built, it will pay for the lowest wage at least eight dollars an hour or sixty-four dollars per day to start. You can raise a family on those wages in Rocadura."

"You campaigned on a platform of economic reform, correct?"

"Yes, I'm in the process of implementing a plan to create thousands of jobs in the Vizcaya Province. My staff and I are working with President Lazaro to put an end to the corrupt federal colonial system."

"I object, Your Honor," Martinez interrupted. "I fail to see the relevance of this line of questioning."

"Your Honor," said Sierra, "I am trying to establish the context in which jobs are created or not created in Vizcaya Province. There are well-paid jobs and there are jobs at extremely low wages. There are jobs with security and marginal jobs with little or no security. The question has direct bearing on the future use of the Calaveras land in terms of its highest and best use and it terms of the best public interest."

"Very well," Judge Marcos allowed. "You may proceed."

"Thank you, Your Honor. Now, Governor Francisco, could you please describe to the court what you mean by the Federal Colonial System?"

"Certainly. It is the old, traditional dictatorship system, where elected officials become corrupt by using their position for personal gain, those who were in office and used government tax dollars to buy businesses and then they drained off a large share of the profits for themselves. When these politicians retired, they had accumulated millions of dollars in foreign banks, and they own huge mansions in the United States and Europe."

"What is the status of workers in such a system?"

"Workers are virtual slaves, working for minimum wage or less. Wages are held down by deals between the politicians and businessmen. Wages are much higher in other parts of the world. The business owners make large profits by exploiting the workers that way. If the workers rebel and ask for a more just distribution of the wealth, the same wealth that they themselves create, they are attacked by organized paramilitary forces. Their protest is put down by local police who are bribed to go along, and all too often, they were backed up with the full military force of federal troops. Private employers had the custom of bribing government officials to not interfere with local policing actions, like the one described by Señor Gonzalez."

"Have you or your elected officials been offered such bribes since you were elected?" Sierra asked.

"Many times," said Governor Francisco, who was visibly enjoying the opportunity to testify, "but, of course, my cabinet and I have refused. This is a special bond among us, because we all believe in an advanced economic arrangement with social justice."

"Were you ever approached by the Calaveras family with a bribe offer for something they wanted?"

"I was never approached directly. Certain members of my cabinet told me they were approached with requests. However, when their requests were turned down, the Calaveras family saw that their subtle bribery attempts would fail and they backed off."

"So, in a word, the Calaveras family tested your cabinet to see if they could be bought?"

"That is an accurate statement."

"Objection!" Martinez said loudly. "This is pure supposition and very misleading."

"Sustained," Judge Marcos countered. "The witness is stating what he heard from others, which is hearsay."

"Were you ever personally threatened by the Calaveras family after their lobbying efforts were rejected by your cabinet?"

"I have received many death threats since I've been in office. We have not been able to trace the threats directly to the Calaveras family. Three weeks ago, before it was announced that eminent domain would be used to buy the Calaveras land for a just price, an attempt was made on my life."

"Please tell the court what happened."

"I was visiting friends, the Webb family, north of El Cedro," Governor Francisco began. "The Webbs' house was located on top of a high hill, just on the edge of town. When it was time to leave, two of my associates joined me and we drove down this very steep hill. My security people followed closely behind. Immediately, the driver realized the brake pedal was going all the way down to the floor. He pumped on it, hoping it would come back, but it didn't. The emergency brake failed. By this time, we were doing thirty-five miles an hour with a sharp ninety degree turn coming up. If we missed the turn, we would go straight over an embankment and crash to our deaths. Fortunately, my driver saved our lives. He made the turn without rolling over and then we were headed down the long steep hill. I knew that by the time we reached the bottom, we would be doing fifty miles an hour and would enter a major intersection with a traffic light—right at the bottom of the hill. Our driver instantly decided to ditch the car rather than face the traffic light. He saved our lives."

"Did you ever find out why the brakes failed?" asked Sierra.

"Yes. The brake system was rigged to fail."

"For the benefit of the court, did you find out who tried to kill you?"

"Yes. It was Victor Saldana. He attacked me and my bodyguards with a helicopter gunship after leaving the Webbs' house. My bodyguards fired back and killed Saldana."

"Were you able to trace these attempts on your life to the Calaveras family?" asked Sierra.

"Yes, Colonel Saldana was once employed by a number of rich landowners to destroy the ethanol facilities in Las Faldas, a new town the Cornerstone Constellation. The millionaire who paid Saldana was Señor Raul Echeverria. This was established by tape recordings of their deal before their helicopter gunship attack on Las Faldas. The Calaveras family has had many long-term business deals with Echeverria and they are lifelong business associates. After his gunship attack on the Constellation, Colonel Saldana escaped and went into hiding. He resurfaced to try to kill me and other officials in the Constellation. We have two witnesses who observed a meeting between Calaveras, Echeverria and Saldana. They mentioned my name in that meeting and then I was attacked twice by Saldana. I think this is evidence of a direct connection since they all had motives to stop the Constellations from continuing its success."

"Objection!" said Martinez. "The witness can not assume guilt by association. There is no proof that there is any connection between the Calaveras family, Mr. Echeverria or Colonel Saldana. Furthermore, the Calaveras family makes business deals every day with many people. There is no proof offered of any special business relationship between the Calaveras family and Mr. Echeverria or Saldana. This is hearsay with no substantiation in fact."

"Your Honor," said Sierra, "I hereby submit as evidence to the court, tape recordings of conversations between Sr. Saldana, Sr. Echerverria and Sr. Calaveras plotting the assassination of Governor Jaime Francisco. I am prepared to bring witnesses forward to testify to these life threatening events."

"Objection denied. The court will hear all relevant testimony."

"It's very curious that rich landowners have paid a hired killer like Saldana to try to destroy the Constellations," said Sierra. "Do you think they're afraid of letting people become worker-owners in cooperatives, so they can make a decent living to support a family and have some control over their own lives?"

"I object," Martinez asserted. "Counsel is leading the witness to conclusions."

"Sustained," said Judge Marcos. "Rephrase the question, Mr. Sierra."

"Why do you think you were attacked?" asked Sierra.

"There can be no doubt about it. Some, but not all of the big land barons will try to kill anyone who gets in their way. They believe they have a right as businessmen to control worker's lives and pay them next to nothing, so the rich landowners of the world can make huge profits and have power over people."

"Objection! Once again, this is unsupported allegation and an emotional appeal to the jury against the Calaveras family."

"Objection sustained. However, at this point, it remains to by seen if these allegations of attempts on Governor Francisco's life can be verified by witnesses who will be forthcoming."

"Thank you, Governor Francisco," Sierra said. "Your candid testimony has explained a great many things about how the property in Vizcaya Province is controlled and how the workers are exploited for profit. I have no further questions, Your Honor."

"Does the counsel for the plaintiff wish to cross examine the witness?" Judge Marcos asked.

"Not at this time, Your Honor," answered Martinez.

Judge Marcos looked at his watch. "This court is adjourned until tomorrow morning at eight thirty."

As Alan Sierra was leaving the courtroom, he was surrounded by a large group of newspaper and TV reporters.

"Mr. Sierra!" shouted the closest reporter. "With Cordoba Motors moving in, they'll create thousands of permanent jobs. How can the Constellation compete with them?"

"Tomorrow," Sierra replied, "you'll hear some answers tomorrow."

"Mr. Sierra!" shouted another reporter. "If the Constellation doesn't win the right to use eminent domain, how will El Cinco build any more?"

"It will be more difficult to build Constellations. It will take much longer without eminent domain, but Constellations will be built," Sierra replied with force and determination.

Sierra climbed into his waiting car as quickly as possible and he and Tomas drove away.

There were over a hundred and forty reporters from around the world covering the trial. As Sierra drove away, they rushed to every available telephone to relay the latest trial news to their newspapers and TV stations.

A reporter to *The Paris Times* called his editor. "Henri? Get the headlines ready for the close of this trial! Yes, it's going to be a major breakthrough—win or lose. Hell, it's a good alternative to this mess. A realist? For Christ's sake, if you want to be known as a realist, listen to reality in the making! They are trying to advance the Third Way. Right now, *any* alternative to global competition will look good!"

Another reporter to the editor of the *Boston Herald*: "Constellation Style economics is front-page news! What? Yes, it goes beyond capitalism, whatever *that* has become. It's strong enough to co-exist with capitalism. The United Nations staff is taking a good look at Constellation Style economics. They're leaning toward it strongly. Get ready to roll with it!"

A reporter for the *Business Street Journal*: "Bill? No, I need to talk with Bill. This is top priority."

There is a twenty second pause.

"Hello, John," Bill answered. "What's so damned important in Rocadura? Are you smokin' somethin'?"

"No, but as soon as I file my report, I'm going for Jack Daniels rocks and a prime rib. Want to join me?"

"That good, hey? What's happening?"

"I'm sending my report to legal. The whole case centers on eminent domain. If they establish a legal precedent here, it will have international implications and really rock Latin America."

"That's interesting."

"Interesting? We're talking about how you can build a new society with a healthy economic system on land owned by the super rich elite, with much more than just compensation, of course."

"Okay. You've got my attention. We'll set up and stand by."

"Bill, this is good. This is *really* good."

"Fine. If it really is that good, you get the front page."

Chapter 17
AN HONEST APPRAISAL

The court reconvened the next day at 8:45 a.m.

"Your Honor, I would like to call Señor Ernesto Pax Santana, the president of Cordoba Motors to the witness stand," Sierra offered.

After Santana was sworn in, Sierra began his line of questioning about the highest use of the land.

"Señor Santana, you estimate that the proposed auto-assembly plant would employ approximately two thousand five hundred people and another five thousand as suppliers and outsourced workers serving the plant. How much will the employees at the proposed plant earn?"

"The average auto-worker will earn about eleven thousand per year, not counting overtime, which can push salaries up to thirteen thousand a year," answered Santana.

"And it is my understanding that these workers pay for their own health care and pensions have been eliminated as well. Is that not correct?"

"Workers make enough to pay for their own health care and they naturally need to save for retirement," Santana answered.

Sierra turned toward the courtroom. "Let the jury note the Cornerstone Constellation has worker-owners who pay themselves an average of sixteen thousand dollars a year to start. By the eighth year they earn an average of $37,000 per year. They also have full health coverage. They have a Home

Ownership Plan that enables them to own their home early in life, when they need it most to raise a family. They retire with a full pension equal to fifty-five percent of their gross salary and a lump sum payment of one hundred and fifty thousand dollars."

The jury was appropriately impressed by the wages and benefits paid by the Constellation, as they broke out in whispers to each other.

"Order in the court," announced Judge Marcos.

Sierra turned back toward Santana. "Three years ago, fourteen thousand workers went on strike in your company. They stated they were being asked to work overtime until their health and safety were at risk. They said Motores de Cordoba refused to hire new workers whenever production demand went up. As a result, employees were asked to work ten to twelve hour days for months. Was this not reported correctly in the press?"

Santana stiffened notably at this question.

"It is the nature of the auto-making industry that supply and demand rises and falls. When we hire new employees, they basically enter into a lifelong contract. It is not our desire to hire large numbers of people and then lay them off when demand falls again."

"So, your solution is to make your regular employees work longer hours until demand falls again," Sierra surmised. "Let the jury note that in a worker-owner cooperative, such as the Vizcaya Constellation, owners do not abuse themselves as workers. They adjust production and sell fewer products instead of trying to maximize profits. People count for more than a few extra dollars of profit in the Constellation. Your local suppliers are contract workers, is that not correct, Señor Santana?"

"Yes. And they are well paid."

"And indeed, they should be," Sierra noted. "Because just like the workers inside the plant, the suppliers and outsourced personnel have no health care or pension plans paid by the company. Our survey of contracted suppliers shows they are paid more per hour but actually make far less per year than regular workers because they have little work when demand goes down. Many contractors can't stay in business and fall into unemployment. Is that not correct, Señor Santana?"

"It is possible that it could work out that way. We can not control market forces. Everyone must adjust to the market."

"Except in the Constellation," Sierra asserted, turning directly to the jury. "Because the Constellation is self-sufficient in basics, these ups and downs of market forces do not effect the basic necessities of life at all. The only adjustment required is with regard to export products, and these adjustments are made with the workers in mind, rather than more profits."

"Well," said Santana, "I don't see how they can conduct business that way. Corporations must earn as much as they can in order to have enough in reserve to meet a huge drop in demand or to produce a totally new product. In order to weather the marketplace, and stay in business, you soon learn you can never make enough."

Sierra smiled and faced the jury. "That is precisely what drives this global economic madness that has caught everyone in its dog-eat-dog trap. But that is not the case for everyone. For over fifty years, the Mondragon Complex in Spain has not only survived in the marketplace, it has grown and thrived. Mondragon is the forefather of the Constellations. The worker owned cooperative in Mondragon taught us how to escape this market force madness. They learned to work diligently and they learned what is 'enough.' Over the last fifty years, they have protected each other from layoffs. Workers who own the business do not fire each other."

Then, turning to Santana, Sierra asked, "How many people have you laid off in Motores de Cordoba over the last twenty years, Señor Santana?"

"I don't know, offhand. It could be a few thousand. I would have to consult our records."

"Well, I'll tell you for the record, Señor Santana. My assistant, Tomas, has just handed me a summary of news reports of layoffs by your corporation dating back to 1980. The number of people 'downsized,' laid off, and forced out, or in plain language, cut off from their livelihood, totals thirty-three thousand. With four persons to a family, that's one hundred and thirty-two thousand lives that were thrown into desperate poverty and hunger by those firings. I offer these reports for the record as exhibit A, Your Honor."

There was a notable stirring in the courtroom as the jury looked seriously concerned by Sierra's report.

"No further questions," said Sierra as he strode to his seat.

At that moment, a legal assistant stepped forward and spoke some words to Alan Sierra. He rose from his chair and approached the bench. "Your Honor, I realize the appraiser's testimonies are scheduled next, however, I have just received some new evidence to submit to the court that has a direct bearing on the appraisals of the land purchase by LSI."

"This is highly irregular, Mr. Sierra," Judge Marcos said with concern.

"Please bear with me, Your Honor," Sierra said.

"Very well, Mr. Sierra, you may proceed. But be forewarned, if you begin to waste the court's time with irrelevancies, I will be quick to act."

"Your Honor, as you can see, my aide is setting up a video screen for the benefit of the court. This presentation will be brief and will speak for itself."

The scene on the screen was taking place in an office.

"Your Honor, and members of the jury," Sierra announced, "the scene before you is a meeting between Jose Calaveras and an appraiser who was asked to determine the value of the ten thousand acres owned by the Calaveras family for purposes of providing an independent estimate to the jury."

The video monitor was large and easily visible to all members of the jury. On the screen, two men were seated at a table. When Jose Calaveras saw himself on the screen his face was a mask of shock. He looked desperately at his father and brothers.

"We believe your firm will be one of those selected to provide an appraisal of our property," began Jose Calaveras. "I understand your usual fee is about fifteen thousand dollars for this kind of work. Is that correct?"

"Yes," answered the appraiser, "that's near the customary fee."

"I believe your work is *much* more valuable," said Calaveras with a knowing smile. "Also, I have no doubt you will find our land is worth a great deal more than the one hundred and twenty million dollars proposed by the province."

"What do you think my fee should be, Mr. Calaveras?"

"Well considering all the work you must do to examine ten thousand acres and several comparable properties, I think it should be at least one hundred thousand dollars, don't you?"

"Oh, that would be a very nice fee," answered the appraiser, smiling broadly. "So, how much do you think the land is really worth?"

"Well, given that it is all in one piece, contiguous I mean, I believe it should be worth at least two hundred and forty million dollars. Wouldn't you agree?"

"Ah, well, now that you put it that way, I can see how it *could* be worth two hundred and forty million. But, there is a problem. You must secure at least two more appraisals near that same value, or I will look like a fool. My reputation will be totally destroyed."

"Do not be concerned. The other appraisers who could be selected for this task have agreed to the same deal. Yours is the last firm they could possibly approach in Vizcaya Province. If you are not selected to make an appraisal and testify, your fee will be thirty thousand dollars. Agreed?"

"It's a deal!" The appraiser exulted, rising from his chair to shake the hand of Jose Calaveras.

Calaveras shook his hand vigorously and laid an envelope on the appraiser's desk. "Here's a ten thousand dollar advance to seal the deal."

"Your Honor," Sierra stated, "the Calaveras family, by their own admission on this video, have attempted to bribe the appointed appraisers in order to double the appraised value of their land."

Jose Calaveras could restrain himself no longer. He leaped to his feet.

"He's a damn liar! I left money to help cover his expenses. It wasn't a bribe! He's a damn liar!"

Judge Marcos responded immediately.

"Bailiff, remove this man from my courtroom. I don't care if you use handcuffs or a wrecking bar. Just get him out of my courtroom and keep him out."

The gallery broke into an uproar and Judge Marcos did not restrain them. He sat in icy calm for a full two minutes while the bailiff removed Jose Calaveras from the courtroom. When he spoke again, his voice was soft and even.

"Order please. We will now resume."

He turned to Alan Sierra.

"You said they attempted to bribe them," Judge Marcos remarked. "It appeared to me that money exchanged hands and the transaction was completed."

"Well, Your Honor, it is true that money was offered to the appraisers by Calaveras. But the appraisers, including Mr. Garcia here shown on the video, never accepted the bribes. Your Honor, I would like to call Mr. Garcia to the stand."

Mr. Garcia took the stand and was sworn in by the bailiff.

"Mr. Garcia," Sierra questioned, "is it true that Jose Calaveras offered you a bribe of one hundred thousand dollars to make a higher estimate of the value of the land owned by the Calaveras family?"

"Yes," answered Mr. Garcia. "It happened just as you saw it on the video. He left an advance of ten thousand dollars on my desk to seal the deal, but I didn't accept the money. I only pretended to accept the money. I gave the money to my attorney so he could put it in an escrow account to be returned after this trial."

"And why did you pretend to accept the money, Mr. Garcia?"

"I and the other appraisers had previously signed a contract with LSI."

At this, the court erupted, since it appeared that LSI had bribed the appraisers before Calaveras could reach them. Judge Marcos had to hit the gavel several times and shout "Order in the court!" several times before the crowd was relatively quiet once more.

"What kind of contract was that?" Sierra asked.

"It was a contract for honest surveillance of wrongdoing," answered Garcia. "All of the appraisers in the province met and agreed it was the right thing to do under the circumstances. We could not accept a bribe for our work. Our livelihoods would be destroyed."

"So," Sierra asserted, "what you are telling me, and the court, is that Livelihood Systems, Inc. contacted you in advance and contracted with you to video tape any bribery attempt by Calaveras?"

"That's right. LSI insisted they would not bribe the appraisers because that would be both illegal and immoral. Instead they offered all of us this Contract for Honest Surveillance of Wrong-doing." Garcia held up the contract for all to see. "The contract states that LSI will pay twelve thousand dollars to each of the appraisers for surveillance services. It requires one of the five appraisers to supply actual proof of the bribe attempt on videotape with an audible recording."

"Thank you, Mr. Garcia." Then, taking the contract from Garcia, Sierra said, "Your Honor, I would like to submit this contract as evidence to the court, as exhibit B. I have no further questions of the witness."

As the courtroom burst into chatter again, Judge Marcos hit his gavel twice, and yelled, "Order! Order!" Then he called to Mr. Martinez, "Do you wish to cross-examine the witness?"

"No, Your Honor," Martinez said, knowing this agony of his client should not be prolonged.

Then, turning to the witness, Judge Marcos said, "You may step down, Mr. Garcia."

Judge Marcos then addressed the counselors. "If there are no further witnesses, the counsel for the plaintiff may proceed with his summation."

Martinez rose from his chair and buttoned his suit coat. He walked back and forth twice in front of the jury box, before he spoke.

"What we have before us is a case of a fine, Rocaduran family fighting for its very life. What one of you, I ask, would achieve as much as the Calaveras family has achieved and let it be stolen from you by billionaires seeking a bigger profit than yours? What one of you would fight for decades to provide a strong economic future for their entire family—nineteen families in all— only to let it all slip from your hands because of a threat by people with more money? None of you would let your families be deprived of your own land and the land of your forefathers. The land that represents a livelihood for all of your families for generations to come. It is unthinkable! It is incredible that you would let all of that slip through your fingers because of a hostile takeover! You would fight! You would bargain! You would do almost anything to protect your families!"

Then, Martinez lowered his voice. He strode before the jury box like a confident matador before the bull.

"It is claimed that the Constellation will create more jobs than the Calaveras family. Well, that is simply not true. You have heard the testimony of Señor Santana, president of Motores de Cordoba, that seven thousand five hundred jobs will be created in Vizcaya when he builds his auto-assembly plant. And this is just for seven thousand acres of land. What do they know of the grand plans this noble family has for the future of the other three thousand acres? It is an insult to say that they can create more jobs than the Calaveras family. Who has employed the people in Vizcaya for all of these years? Who will go on providing more and more jobs? I do not have to tell you, because you already know. It's the Calaveras tradition to employ as many residents of Vizcaya as they possibly can. And I know for a fact that their plans for their land are wonderful. They will create tens of thousands of jobs for you and your children. I ask you to place your trust in the people you know. Do not trust the people who come from the sky and make promises they cannot keep."

Then, Martinez turned to Judge Marcos and said, "Your Honor, that is all I have to say."

Judge Marcos said, "Thank you, Counselor Martinez." Then, turning to Alan Sierra, he said, "The counsel for the defense may address the jury with its final summation."

Alan Sierra rose to address the jury regarding the valid public purpose of the land. He walked in front of the jury box and looked at the jury with confidence. It was clear he was absolutely respectful of them as persons about to render a very important judgment.

"I'll make my summation very brief," Sierra began. "The first point is the Constellation's potential for job creation versus Calaveras. The Cornerstone Constellation has created forty-nine thousand jobs and is creating jobs at the rate of about seven thousand, or more, per year as the Cornerstone builds out. It is important to note that these are permanent, sustainable jobs. The Constellations put people above gaining more and more capital. They are worker-owners and there are few layoffs, and only then for very good reason.

The rate of new employment in the Constellations will increase. It is projected there will be a population of sixty thousand or more, and forty thousand jobs in each of the seven new towns by 2020. That's a total of two hundred eighty thousand jobs in just ten years."

Sierra paused for his message to take effect with the jury.

"Today, Calaveras employs about twenty-five hundred people, but that's after they kicked the three thousand tenant farmers off their land. They used to hire temporary labor to harvest the sugar cane, but most of that is done by machine now. Their history is one of decreasing employment. Even given the benefit of the doubt, let's assume that Calaveras will create a total of twenty thousand jobs compared to two hundred and eighty thousand jobs in the Vizcaya Constellation. And tax revenues to Vizcaya Province and the federal government will be much greater because there will be so many new jobs. This second point is very important because the government will have more revenue to provide health care, food, sanitation systems and purified water for the poor. No one can work when they're sick and weak from disease and poor nutrition. However, with these increasing revenues from the Constellation and the government, Governor Francisco will be able to keep his promise to provide health care and help the Constellation to build new roads and rapid transit systems. The worker owners in the Cornerstone also care for those who do not yet have jobs. They show their solidarity with the community by giving ten percent of their profit income to those who need it the most—just as their forefathers in Mondragon, Spain taught them."

Sierra paused again to let his points sink into the minds of the jury.

"The third major point is job security. Constellations build permanent livelihoods that are sustainable because families are insulated from the massive layoffs of the market economic system. There are no layoffs because the Constellation make themselves self-sufficient in the basic necessities and they care for one another. The Calaveras empires of the world always blame market forces for cruel layoffs and declining wages, even though they are caused by corporate decisions, motivated by serving shareholders and lofty compensation for managers."

The jury could not contain itself passively after this point. Too many of them had experienced the pain and anguish of being fired for no just cause. There were murmurs and head nods as Alan allowed the jurors time to recompose themselves.

"The fourth point is about education, pay and purchasing power: after vocational training, the entry level pay in a Constellation is sixteen thousand per year, plus health care on pension benefits. With a college degree, the annual salary starts at thirty thousand dollars plus full health care and pension benefits. And by the way, the Constellation provides an economic ladder for students to work their way through vocational training or college."

Alan paused to let that last message sink into the hearts of his audience. The jurors looked at each other, thought about their children's future and were deeply impressed with Alan's words.

"The fifth point: quality of life. The Constellations provide solidarity, a wonderful sense of community, and everyone is working to advance the forward days of all Constellations, and especially the lives of their own children. They are working for something that transcends themselves. They are in union with spiritual reality, which is to love God and your neighbor.

"The sixth point: the Constellations are kept in harmony with nature, using ethanol and solar cells for fuel and electricity, while the Calaveras land barons of the world are polluting the environment with a polluting old incinerator. Constellations are planned with sensitivity to the environment. They are planned with care for Mother Earth, which sustains us all, and for long lasting, sustainable development for our children.

"The seventh and final point: at Cornerstone enough ethanol plants were built to supply not just the Constellation's needs but the entire country's energy needs. El Cinco invested two billion dollars to make Rocadura free from oil imports and totally energy self-sufficient with ethanol and solar cells. The federal government saves over one billion dollars per year on its balance of trade ledger, and the more constellations we build, the better it gets! These are the public purposes of the Constellations! Economically, nationally and locally, and in every other way, there is no contest here." Alan's eyes searched the jury. "No doubt, some good forms of capitalism will survive if they begin to serve human needs well. But Calaveras style capitalism is dead. Cut throat capitalism is no longer competitive. It can't deliver the most fundamental public purpose: human survival and well-being. The so-called 'free market' is simply a group of rich men paying themselves four hundred times more than those who produce the products. Thank God we have an alternative! Constellation Style economics brings people into right relationship with each other so they can give of their gifts while earning a living and be in right relationship with nature, and most importantly, with God."

Alan Sierra paused to let the jury ponder his summation. He took a drink of water and sat on the edge of the table.

The jury took forty minutes to discuss the case and reach a verdict. They voted unanimously in favor of eminent domain by Vizcaya Province and the Constellation. The gallery broke into animated conversation.

After a minute, Judge Marcos said, "Order, please."

He then set the stage for the determination of the purchase price of the land. "The court will now hear the testimony of three independent appraisers who will provide the jury with the appraised value of the land."

The first appraiser estimated the price at one hundred twenty-one million dollars. The second appraiser estimated one hundred twenty million dollars and the third appraiser estimated one hundred twenty-three million dollars.

Judge Marcos read the final decision. "The jury has set the price of the land at one hundred twenty-three million dollars. This court is adjourned!"

Alan Sierra was immediately surrounded by Conchita, Fredrico, David, Carlos and the LSI staff.

Fredrico hugged him and said, "Alan! Fantastic job! This is a decisive human event!"

"Fredrico! You old fox!" Alan shouted. "That contract for honest surveillance was inspired. Talk about beating the bribers at their own game!"

"Yes, it was the most fun I've had in years. But all the credit goes to this man." And he brought Tomas Xavier forward to meet Alan.

"So, it was your idea?"

"If Fredrico says so," Tomas answered with a big grin. "We sort of worked it out together over a vodka and tonic."

Alan laughed and smiled, hugged Tomas, Conchita and David and shook hands with the LSI staff for five minutes.

"You know," Fredrico said to Alan, "I'm sure that the bribe bit helped our case emotionally, but you still had to win on the points of law, and you did! *Maravillosa!*"

"I can't wait to read the morning papers!" Conchita exulted. "This is already hitting the international wire service. It's a landmark opinion! Let's go party!"

"Where shall we go?" Fredrico enquired.

"La Ronda! Where else?" Tomas shouted.

"All right! Let's meet at La Ronda," Conchita agreed, as she seized David's hand and led him out of the courtroom. On their way out the door, Conchita called over her shoulder, "I'll go bribe the maître d' for a table!"

They gathered at La Ronda, a large, festive restaurant with two dance floors and a European band. As David and Conchita walked through the foyer, they were met with the unexpected: the band was playing an old Mid

East belly-dancing classic called "Port Said." There was a large crowd and the dance floor on the lower level was filled with bouncing heads and swaying bodies. They were directed toward the upper second floor level for seating.

La Ronda was constructed in the round. The upper level had a continuous sixteen foot wide balcony overlooking the huge dance floor below. Tables were set against the inside wall, leaving a service aisle and an eight foot wide dancing area. David and Conchita were seated in an empty section. They danced to the railing to look for the rest of their party. Soon Alan, Fredrico and Tomas appeared on the lower level, followed by the rest of the LSI contingent. David waved to them to come upstairs.

Tomas rushed to David and shouted over the music, "We blew 'em away! I love it! I'll never forget the look on old Calaveras' face when we showed the bribery tape!"

"That was a beautiful trap you set, Tomas! A contract for honest surveillance! *Dios mio!* What a trip!"

Tomas held out both hands to Conchita and gave her a heartfelt hug.

They all joined hands and danced together, free-styling their steps, moving in a circle clockwise to the upbeat, raucous old tune "Port Said."

"Fredrico," smiled Conchita, "I didn't know you were such a good belly dancer!"

"Neither did I!" Fredrico shouted back.

And so the evening went. Carlos arrived with his date. She was a Latin beauty with long black hair and teasing brown eyes.

"This is Linda Alvarez," Carlos introduced. "She's a wonderful dancer, currently appearing at the Club La Joya."

Conchita danced with Alan, then with Fredrico and David. At eight o'clock, they all retired to one of the more intimate dining rooms for the evening meal. They ordered supper and a carafe of Chardonnay. Alan Sierra rose to say a few words.

"There aren't too many times in a person's life when they feel this good," said Alan. "There's nothing like going into a really dirty fight and coming out clean...a winner! Well, I owe all of you a huge debt in bringing off the win. I couldn't have done it without you."

Conchita rose from her chair to say a few words.

"El Cinco could not be here tonight, but Padre Parejo called me to say that they will arrange a party for us to celebrate our victory. He said, this is a powerful advance on the spiritual journey. We can now give hope to millions of people in thousands of villages around the world."

Dinner was served and the conversation was warm and lively.
Fredrico rose from his chair with glass in hand.

"Here's to David and Conchita. I know you two are kindred souls."

Everyone toasted the couple, as their love for each other was obvious to all.

"Tonight," Fredrico continued, "we're blessed to celebrate a victory of the unseen over the seen. The Constellation is still very new to many, but by tomorrow the news will be out. Reporters from around the world have camped out on this trial for days. For those people who care, their eyes will be opened to understand what Constellation Style economics is for the first time. It is a new kind of globalization—family style."

"To globalization—Constellation Style!" Tomas toasted.

"To the four-day workweek!" Carlos toasted.

David rose and offered a toast. "To *real* freedom. Here's to people taking charge of their lives."

The following morning, Conchita rushed to her favorite newsstand and read the headlines. She was not disappointed.

THE BUSINESS STREET JOURNAL

LANDMARK DECISION
IN ROCADURA ON
PROPERTY RIGHTS

Eminent Domain Can Be Used
To Build New Towns To Create
More Permanent Jobs

EL DIARIO NUEVO

!CONSTELLATIONS ARE VICTORIOUS!
El CINCO WILL BUILD 7 MORE
NEW TOWNS IN VIZCAYA PROVINCE.

Governor Francisco Predicts
Huge Increase in the Standard
of Living in Vizcaya

THE PARIS TIMES

CONSTELLATION STYLE ECONOMICS BORN IN ROCADURA

7 New Towns Are Economically Integrated To Be
Self Sufficient in Basic Necessities.
Regional Trading Blocks Are Established for
economic permanency.

European Parliament Member Celebrates
Freedom From Market Economy Entrapment

THE BOSTON HERALD

CONSTELLATIONS IN ROCADURA OFFER AN ALTERNATIVE
TO GLOBAL ECONOMIC COMPETITION
United Nations Development Division
To Send Team to Rocadura

Chapter 18
DOUBLE DOWN, DOUBLE UP

David and Conchita settled in on the couch to watch a video. He positioned himself with his back against a large pillow at the far end of the couch. She positioned herself with her back and head against a small pillow placed against his chest. Occasionally, he embraced her shoulders, her arms, and gently stroked her cheeks. Once in a while, he nuzzled her hair and brought his arms together on both sides of her face to caress her. If the music was couch-danceable they creatively swayed to the rhythm. But mostly, he just held her.

For her part, she just soaked it up. For his part, he enjoyed it all as much as she did.

"A man who loves his wife loves himself."

"But I don't see any ring on my finger."

He reached into his pocket and pulled out a little black ring box. He carefully, slowly, placed it on her belly. Her eyes opened wide as she looked at the box and quickly opened it. It was an engagement ring with three rows of small diamonds. She quickly jumped up from her slumbering position and looked David in the eyes. He was smiling his teasing Irish smile.

"For the last six months, I've felt like you are my wife. Will you marry me?"

"Oh, yes! Yes!" she shouted as she threw herself full length on his body. "Oh, yes! I felt married to you after the first six months!"

"Well, if the truth were known, I knew you were inescapable that night at Diego's fire."

"Oh, yes, I remember. Captain Kirk said he was entering the Mysterious Romantic Zone and he was going in all the way."

They held each other tightly and kissed with a full expression of their feelings. Their passion soared to a new level, then a higher level. She knew that he adored her and she loved him with all her being. It was a night that they would never forget. They spent the next day playing together and the next. It was a Sunday evening when David and Conchita were once again ensconced on the couch watching a movie that David's delight in Conchita was broken by a totally unwanted realization.

"Darn it. I left my new video at the office."

"Oh, no, honey, I'm feeling so mellow. Can't you pick it up in the morning?"

"My flight leaves for the States at 7:00. I'll never make it. I have to get it tonight."

"One of these days, the Constellation will have to take a back seat so we can have a life together."

"You're preaching to the choir, honey, and you're just as guilty as I am."

"I know. But I want you with me tonight."

"Please don't make it any more painful than it is. I'll be back in thirty-five minutes."

"Okay. You're right. You've gotta be good out there and recruit the village builders of tomorrow."

David drove to LSI headquarters. It was a fifteen minute trip. He rang the door buzzer and was let in by the security guard. At the elevator, he spoke his voice I.D. and waited for the door to open. He entered the elevator, exited at the fifth floor and walked down the hall to his office. As he was about to enter his office, he was surprised to see Carlos seated in his chair. The door was open and David could hear Carlos carrying on a video conference. David stood motionless in the doorway.

The caller was talking on the video screen. He was a tall man with an aristocratic air. His image was obviously well-polished and diplomatic while being very direct.

"Yes, the papers are ready to be signed, as agreed. As vice president of Strategic Planning, you'll staff the Executive Committee. You'll have a five-year contract for five million dollars. We have every confidence you can deliver on your promise to position Avar Oil to gain the largest market share of ethanol production in the world."

Carlos answered, "Given Avar's existing transportation and storage facilities we have a head start. The task will be to build ethanol aerobic digester facilities at mega-speed. Simultaneously, feedstock supply must keep pace. We'll make it happen. I know how to write contracts they'll be hot to sign." Carlos smiled.

"You're definitely our man. Oh, and by the way, the Executive Committee loved how you negotiated Warner into our camp. They all said it was a really nice piece of work."

"Thanks. I read him pretty well. He wanted a quicker solution than the Constellations could offer."

"That's a key point to remember in the future. I'll put that little saying on my wall. See you tomorrow. Have a great flight."

Carlos spun around in his chair and saw David standing in the doorway. For a moment, he froze in disbelief. Then, he lay his head back, put both hands on his forehead and slid them very slowly down his face, as if to wash away the vision and the pain.

David was stunned by the betrayal he had just witnessed. He leaned against the doorway and waited for Carlos to speak.

"I'm going to miss you, buddy. You're the best friend I've ever had. Please don't hate me for this. I don't want to see the Constellations go down. They're good. But I've been offered a deal I can't refuse."

"Don't sell your soul, Carlos. They'll take all of you if you let them, and from what I've just seen, you're well on your way."

"If it gets too rough, I'll get out. But I like this kind of creative challenge. It just suits me too well."

David reached into his desk drawer and pulled out a bottle of Jameson Irish whiskey. He took two glasses, filled them each two fingers high, and handed a glass to Carlos.

"The truth is I'll miss you too," David said. "We could have a helluva good time together, playing around the world. We have the power in our hands to give millions of people a whole new life."

"Nothing has changed between us. I just have my unique package to unfold, just like you have yours. You're a standup guy, and so am I."

David took a sip of Jameson, set his glass down, and folded his arms across his chest. "Everyone has their own mysteries and their own dreams to play out. I just wish it were different."

"Look at it this way, now I'm a double agent for you. I'll guard your flank better than anyone can because I'll be on the inside."

"You will do that, won't you?"

"You know damn well I will."

"If they find out they may try to kill ya."

"I'll have to play it close to the chest, but you have my word, I'll keep you posted where it really counts."

"It was Che Guevara who said: 'You're in the heart of the beast.' Be careful!"

"Well, I can tell you this. I won't be communicating by video phone. You'll know when you get specially coded e-mail from complete strangers. I'll create some new identities. Only you and I know about certain personal experiences. That's how you'll know it's me and vice versa."

"Like, for example, when was the last time you saw a slimy bullfight?"

"Yeah, and I went to the zoo the other day. Damn those vipers were big!"

"We'll meet secretly from time to time, and our first meeting will be at Belmont. Race tracks are great places to conceal conversations. You come as you are, if you like. I'll be disguised, because FBI agents cover the tracks like a blanket."

"Are you in their files?"

"Yeah, I made a stupid mistake when I first graduated with my B.A. I actually interviewed for a job with 'em. Well, you can see that I have a predilection for being a spy. It's exciting. Any how, the FBI does a monster background check on people who interview. They go to the towns that you lived in and ask all kinds of questions. They check out all of your family members. If they find a bad apple they think could influence you to the criminal side, they reject you. Well, guess what? I forgot one of my friends got caught breaking and entering with a couple of his buddies at age eighteen. They got high and thought they were just having fun. They sent him to a 'reform school.' He was very sharp and very athletic. He hated being penned up. So, within ten months he escaped."

"No kidding! That's a tough deal to pull off in any age."

"No doubt about it. I was amazed when he showed up at one of our favorite bars. In those days, it was easier to create a new identity. They never caught him. The statute of limitations ran out and he lived a normal life. But he was still in the FBI files."

"So they didn't hire you?"

"Not a chance. It was hard for me to understand at the time because I had no record and I forgot about his. It took me awhile to figure it out."

"They don't take any chances, do they?"

"Thank God! What an incredible mistake that would have been for me, to join the FBI!"

Both men took another sip of Jameson.

"I'll never forget the interview with the regional FBI director. As soon as I walked into his office he held his right hand up shoulder height and squeezed it like he was crushing a tennis ball, a weird-looking gesture. It occurred to me that he was testing me, maybe for malleability or nonverbal communication. So, I held my hand up and gave him the same gesture back, like a greeting."

"That sounds weird all right."

"Then, he said that to be in the FBI, you have to be as pure as Caesar's wife. I guessed Caesar's wife must have been pretty damn pure and I figured since they had done a thorough background check and I'd reached the interview level I was considered okay."

He said they had to be very careful so no one could blackmail an agent. He asked me if there was anything in my past that I felt I needed to tell him. The only thing I could think of was gambling, so, I told him I used to play the ponies. He asked if I made any money on the horses. Well, I told him that I had played a system given to me by a master handicapper and paid for two years of college that way."

"Was that the truth?"

"Oh, yeah. I never told you about that?"

"Never crossed my desk."

"Hmph. Well, he lit up like a Christmas tree and revealed something I'll never forget. At the time, the infamous J. Edgar Hoover was the head of the FBI. He said Hoover himself enthusiastically played the horses and encouraged his agents to enjoy the fun as well. That's how I know the tracks around the country are well-covered by the FBI. They're looking for high rollers that bet at the fifty dollar window and cash out at the U.S. Treasury window. They're looking for mob connections and people who are in gambling trouble who might commit a crime down the road to pay off their debts before they get their kneecaps busted. There are agents who are assigned to spend the entire day at the tracks around the country and they can gamble if they like. Agents collect so-called successful betting systems so they can make a little bonus now and again. They can also intercept inside information from their national phone taps on high rollers and the mafia. That's why his eyes lit up and then he asked me how my system worked. So I told him. He was impressed. I'm sure he dictated my system to his secretary as soon as I was out the door!"

"Do you think this is still going on?"

"What do you think?"

"This guy had no intention of hiring you when he interviewed you."

"That's right. They just wanted to round out the file on me!"

"There's nothing quite like being on the inside, getting special information. An old-timer told me a story about how he got a horse tip one day. He had been helping an invalid friend who was confined to a wheelchair. It turned out the guy was a top-flight horse trainer most of his life before his auto accident. He still had many friends who wanted to pay him back for tips he had given them over the years. They felt sorry for him. So, one day, he got a call that there was a horse named Bug Brush that was primed to take the race. Bug Brush broke the track record that day at really good odds and that record stood for over ten years. David, I'm the same guy you've always known. I just have to take a different path for now. I hope we can join up again, down the 'roadski.'"

David was still reeling with the betrayal, wondering how he could ever trust Carlos again. "What did you tell Avar Oil about the Constellations?"

"Nothing they haven't read in the *Times*, except...I told them about ethanol, how we produce it with the Ingram process, and how we set up feedstock supply lines. They really don't care about the Constellations. You heard what Carson said about positioning themselves to capture the largest market share in the world. I'll show them how to take the lead in ethanol production worldwide."

"The Constellations are the lowest price producers, right now. That could eventually reduce our income from exporting ethanol to other countries."

"Not really, David. If you think about it for just a minute, the market is global and totally elastic. The only reason everyone isn't filling up their tanks with one hundred percent ethanol is lack of accessibility. It will probably take twenty years or more to meet global market demand. Hell, David, you know this is really good for the environment. Big Oil should have shifted to an ethanol mix with gasoline a decade ago to decrease fuel prices and global warming. They won't be concerned about Constellations until they come to the U.S. and that's a long way off. No, the Constellations are safe. I thought that one through to make sure."

"So, what happened to Sheik Amad's deal with Warner?" David asked pointedly.

"Warner was pretty desperate. He knew he had to get out of oil and into ethanol. The thing that appealed to him most was staying on as general manager in a Constellation. I told Avar and they made him an offer to come to work with them in thirty days to manage a big part of their ethanol operation. He jumped at the chance."

"The African Constellation lost a potentially good partner there."

"Not really. We were setting up a deal to bail *him* out. The Constellations don't need him as much as he needed them."

"Okay, I guess we're still buddies."

"Good. I know it's a shock. You have to be hurting. But think about it. You really need me on the inside more than here now!"

"Double agent down, double agent up. You son of a bitch! You *are good!*"

They gave each other a strong Spanish hug.

"Time to go."

"Yeah, time to go."

Carlos walked to the elevator. David stood in meditative suspension, his mind still reeling from the experience. He thought about calling Conchita to let her know he was okay. It was late. He decided she would have called him if she was worried because she knew where he was. She was asleep by now, and it was probably best to let her rest. He joined Carlos at the elevator and they rode down together.

"Are you taking Linda with you?"

"I have to get things set up first, then I'll fly her up to stay."

"Good. Sounds like you've got your act together."

"Hey, buddy," Carlos smiled, "we're planners, remember?"

"You know, there was an internationally famous assassin and man of mystery named Carlos, alias 'The Jackal.' A human jackal is one who does mean work for another's advantage."

"True story. Not my style. I'm a lover, not a killer. My work will benefit humankind nearly as much as yours, but not quite."

"I'm glad you still see the value of Constellation-style. After you've made your first billion, you might want to start up another group of wise capitalizers."

"That will be very tempting. But first, I have to make the billion as my entry fee into that elite group of wise guys."

David laughed and felt a great release of tension. "Go. Get out of here. Make your billion and join me down the 'roadski.'"

"Down the 'roadski' it is. Bye for now."

Chapter 19
THIRD WAY DESIGNERS UP FRONT

David and Conchita married and settled down to teach at New Town University in Las Faldas. It was the first university to be dedicated to the planning of Constellations. For the first time, Conchita and David began working a four-day week. Two days a week, Conchita taught courses in Constellation Financing and a course in Communications. Two days were spent traveling to increase the number of investors. David taught courses in Constellation Planning. Every year, he made several trips to the U.S. to recruit more students to build Constellations.

The Cornerstone Constellation and the Vizcaya Constellation had reached maximum buildout and Trinity was almost complete. They now had built twenty-one new towns, and they were fully self-sufficient. The Home Ownership Plan had achieved its first full cycle. Those families that had saved in the plan had bought their first homes. This enabled David to make a Life Cycle Chart, showing how families in Las Faldas had achieved a new level of self reliance and economic security.

It was travel time again, and David had arrived at the University of Cincinnati to recruit more architects and planners. Now, he could prove empirically what he could only project before. This gave his lecture at the university a new dimension of vitality based in fact and the good life in the new towns. It gave him hope that one day, Constellations would be built in the

United States. Once again, he recalled Padre Parejo's vision of how north to south investment could bring huge rewards to the U.S. and Canada in terms of revitalized human values, dignity and real economic freedom.

David stood on the campus stage with a huge chart cast upon a screen behind him.

"Good evening," he said. "I'm David O'Laughlin and I'm a professor of planning at New Town University. I live in Las Faldas, Rocadura, part of the Cornerstone Constellation, the first of its kind to be built in the world. Las Faldas means the foothills or skirts of the mountains. The whole name of the city is Las Faldas del Cielo, which means the foothills of Heaven. To me, it is a piece of Heaven. I'm here to give you a good understanding of what it's like to live, work and play in a Constellation. We're looking for new planners, architects, engineers, economists and many other professionals to join us in building new towns around the world. I've had planners and engineers tell me it's the best kind of work on the globe and it's self-fulfillment at a very high level. At the end of the presentation, I'll be happy to give you materials to help you decide if this kind of work is for you."

David paused and looked around the room. It was a good turnout of four hundred students.

"There are mikes spaced around the aisles so we can have a good chat together. Please don't be bashful. Just jump right in and I'll try to answer those probing questions that only college students know how to ask."

There was a chuckle of recognition, around the auditorium.

"I'll start by asking the two biggest questions of all: first, what will my paycheck look like? Secondly, how does a worker become an owner in the Constellation?

"This is a Life Cycle Chart," said David, as he turned to the projection on the screen. "It shows how a family's wealth increases over their life span. It also shows how the Constellation is financed internally, by the worker-owners themselves.

"The Constellation has a very special feature that will enable you to buy your own home in the first five to seven years of work. It's a really simple plan: instead of putting dollars in a pension plan, you can begin saving money in the Home Ownership Plan to buy a home. You save eight percent of your gross pay and the Constellation matches it with eight percent. These savings are totally tax exempt. Charles Schultz, the author of the *Peanuts* comic strip, said we ought to issue every kid a dog and a banjo. We think it should be a dog, a banjo and home ownership when your young.

"If you are single it will take you about six to seven years to save enough to buy a home with thirty-eight thousand dollars, or more, of equity. I call that the Lonely Path. Now, let me tell you about the Lover's Path," he smiled, as he flashed another slide on the screen.

"If you should meet that very special person and marry, both of you can merge Home Ownership Plan accounts and buy a home, together. In seven years, you can have eighty to one hundred thousand dollars in equity when you merge accounts."

There were "ooohs and aaaahs" from the audience. As always, David noticed the merger feature of the plan was especially appreciated by the coeds.

"I know it's amazing, guys, but that incredibly strong hormonal surge you are experiencing can actually work *for* you. Getting married can be rewarded handsomely with the Home Ownership Plan. Big equity in your home eliminates many financial problems because you can borrow on it if you need to meet extraordinary expenses. It gives you personal financial security, which is really good to have when you start married life. Don't leave your rental apartment without it."

That brought a few chuckles from the audience.

"Now, here is a really neat feature: after you purchase your home with the HOP, your monthly housing costs drop by one-third. This totally offsets the twenty-four hundred dollars you pay each year on your loan to become a Constellation co-owner. Your disposable income actually increases each year, because you receive a five percent pay increase each year between the fifth and twelfth year. When your owner's loan is paid off, your disposable income increases by twenty four hundred dollars that year.

"Assuming you very wisely took out a fifteen-year mortgage, your home is completely paid off by the 20th or 22nd year of work of designing and building Constellations. With no mortgage, your disposable income increases by as much as thirteen thousand dollars more per year. Now, you're about forty-six to fifty-five years old. You are still a veritable spring chicken. It's big vacation time!"

There were more affirmations from the audience.

"Between age forty-six and age fifty-five, you and your spouse can tour the world with three-week to four-week vacations. By sixty you retire with a full pension at seventy-five percent of your gross income and a one hundred and fifty thousand dollar lump sum payment. Then is the time to take a refresher course in romantic dancing together. This is a life with a solid economic future. There are no layoffs. I'll explain how that works later. There is no

'Chainsaw Al' corporate director to destroy life as you know it every five years or so. As I said earlier, you can own your own home early in life. Your income increases steadily over your lifetime. You have a comfortable retirement to enjoy. How do we do that?" David paused. Then he softened his voice slightly, just above a whisper and said, "We do it by *design!*"

The applause was instant. "Oh, yeahs!" and other comments were heard up and down the rows of students.

David paused and walked around the stage looking into the audience. He smiled knowingly and nodded recognition at their responses.

"Please note well that on line fourteen of this chart it says 'profit sharing bonuses not counted.' That is a 'biggy.' My annual bonuses have run between $3,000 and $5,000 per year. Bonuses increase when worker/entrepreneurs produce more and—automatically—distribute the profits to themselves! What a concept, hey?"

The audience applauded and stomped on the floor for thirty seconds.

"As good as they are, these are just the surface statistics. What the chart shows is a good solid economic life. Rising incomes, homeownership early in life, three days off each week, large vacations and early retirement while you're still young enough to really enjoy those energetic, fun-lovin' vacation trips. But, there's a lot more to that chart than meets the eye."

He flashed another chart on the screen, and then guided the audience through the points on the chart.

NO LAYOFFS. NO "DOWNSIZING."

"In the Constellation, you can be a cocky worker and a humble boss," said David. "Worker-owners simply don't fire each other. In recessions, some folks are shifted into advanced training courses to boost the next round of productivity. Some folks shift to research and development to provide creative advances in technology. But through the worst national recessions, the Constellation is designed to deliver the basic necessities of life: food, housing, energy, clothing, transportation and a few luxuries provided for the whole community. Constellations have their own trading blocks which maintain a healthy balance between the prices of goods and incomes. How do we do that?" David softened his voice again, and said, "We do it by *design*."

ESCAPE FROM THE RAT RACE

"Working in the Constellations, you become part of the self-sufficiency revolt. I've learned that a revolt is a successful revolution. The Constellation is that revolt. In the Constellations, you are on a journey of self reliance and community freedom. You produce your own housing, food, clothing, energy, transportation systems and most of your luxury items. Because you produce it for yourselves, you do it as good or better than others do! You export products to buy the items you don't care to produce yourselves. You have escaped the rat race of classical economics."

David was interrupted by applause.

"You will grow and create your own market economy, outside of the control of corporate command and control structures. I once read that in 1997, seventy percent of the world's goods and services were produced by five hundred large corporations. They tell people how much their pay will be reduced, who will be fired and how much the stress level will be increased tomorrow—if you want to keep that miserable job with a soulless corporation. That kind of dictatorial power has been abused far too long. Escape from the Rat Race, without becoming a starving artist, is now a real economic alternative."

DEMOCRATIC WORKPLACE

"The Constellations offer a clear alternative with democratic governance with one person, one vote. In the Constellation, you all join in community to do what's best for the community with freedom of expression. It's a tough balancing act and it's challenging—but most of all it is incredibly invigorating to know your vote really counts. We work diligently. There is peer-group pressure to carry your own weight. Your salary is on a rising curve but you and your peers determine each other's bonuses."

Again the applause broke out and David knew his audience was with him. A student rose to the microphone to ask a question.

"How can the Constellation completely escape the market economy, the competition from globalization, the market forces of supply and demand, business cycles and inflation?"

"It's pretty easy," answered David, "when you understand that you can organize your own production and distribution system *within* twenty-one new towns. Remember, these new towns are designed to produce all of the basic necessities of life, and quite a few luxury items. We have an internal trading block of one and half million people. As the Constellations grow, the internal security of this ever-increasing trading block grows. Now, we are developing sister Constellations around the world. Global Constellation trading partners. We control the price and wage structures. We control supply and demand, which controls business cycles. What a concept, hey? Those mysterious market forces that are supposedly the cause of all of these corporate layoffs by the tens of thousands are a lie! It doesn't have to be that way!"

There was a rumble of conversation throughout the theater.

David continued. "Recessions can happen, from an act of God. For example, a monster hurricane wiping out crops in one place is counter balanced by growing more than enough crops in another Constellation."

The students took this all in and one of them asked another question. "But what happens when the national economy of Rocadura goes into recession, or inflation turns money into trash?"

"Again, the Constellation is internally self-sufficient. We own our banking system. We maintain capital reserves for hard times. Within a very few years, a national recession can no longer occur in Rocadura, because the Constellations will be too strong to be affected in a major way by the global market economy. Constellations now comprise thirty-five percent of the Rocaduran market. When we reach seventy percent, only government, the military, health care and some independent commercial activities will be outside the Constellations. We will have stabilized the Rocaduran economy. Inflation can soar outside of our system, but the Constellation knows how to maintain a healthy production-distribution balance *internally*, with enough for all."

David paused.

"And?" he asked. "How do we do that? Anyone?"

"By design!" shouted half the students.

David looked out over the audience and was elated. He had never struck such a strong understanding with a group of people so quickly. His heart soared as he continued to answer the student's question.

"You planners, engineers, architects and economists are the designers!

You take control of your own lives and your community while you give life to millions of people! You are the talent of the future. By taking your master's degree at New Town University, you will gain the professionalism to create Constellations that are not imagined today. You'll join us in what we fondly call The Sandbox. To borrow Lawrence Halprin's wonderful phrase: 'We work and we play and we seldom know the difference.' It's creative Heaven. Where the daily question is: How can you make your life and everyone else's even better? And of course you know how that's done."

"By design!" came the happy refrain of four hundred strong voices.

"That's right! By your happy, insanely creative, hard-working design!" shouted David. "Because the market economy is a fraud and a killer of livelihoods—by no design. By the complete lack of design. It's that simple! You can design a far happier economy than I can conceive of today. I'm convinced that this group has the spirit to do the job."

David flashed a new chart on the screen, and said, "This one is self-explanatory."

FOUR-DAY WORKWEEK

- Minimal stress = a healthier, longer, and happier life.
- You have time to be who you are.
- You have time to make a better community with healthy and self-fulfilled neighbors.
- Play. With minimal stress you can become as playful as a child. You can create new social events in your town because people have a strong sense of community.

Another student rose to the microphone.

"What you are describing sounds like a whole new world. It's very inviting. But, I know there will always be some problems for the Constellations to expand, because they need plenty of land. Two percent of Brazil's landowners control about sixty percent of the land. How will you deal with that problem?"

"You may have read that in Latin America, the Constellations can expand by eminent domain in most countries because they can create more good paying jobs than any other land owner. We create permanent jobs with excellent benefits. National governments see the value of our expanding tax base where little or no tax base was before. And by the way, I like it that two percent of Brazil's landowners control about sixty percent of the land. Fine.

There are fewer owners with which to negotiate! Many land speculators will settle for a good price because they need a buyer. It is astonishing how much land is owned around the world that is lying idle. Huge amounts of land are under poor management. But, that is where you come in: you can take that land and apply creative design to bring millions of poor people out of poverty. Your God-given talents are desperately needed. You are the difference. The land will lie idle or mismanaged until you turn it into something worthwhile!"

David paused and took a drink of water.

"Building Constellations is not entirely a trip into Utopia. We have many problems and frustrations to overcome. Democracy is messy business, primarily because we have been brained washed to believe in selfishness, rather than cooperation. Enlightened self interest has just been moved to a higher level in the Constellations, where self love and selfish interests are transformed to understand the cooperation gives us all that we really need. Land purchase is an ongoing challenge. Government red-tape is something we all suffer with until we find a way to reduce it to rational levels. I repeat, the Constellation is not a Utopian dream. It still requires hard, diligent work to make a better work-play community in the world. But hey, why work your heart out for less?"

The audience burst into conversation. Each person had something to say to the person next to them. David let them talk for over two minutes. Then he spoke again.

"I'll take one more question before I have to leave," he said.

Another student rose to the microphone.

"How can the Constellations keep abreast with the rapid changes in technology that the top five hundred corporations introduce every year?"

"We have our own research and development centers. It's important to note that most of the technology research in the U.S. is misdirected to military, luxury products and frivolous gizmos. Many of the technology advances you see today are for sale to corporations for advancing business operations and profits. And who are they selling these expensive new technological inventions to? Naturally, to those who can afford to pay the price. But these are luxury items or very minor improvements that now add little to our lives in terms of real satisfaction. They clearly don't add personal financial security. The biggest technological advances in the twentieth century were in computers. Americans were told they would have to work fewer hours, maybe even achieve the four-day workweek because of computer technology advances and newfound productivity per worker. So, what happened? People worked harder and more productively than ever before. Corporate profits soared and wages stagnated. Corporate revenues soared and they put the cash in *their* pockets, not yours. In the Constellations, worker-entrepreneurs benefit directly from their own productivity gains and our wise use of technology allows us to have a four-day week and job security."

When David paused, the audience spontaneously shouted, "By design!"

"Thank you. Thank you, my friends. Now, I know you understand!"

David smiled from his heart, shook his head slowly from side to side and let the audience know his feelings by circling his arms together as if to hug all of them. "Now, you're gettin' to my Irish heart."

"How did the Constellations get started?" asked a student. "I mean from the beginning?"

"Well, first there was the Prime Mover who set everything into motion."

David paused only briefly before the laughter started, and someone groaned, "Oh! No!"

"Okay, I'm sorry, I didn't mean to go *that* far back. That was paraphrasing a line in the movie *Airplane*, which was way before your time, and don't ask me how old I am."

"How old are you?" came a girl's teasing voice from the audience.

David looked at his watch and answered, "Old enough to realize that I'm talking too long and it's cutting into my playtime. And in closing, I'd like to say that we work diligently and play hard in the Constellations. We've learned that in design, as in living, the path is play and playfulness. That's how we arrive at our best solutions to difficult problems. We play together. We concentrate our research and planning on making people happier in a playful community life.

David paused to let all that he had just offered be taken in and reflected upon for a minute.

"And now, it's my turn to ask a question," said David. "What can prevent the playful human soul from leaping into the design of a kinder economic arrangement that's closer to the human heart?"

There was a long pause. There was silence for thirty seconds.

"I'm personally convinced that nothing can stop human creativity, and when it's at its best, it's totally playful. Many of the problems in the world are simply design problems that we know how to solve with play-work. Now you know why the planning offices in the Constellations are affectionately called The Sandbox."

David raised his voice to speak over the rising applause.

"I'd like to leave you with one last thought."

The audience slowly fell to silence.

"The global economy needs to shift its focus: if you have everyone involved in human development we won't be involved in war, because the prospects are far more promising with human development for everyone. We must focus on human development in all of our creative thinking. I want to thank you for coming this…" David said as the entire room erupted in a standing ovation.

He felt the moisture growing in the corners of his eyes, but he resolved not to wipe the tears.

"I hope to see many of you in my classes at New Town University, working for a master's degree in Constellation Planning. I hope you will answer the rest of your questions there, in the Sandbox. I know that you'll enjoy the beautiful new town of Las Faldas and the people there. But now, I have a plane to catch. So, please pick up a packet in the foyer and contact LSI to make arrangements for enrollment."

As David flew to Las Faldas del Cielo, he wondered how long it would take before a Constellation could be built in the U.S. He longed to see that happen. Yet, he knew that decades of indoctrination in so-called "free enterprise" economics would prevail for a while longer. It would be interesting to see when the American heart and soul would listen to a new song and spring into action. That thought brought Carlos to mind. After he arrived at the airport and confirmed his reservations, David decided to give his old friend a call.

"Hello."

"This is a voice from the past," David said. "Seen any good bullfights lately?"

"Hello there! Glad you called. This line has incoming calls all of the time. Could you please call back on my private line?"

"Sure, let me get a piece of paper. Ready."

"It's 202-999-455-9000."

"Okay. I got it. Call you back right away."

David felt a surge of anticipation as he dialed Carlos's secured number. He knew they could talk freely once they were connected.

"Hi, buddy," said Carlos, "it's been way too long since I had a David fix. How the hell are ya?"

"I'm floating around on a whole new natural high. I just finished a presentation at U.C. and I can't believe how well the students connected with me."

"I know, I was there."

"You were there? Really?"

"Oh, yeah. Linda and I are visiting friends in Cincinnati. You were something else, man. Hell, you even sold me!"

"Carlos, you're tearing my guts out. Are you comin' back?"

"Hell yes! Linda and I have been talking about it for weeks. She was there with me. You took us both over the top. We're definitely comin' back!"

"God love you both, this is great news. I've missed your hard-nosed insights and the fun we have together. We play together real well, you know."

"Yeah, but mostly in The Sandbox. I want to play outside of all that serious stuff too."

"You get your furry little buns down here and we'll play any way you want to."

Then David thought about what they were saying to each other. This conversation could jeopardize Carlos if his line was tapped.

"How long do we have before the wire can be tapped?"

"It's already happened and I don't give a damn."

"You really have decided, haven't you?"

"Just get out that big, beautiful paella pan of yours, and plan to serve me and Linda in the very near future. Okay?"

"You name the day."

"See you soon, buddy."

"Okay, bring a bottle of Gran Sangre de Toro."

"It's a deal, but only if you make paella," said Carlos as he hung up.

As David flew back to Las Faldas his mind was filled with the good times and the bad times with Carlos. He was awash in emotions that swept over him in uncontrollable waves and he was loving the whole, awesome, mind bending experience.

Conchita met him at the airport. He told her everything and she was as elated as he was. They just looked at each other during the drive home.

Finally, David said, "If it walks on water and smiles directly at you..."

"Let's go out and celebrate."

"Where do you want to go?" asked David.

"Let's go to the Cuddle Zone and shoot pool."

"Oh, you *are* a cheap date. But I'll only shoot three games because I want to get back and cuddle you."

"Okay, but you have to lose two out of three."

"I'll do my very best to put the eight ball in and scratch, as is my custom."

"I love it when you say those sweet things."

"These are going to be fast games."

* * *

The years rolled by quickly for David and Conchita, Carlos and Linda. New Town University was filled to overflowing with a steady stream of students who wanted to enjoy the life David described to them. They were not disappointed. Word of mouth traveled back to students in the United States at an accelerating rate. Students poured in from Latin America, Canada, Mexico, and all parts of Europe and Japan. The University expanded twice before El Cinco decided it was time to build a second university in the new Trinity Constellation. The Trinity Constellation joined Cornerstone and Vizcaya to complete a large regional trading block of twenty-one new towns, with a population of 1,260,000.

David and Conchita were asked to teach at Trinity University, and a new member was added to the family. David bought a Shetland sheepdog puppy and named him Vienna, because he loved to feed his dogs Vienna sausages for breakfast. David no longer had to recruit students. The flow was continuous. Ten years later, there were twenty-two additional new towns built in Rocadura and twenty more were under construction.

Six years passed and it was announced, on global television, that Rocadura was approaching completion of all its Constellations, and an International Feria of Constellations would be held in El Cedro, the capital of Rocadura.

On the eve of the International Feria, David took a walk in the cool fall air. He strolled along the edge of a small lake on the campus grounds and watched the breeze make gentle ripples across the sun-lit lake waters. Many small clouds, like fluffy cotton candy balls, marched in loose formation across the light blue sky. His mind reached back to the early days with Fredrico, and how the secret of Mondragon had so deeply impressed him. How Mondragon lay in quiet hiding for so long, ignored by most of the world. Strong, resourceful and expanding. Mondragon performed quietly, just off the world stage in the wings. Then, with the emergence of the Constellations, it took center stage as the original source of a new way of life.

David remembered how people yearned for so many years for a caring economic system, and sustainable development that was friendly to Earth. People had longed to live in a town with a sense of community. They longed to have time to be who they really are, to have a place to unfold that special, unique package that we all bring within us when we are miraculously born into the world.

David believed men and women were given the creative capacity to design their own workplace, to make life what it was meant to be: economically secure, with worker-entrepreneurs building a future for themselves and their children's children.

He passed a tree which was clearly reaching and straining upward toward the sun. He envisioned how time lapse photography would record the event: a seed put into the ground, a sprig, a sapling, an adolescent tree, an adult tree springing up powerfully now, continuing to grow, throwing off many seeds to start more saplings. The tree was bursting with creative energy, as were the Constellations. And David took deep satisfaction in the fact that he was part of that incredible rush of creative energy. He was an active participant in something much larger than himself. He might only be a micro-burst of energy in the birth of the Constellations, but he was part of the whole enterprise as it magically came up from its roots. To make a contribution, he had harvested from the labors of many, and labored himself, knowing he would never see all of the fruits of his young recruits. For he knew, the real power of the Constellation lay well into the future. But his contentment was abundant as he recalled the words of Christ:

"*Do you say*
there are four months
and then the harvest cometh?
Behold, I say to you
lift up your eyes
and see the countries
for they are white for the harvest.
And he that reapeth receivith wages
And gathering fruit unto life everlasting
that both he that soweth
and he that reapeth
may rejoice together.
For in this is the saying true
that it is one man that soweth
and it is another that reapeth.
I have sent you
to reap that in which you did not labor
Others have labored
and you have entered into their labors."

David strolled back to his house looking forward to a quiet evening with Conchita. As he entered the door, the phone was ringing. As he approached the phone he hoped that it would not be a call that would force him out of his mood.

"Hello."

"Hi, David. How are you doing?"

"Padre Parejo! What a surprise. I'm fine. What's happening in your young life?"

"Well, David, El Cinco and Erikson have given the green light to start a Constellation in the United States and they want you to be the planner in charge."

"Padre, I am humbled. That's wonderful! What location have you picked?"

"You know the U.S. better than we do. It's your call."

"Padre, please start praying for me. I know I'm going to need everything providence can deliver."

"Peace. The saints don't take this life so seriously. They know a little more about where they are going and it's beyond the dreams of most men and women. They know, that whatever severe pain and suffering that happens, God is at the very center of their being, holding them close to His eternally loving heart."

"God, what a precious understanding to hold. I'll try to hold tightly to that in the heat of battle."

"David, my prayers are always answered. You and I are in the hands of the Trinity. Given that enormous gift, may I ask, how can we do any harm? We will do good things together, you and I. Just go in peace and serve the Lord."

"That benediction always gives me great comfort, Padre."

"Bye for now, David. I'll see you soon in the U.S."

"You mean you're coming here to help me plan the Constellation?"

"Yes, I am."

"Well, with a living saint by my side, I think I've got a shot! I take heart!"

"It's providence at work. We'll play together to create God's New Towns."

"I'm really looking forward to our kind of play."

"Me too. Bye for now."

"Bye, and thanks for everything!"

Printed in the United States
65000LVS00004B/229-321